# NEVER
# THROW
# STONES
# GOD AT

# NEVER THROW STONES AT GOD

AZIM MUJAKIC

**To order additional copies of this book, contact:**
Xlibris
1-888-795-4274
www.Xlibris.com
Orders@Xlibris.com
798473

# DEDICATION

---

This book is dedicated with love to my family and friends who helped me escape the war evil and find a peace and freedom!

# WORDS ABOUT BOSNIA

---

All the time we are on someone's boundary, always someone's dowry. Through the centuries we were looking and recognize ourselves, soon we will not know who we are. We live on the border of the universe, on the border of the nations, always blamed of someone.

Over us the history waves broke us on the reef. We're torn away, and unaccepted.

We are as a stream that the torrents have separated from the mother, so there is no flow, nor the firth, which is so small to be a lake, to great that the ground can't soak us.

Mesa Selimovic

# CONTENTS

# INTRODUCTION

No matter how warm and safe I was in my bed in Missouri, I couldn't make the dreams of the old country stop. The dreams of the war, of my home, and the castle.

*The frightening dark, the rain, and the night shadows killed my patience on that winter night in 1993. I lay in a freezing cold trench in Pecigrad, at the edge of a forest. The quiet, that uncertain quiet, made me grip my rifle harder, ready to fire at any movement or shadow. I couldn't feel the feet. They didn't care anymore about the mud, the stones, or the snow, or about the dampness and stink.*

*"Am I a fool?" I wondered. "Cold, wet, scared, and staring into the gloom— for what? I didn't ask for this. I'll either get sick or killed. Either way, I'll be dead."*

*Machine gun fire lit the night and broke the quiet at the top of the hills—the tallest was called Metla.*

*"They're coming! Open fire!" somebody shouted and began shooting from the closest trench.*

*I didn't see anything, nor did I shoot because I didn't want them to notice my trench. The soldiers from the other side didn't fire in order to spare their bullets. Sometimes, they came to our trenches to cut our soldiers' throats with wire. I shivered thinking of it. The winter's rain was all over my face, letting me moisten my dry mouth.*

*Then I heard the explosion and saw the fiery red ball, like a setting sun, flying toward our trenches. Where would it fall? Questions flowed through my head like bullets, and I prayed to God to save me. The fiery ball hit a storage house, its brick wall visible just before and after the hit. The loudness and power lifted me from my trench, and I flew through the air, hitting the sidewall of a long-abandoned barn.*

*Pain ran from my head to my toes and back again. I felt faint, yet I tried to touch my hands, legs, and head to make sure I hadn't lost any parts. I didn't cry or sob because in my lungs there was neither air nor gunpowder. They were filled instead with the powder of homemade explosives. I felt as if my chest would burst. Finally, I caught my breath and hollered loud and long for help.*

Opening my eyes, I saw my bedroom walls with sunshine entering the room through the blinds. I was all sweaty. Pulling up the blinds, I saw my cherry-colored car in the parking lot where I had left it at midnight after the second shift. The beautiful green-leafed oaks of Jefferson Barracks Park shaded the first row of cars until noon. Playful squirrels were always there, running up and down the trees, easily and gracefully, like shadows jumping from branch to branch, and I liked watching them and listening to the singing birds of many shapes and colors.

I'd fallen from my bed to the floor, but that pain was nothing because I realized I was far from the evil of that war.

"This is my country now; I know that for sure," I thought.

I splashed cold water on my face and heated the coffee my wife had left for me because she was working the first shift, starting at 6:00 a.m. For breakfast, I fried a little salami and eggs.

I got dressed and ran out of the quiet, two-story building to Jefferson Barracks Park, where I exercised on the bank of the Mississippi River.

Walking and running, I met people of different ages and genders, and we greeted each other with "Good morning." I liked it because no one cared who I was or where I was from even when they knew I was different from them, if not in my outlook, then in the accent they heard when I greeted them.

On the side of the path, deer grazed, rabbits ran with squirrels, and the green meadows and small green hills all together made a beautiful composition of nature.

I entered the gate. After about a hundred steps, I was directly above the silent Mississippi River. I did my exercise from head to toe, as I did so often with my students during school physical education hours or during the wintertime in the still-cold morning classroom to heat my students' hands and bodies before their writing or math lessons. Then, I sat on a wooden bench decorated with many names, enjoying the view of the blue water. The hills across the river belonged to the state of Illinois.

At that moment, I wished I could see the castle of my ancestors who built it but never enjoyed it. It was my castle now. I had seen it so many times from the hill of Hrabljenovac, above my native village, and wondered what my ancestors looked like.

"I don't need that castle," I said aloud.

The noise of a car woke me from my thoughts. A blue car parked and out came a husband, his wife, and their daughter, carrying food, drinks and a blanket. They spread the blanket on the freshly-cut grass, under a giant oak tree. They enjoyed the food, drink, fresh air, conversation, and happiness they were born to here, in the peace and wellness of their beautiful country.

"Now, it is my country, too," I thought, sharing their happiness.

"Good morning," I said to them, smiling, and I left them to enjoy their day.

I savored the smells of morning, the birds' songs, and the beauty of nature all the way to my apartment. My morning exercise often took me back, in my mind, to my native country, in which I believed I should have lived my entire life in peace and freedom, surrounded by people I knew and understood, and who knew and understood me.

Learning and working hard made me love the life around me. I thought happily about how both school and life had educated me. I had been happy throughout my childhood, schooling, and working years. I loved to sing songs and listen to music. I sang for the parents during many school festivals and special occasions. Simply, with all these songs, I got in touch with my happiness. On those hard or sorrowful days, the poems I wrote made the troubles vanish. All the days and years were like a huge album with lovely pictures. I could feel my youth and find beauty in anything I saw, heard, or felt. I tried to remember only the beautiful pictures and times.

I ran on the track, taking care not to step on any baby squirrels because they were the main tenants in the park in all seasons. There were a lot of singing birds, deer, lost cats, raccoons, and skunks. The raccoons dug for food around the trash containers during the night. Sometimes, I awoke during the night, checked our car in the parking lot, and noticed whole families of raccoons and skunks. People left expired food outside and around the trash bins because if the trash container was empty, the raccoons were caught inside. A couple of times, we propped a long piece of wood inside the smelly container to help raccoons climb out.

Back in the apartment, I drank orange juice and took a shower. I left the water running until it felt cold. After the shower, I had a cup of coffee, thinking about what to do before my second shift began at four o'clock. Auto-Auction, my employer, was miles from St. Louis, in St. Charles County, and I had to leave home early to avoid the traffic on the highway. The whole apartment building was silent because most of the tenants worked the first shift, and their kids were in school or daycare. I decided to study some English words. I knew that I could not live well without being able to communicate with people around me. It was very hard to learn English after learning three other languages. I had trouble with the long and short vowels. Every day, I carried my dictionary to work.

In that company, were many people from my country, and through those connections, I got a job there, too.

They advised me, "You had better get a job before December because jobs are very hard to find at the beginning of a new year."

I wasn't thrilled with this job, but everything was fine because I was just trying out this life. The workplace was hot and wet in summer, and during the winter, it was very cold. I learned there that it is not good to work with people from the same country.

I hoped that after learning the language, saving some money, and waiting until I was used to American culture, I'd find a cleaner and better-paying job.

However, I liked one thing about that job; the hours passed very quickly. On the other hand, I didn't like driving 28 miles on three busy highways to get there. Until I bought my first car, my cousin who also worked there drove me every day. I paid him, but it could never be enough because of the very busy traffic.

When my wife and I saved enough money for the down payment, we bought a used Mazda. We were happy because it was our first car since the car we had left on the Hukica Brdo road during our escape. All around us had been shooting. The street, Velika Kladusa-Karlovac, was jammed with cars, tractors, horse-drawn carriages, men, women and children. Around the whole city, bullets were flying. We left that car full of food, clothes, and blankets.

*Terrified people were fleeing the city and country, fearing that the army would beat them. There was no justice, only rifles and soldiers' laws. In the summer of 1994, with an apartment and a job, I was happy if only because I was not in a trench. I considered the war as "the exchange of capital from the rich people to the poor people," and added, "from rich and good people to war criminals without souls." I heard many sad stories from old people about World*

*War II, and the Cazin Revolt, about what had happened to the people who were there. That was the reason I tried to stay away from it all. I grew up like that; they taught me that if I couldn't help, I shouldn't make it worse. I tried not to put my nose in others' business. I tried to survive the war healthy and to keep my family close because during the war years, I saw how even people that you were kind to, tried to kill you if you had something they wanted.*

*I had turned toward the old castle and saw its soul full of sadness because it did not have the legs to join us, nor could it protect us within its walls. Many times, I had gazed at it from Hrabljenovac Hill, standing and admiring it until the kids who wanted to play arranged their games around me. I liked the power that it had, persisting there through the centuries, all the way from my ancestral Hrnjica and the little village Kladova.*

Built in 1637, the castle was renovated during the 1980s, when my city had jobs and extra money. It was a symbol. It had survived invading armies representing empires and their rulers, wars which came from its west, Austria-Hungary, and Germany. This new war, sadly, came from the east of it, and only because two human heads refused to come up with a way to compromise. Often people want to be famous or big names in history, even when they don't know that history well. If they had understood the life of my ancestor, our common ancestor, the knight Mujo Hrnjica, there would never have been mile-long lines of good people leaving warm homes built with love. People who wanted to live in peace with their neighbors.

But I came from there to my present happiness, the joy of living in this beautiful city in the United States of America, a big, peaceful country which welcomed me as it did everyone else. This country gave me peace, employment, and the same rights as those who lived here even before we knew that this wonderland continent existed.

This was the life I had dreamed about during the war and that I imagine my ancestors dreamed of and wanted in my homeland. I now know their dream was impossible, despite the efforts of Mujo Hrnjica and the long line of heroes from Krajina who tried to protect and better the lives of their people.

The telephone rang, interrupting my thoughts. On the other end was one of the women who rode with me to work asking about the carpool.

That's how I started my working life in September 1999. I had worked part-time and full-time jobs in Germany from May 1995 to the day I had to leave: July 12, 1999. It was hard leaving friends who were fellow refugees and even harder to imagine traveling so far from home. I had never flown in an airplane and was scared. My only brother was already living in the United States by then. From phone conversations, I gathered that he had a good place to live and was happy in the new country.

From the big American airplane, I saw endless meadows with neatly plowed fields and forests. The tiny lines were in fact wide highways. My wife, my young son, and I, along with many other Bosnians on the same plane from Frankfurt, arrived at O'Hare International Airport in Chicago carrying white plastic bags, which signaled the people waiting for us. They told us which gates led to our final destinations. Thousands of people of different colors and nationalities milled through the corridors of O'Hare, where even English-speakers can get lost. We didn't get lost because working at the airport was a man named Subho. I knew him from our high-school days.

"Man, where did you come from?" I said, marveling.

"I work here," he said. "Where do you need to go?"

"To St. Louis because my brother is there."

"Don't worry, I'll take you where you need to go, and then you can fly to St. Louis," said Subho.

I was charmed that in such a short time, a fellow refugee could get a job in that amazing airport. I had only a little time with Subho because we had to pass through the other control gate where a man from Naturalization gave us our ID cards, the first refugee documents with our photos and personal information and the allied numbers. The same man took us to the departure gates. The departure screen showed us that our airplane would be an hour late.

We enjoyed the spectacular view airplanes taking off and landing at the airport almost every minute. We were free from the anxiety of flying which had tormented us in Frankfurt. Nevertheless, the flight from Chicago to St. Louis was so scary that the angst came back and we prayed for a safe landing.

We landed among millions of lights, like giant hands that welcomed us and gave us a warm hug.

At Lambert Airport in St. Louis were, besides my brother and sister-in-law, my middle-school friend Serif, my cousins Razim and Zemir with their wives, and some other friends of my brother, whom we hadn't met. There were lots of hugs and questions. My son was very happy in the arms of his uncle because they hadn't seen each other since they had been separated in Kuplensko, the refugee camp, four years before. We found our luggage and headed to the big garage, and from there toward my brother's apartment. Riding toward downtown, I was able to see for real what had looked from the plane like long wide lines. We passed by the Arch and many tall factory chimneys, which seemed to promise work and wealth.

My brother made us a welcoming party and filmed us with his camcorder, so we felt like special guests and future inhabitants of this shiny, big city with the biggest gate—the Arch—we had ever seen. We had drinks, roasted lamb and cakes; more than enough. Seeing those, we realized that even Bosnians here had good lives.

"Let's call Mom and Dad in Bosnia," said my brother. We gave the phone to my son because our mom and dad love him possibly more than they love us. He was their first grandchild. My mother answered from the other side of the world. We talked for a very long time because here we did not have to save phone minutes as we did in Germany and Bosnia. Mother cried, sad that we had all left her and our father alone in our family home. They had returned there from Kuplensko, the second refugee camp we lived in, for four years of the evil war. It had been hard to leave them aging and alone there. I had also left other relatives and friends, and the language that I speak the best, and the diploma that I had earned, and the house I built with love, after having saved up for it for seven years. I had left my parents and all I had dreamed of for this new life.

The war took everything and forever separated us. Adults, little ones, old ones, all were forced with bullets, grenades, knives, and wires from what we called life, love, and happiness. Because of that evil, I flew unwillingly ten hours away, "across the world," as my mother said because she did not know exactly how far away or where I was, only that I was very far away at "the end of world."

Everything was new around me, and I felt as if I had just been born. Still, very often my dreams took me back to the past. I also spent some happy times with fellows from the old country because through our conversations, we kept our homeland alive. Freedom and justice were new, Missouri was new, St. Louis was new, the English language was new, and I quickly traded my German driver's license for a Missouri driver's license for only seven dollars. I had a new work place, and there were new customs.

This is the land of fairy tales. I hugged my family, and whenever I saw the new red, white, and blue flag, I felt the desire to be, to believe, work, love, and to make my own way for my family, so that in this new country they could be happy and proud along with me.

# PART I

## Hurem-aga 1637

"By the order of Mustay-beg Lichki," said Hurem-aga to his sister Fatima and her three sons, "you are to live here. Your daughter, Ajkuna, can stay with us until you are settled."

They were in the hills above Mala and Velika Kladusa, by the little running spring that would later be called Hurem-aga Spring, or just Hura. Fatima and her boys drank the cold water from the spring that sunny day in June 1637 because they were tired from the long walk from Lika.

There wasn't a house, no village; nothing, but high grass and unfamiliar trees.

The three sons, Mooyo, Halil, and Omer, listened while their mother cried and said, "We do not deserve to be treated this way. My husband and the head of my family died somewhere in Principovina for Mustay-beg Lichki, who now does us wrong. But there is a God. He sees everything, knows and hears what is happening, and I hope He will punish Mustay-beg Lichki."

Hurem-aga said, "These are his orders, and he will behead me if I don't carry them out. I am so sorry I can't give you some cattle and horses to start your new life. But, dear sister, take these gold and silver coins and do your best. Your boys are now grown and smart. Together you can start a new life here. Your nephew Osman-bajraktare, when he hears that you are here, will help you right away."

Fatima said, "Tomorrow I will send Mooyo to Banja Luka where he can buy a cow for milk and to plow these meadows, so that when winter comes, we don't have empty boxes of flour."

Hurem-aga filled his pouch with cold water, hugged his sister and nephews, got on his horse and headed back to Lika by way of the village Shturlic. Fatima watched the hills and trees swallow the horse and rider. She felt as if her soul were being torn from her. The brothers wouldn't look at their uncle, thinking that he had planned to get rid of them. But it could have been much worse; they could have lost their heads for no reason, without any justice. Others had been exiled to Anatolija.

Mooyo, the eldest son, said, "We need to eat something and sleep somewhere tonight. Stand up, brothers. I will try to hunt, so we can eat, and Halil needs to cut some branches and young trees to make shelter. Omer, collect some dry branches and stones to make a fire. Mother, don't worry. We'll survive without Uncle and Mustay-beg. The day will come when they'll hear about of our success and wealth."

Mooyo hunted in the forest and caught a deer. Halil made the house from sticks. Omer collected stones and sticks for the fire.

Halil was a big eater, so while his brothers were building the place to sleep, he skinned the deer, and then on the wooden sticks, added many parts of the animal on the fire to cook their supper. Their mother made a small loaf of bread.

At sunset, they were all tired and hungry. Without many words, they ate their meat and were ready to sleep. Because they were all alone, they did not need to stay watch. Nevertheless, their mother slept with one open eye as she was not comfortable in this strange new home.

The sun's rays were shining through the stick house. They needed to hurry. The brothers blinked and saw Fatima with wild strawberries, which she had picked from the surrounding meadows.

"How did you sleep, dear mother," Mooyo asked.

They sat around the table that Omer had made from the pieces of collected stones. For breakfast, they ate a little flat bread and the wild strawberries.

After breakfast, the brothers wanted to mix mud and dry grass to build a new concrete house.

"I will be happier if you go to Banja Luka and buy a cow first, and when we have milk, cheese, and butter, it will be easy for me to cook for you, and we can plow this hill and valley to plant some corn," said Fatima.

"I know it, dear mother, but I cannot live in this cabin of sticks. Rain can come, and we will be nowhere. Today and tomorrow we will build, and when I am sure we have a good shelter, I will go to Banja Luka right away," said Mooyo.

The old woman agreed with him, so they hurried to dig the foundation, mixed mud and dry grass, collected stones that were all around the meadows and forest. By noon, they had built four walls one meter high, and they had a big pile of different sized stones.

The hard work and the smell of baked deer meat told them it was lunch time. They sat around Omer's table, ate lunch, and drank cold spring water. After the break, they worked harder and faster, until the walls were tall enough that the tall young men could walk under the doorway without shaking them down. They left small openings for the windows.

Omer cut a chestnut tree for the door, so before night, they had strong walls and a safe place to rest. Tomorrow, they would add the roof.

The water from the spring filled the hole that they had dug and made a small pond. They could use it to wash up. During Omer's part of work, he made some traps for wild animals. In the early morning, he collected three rabbits, a fox, and some wild chickens.

He set them on the sun to dry, then gave their mother meat to be cooked on the fire. The whole next day, they continued building the roof with dried chestnut logs, grass, fern, and long swamp grass that grew around the spring.

"My son, tomorrow you will go to hunt, Mooyo will go to Banja Luka, and Omer to his sister to announce what has happened with us." Fatima made her plan to protect her youngest son, Omer, who was more an artist than a knight. He was good at making furniture and sculptures of dried wood with the faces of humans and animals. The other brothers were good with guns, swords, and other weapons, riding on horses, and fighting.

Fatima always told them, "someones' who kills with a sword will one day be killed with sword." She did not like brutality, and she taught her sons to never start a fight. Nevertheless, the boys were drilled in the military disciplines of how to fight with a sword, long arrows, and rifle with long pipe as a part of the Ottoman army.

After dinner, the older brothers were working on the roof, and Omer was working on beds. Their mother was busy sewing cloth and filling it with the rest of dried grass for the mattresses for their beds. All around the valley and especially in the house, there was a smell of dried clay and grass.

When the sun was setting against Zagreb, the family Hrnjice had a real home with a roof and warm hearth from where the smell of rabbit stew and fresh bread came all around the valley.

"I give you thanks for this hard work on our home. Always stay together and listen to each other, and I will be proud of the milk I fed you when you were small and every minute I stood awake long nights with you." Fatima smiled and hugged her sons. "Now, let's go celebrate this new home with a nice and warm dinner."

She put clay dishes on the wooden table, and they all sat around the table feeling in their hearts that the whole Ottoman Empire belonged to them.

They knew that the next day they needed to work hard to prepare for the winter and spring with enough food and wood. They slept without worries because they were away from Ottoman laws, and they were in the Balkan forest by the main roads where traded goods passed by so often. Although there were bandits, many of them were in prison.

# CHAPTER 1

## Mooyo's Adventure

The first rays of sun shone through the small windows. Fatima awoke, added wood to the fire, put water in the pot for tea with a pomegranate she had found on the hills that they had not yet named. She did not wake up her sons, knowing that there was another hard working day for all of them. Soon, she saw Omer up. He had placed flat stones around the spring yesterday, so they were able to have fresh water.

"Did you sleep well, dear mother?" Omer asked.

"You know that nights are always long to me," Fatima replied.

"The tea is ready. I will call your brothers too. It is time to wake up, and we will all sit, drink the tea, eat something for breakfast for the hungry heart."

"I am going to see the traps, if something is in them. I will be back by the time they are washing their faces," Omer said and ran to Kresha. He returned fast with two big rabbits in his hands. His brothers were sitting around drinking tea. Mooyo was already dressed in his best clothes, white pants and a long sleeved shirt. Mother was putting some bread in his handkerchief for the long journey to Banja Luka.

"Rabbits again? I'm tired of only little rabbits," complained Halil.

"Better something, than nothing. I found something else. In the bushes, there is a turkey laying on a full nest of eggs, and where there is a turkey, there is a male turkey somewhere in the nearby forest or bushes." Omer continued, "There will be a lots of dried turkey for winter because the nest is full of eggs, and you will be happy with my hunting, my fat brother."

Mooyo interrupted, "My brothers, I am going to Banja Luka today, and two of you need to watch our mother. Do not go far from this valley. Before I come back, you need to build a barn for the cow on that side of valley, so it will not mess up with our spring, and dig two escape tunnels for protection. One tunnel needs to be connected to the barn."

"Dear mother, I had some bad dreams last night. Let's not let Omer visit our sister and Arnaut until I return from Banja Luka," Mooyo advised.

"Whatever you say, my son. I wanted to tell them, we were here, but we can wait," replied Fatima. Mooyo knew that he and his brothers could survive any danger without anyone's help. He loved his brother-in-law and his nephew Arnaut-Osman, but he preferred to stay a little distant from them for the time being.

Mooyo hugged his brothers and mother and was ready for his journey of one hundred and fifty kilometers, which he planned to cut in half by going over the hills, forests and valley to the city on the Vrbas River.

Fatima handed him the kerchief with the bread and said, "be careful my son because there are many bandits on the roads. Do not go close to the castles. Be careful when you walk through the forests and meadows because snakes can bite you. God watch and save you. Always watch before you walk over the clean meadows. Do not touch something that is not yours, and help if someone is in need, but be careful."

All three of them stayed to watch as Mooyo walked toward the East and the River Una.

When the sun was high, he knew it was noon, and he was close to The Una River. His goal was to cross the river and climb the hills above it. On his way, he did not see anyone besides some deer or foxes, which got scared and ran to the nearest bushes.

When he came to the Una River, he stopped briefly to enjoy the clear water, which looked like a silver chain between willow trees, whose branches dipped into the water. He drank some water, washed his face and neck, and decided to eat there, cooling his feet in the water. He was enjoying his mother's fresh baked flat bread in the shadow of the willow trees, when he saw a large nest on top of the water. A big stone was in the water like a small island, cutting the water in two, and the nest bumped into Mooyo's feet. In that moment, he saw two little birds, with downy feathers. Swiftly, he stopped the nest and put it on the ground beside his meal. Who knows how it got in the water, and how it fell off the high oak trees?

"Is this a lucky or unlucky sign of my journey?" thought Mooyo. With a piece of dried wood, Mooyo dug into the dirt on the bank of river and found three worms. Then with one hand, he opened the birds' bills and gave them worms to swallow in a moment. Mooyo knew for sure they belonged to a big bird because they ate only meat. He realized that if he left them on the river bank, they would die because they did not know how to feed themselves, so he decided to take them on the rest of his journey to Banja Luka.

He took off his white pants and shirt, tying them around his neck with the cloth where his mother packed his food to swim in the cold river. He then continued to Kamengrad. When he climbed on the top of the deep canyon, he saw lots of smoke in the direction of Ostrozac. The little birds must have fallen off a burning oak tree.

The sun was very hot, but Mooyo wanted to sleep in or close to Kamengrad because tomorrow night he wished to be close or in Banja Luka. He was walking when he saw a thin line of smoke. That meant there must be someone nearby. It was in the direction he was going, so he carefully walked through the forest. He did not want to be seen by anybody especially bandits or road robbers who had soldiers looking to kill them or to put them in prison. They were against the Ottomans' justice. They robbed travelers and caravans with goods from the east, and they sold them in these cities and villages.

When he came very close to them, he smelled sheep roasting on a spit. He was able to hear what they were saying. The bandits were drunk, so he assumed they had walked from the place where they ate and drank where their horses were tied.

"We made a good profit with our last robbery, but this is not a good place to stay," said the loudest man, who Mooyo guessed was the boss.

"We do not have an army, and these forests are easy for the Ottoman soldiers to cross. We need to stay by the Canyon of Vrbas, between Banja Luka and Jajca," added the next bandit.

"In that place between Sarajevo and Banja Luka caravans so often cross the roads all the way to Lika. There are many soldiers in the Lika castles, so it is better for us to stay away from Sarajevo and Lika, somewhere in the middle of these two regions," said the bandit.

"What are we waiting for? We are full, and our horses are rested. Zoko, bring them here," said the boss to a young boy. The boy brought the horses to the bandits.

The bandits got on their horses and galloped in the direction where Mooyo needed to go. He waited in the bushes until they had passed, and he went to their camp, where the spit still held one fourth of a sheep, ready to eat. He took his pocketknife and cut a big piece of sheep meat and put it on his last piece of flat bread to be heated.

When he was done with his big sandwich, he found some worms and water to feed the birds. For the rest of his trip, he cut another big piece of meat, and he put some dirt over the fire, so it wouldn't start a fire in the woods to hurt other birds, animals, or nests.

At dusk, he entered Kamengrad, a little village with a few houses and castles. There was rest for traders. The castle had a restaurant, beds, sleeping rooms, and barns for tired horses and mules that carried cloth, spices, and other goodies. For a coin or two, they all were refreshed, fed, and ready for the trip to the next castle or city. Soldiers were protecting the roads from bandits, and collecting taxes from the local people. They also were a part of Ottoman justice and hierarchy. The laws were always on their side. The people from this region knew the saying "A Judge will charge you and judge you." That was why the people tried to stay away from Ottoman justice, paying their taxes in the hopes of living in peace.

Mooyo greeted some men he found sitting around a wooden table and a well which was in the center of the city where young men and girls had a meeting place while girls were getting water for their homes. It looked as if this place was hidden from the world and main roads.

"Where are you going, hero?" asked a tall man in white pants, shirt, black vest, brand new shoes, and a round, red hat on his head.

Mooyo nodded. "Hello, friends. I want to go to Banja Luka, but night is falling fast, and I need a place to sleep tonight."

"I will let you sleep in my house. I will give you a nice dinner and a bed. If you want to be in our group tonight, you can help us pull the rope because a strong gang is coming from Podbrezici," said the guard.

"Thank you kindly, and in exchange for dinner, I offer you some flat bread my mother made for my trip to Banja Luka," Mooyo said to the men.

After ten minutes, they heard the gallop of horses. About ten young and happy men came to the well. In a short time, from all sides of the city came kids, old men, women, and many young girls. A man blew a horn and began to draw a line. Then he set a rope with a white line in the middle. That meant the side that could pull the white mark over the line on the ground three times would be the winner. On the middle of the line, they brought a young bull and the man announced: "he who pulls the rope with the white mark three times over the line will win this bull."

The players started to tie their shoes and pants, roll their sleeves, and talk about strategies with their teammates. The crowd was starting to wind up. The men from Kamengrad put Mooyo on one end of the rope. The announcer blew his horn. Both teams pulled very hard, but after a while, the white mark on the rope got on the side from Kamengrad. A cloud of dust rose into the air because the men from Kamengrad stood stronger than the men from Podbrezicani and easily won the game. The Podbrezicani gang cried and argued about how they lost the game of tug-a-war. They caught their breath, rubbed hands, took off their shoes because some of them were torn apart, and prepared for the next round, having been surprised about losing the first time. When the announcer blew his horn for the second round, it was silent and all eyes were glued to the white line. Both teams pulled the rope to their side, so the white mark on the rope crossed the line on the ground many times.

The audience shouted: "Go team, go team!" The white mark on the rope finally ended on the side of Kamengrad, and the team from Podbrezicani fell onto the dusty road. The public went crazy, lifting their players in the air, kissing and hugging all of them. The mayor of Kamengrad gave the command to make a fire in the center of the city and bake the bull on the stick. It became a festival, and everyone started to dance, sing, drink, and eat baked bull. The festivities lasted until nearly midnight. Everyone went to Mooyo, the newcomer, and shook his hand with kind words of congratulations. The mayor told him that any time he traveled through their city, he would have a place to sleep, drink, and eat.

"Great job, great job, hero."

Everyone wanted to shake Mooyo's hand. Many young girls fell in love with him at first sight, and they wanted him to ask them for their hand and a chance to join him on his trip.

When he woke up the next morning, the sun was high in the sky. Mooyo was tired from too much eating, drinking, and dancing, but he knew he needed to continue his journey. Breakfast and hot black coffee were on the table. His host's wife filled his bag with hot flat bread, leftover meat, cheese, milk, and water for his little birds. They seemed much bigger than the day before.

Mooyo thanked his host and hostess and said, "I do not have enough words to thank you for such good hospitality and for everything else." They walked under the ripening cherry trees.

The man smiled broadly. "Thank you. You helped us to win, and you deserve much more than we gave you. I hope that God will always make your road short and easy for your feet and that you will always have a good horse," said the man. "Walk in the direction of these hills, and you will be there much earlier than you think."

Mooyo was in a hurry to make up the time and to see the castle Kastel before dark, so he could arrive at the market to buy a cow and quickly return to his mother and brothers.

All the way to Banja Luka, Mooyo enjoyed the beautiful scenery of Krajina and scared the animals, which were not used to humans. He took only one break to eat and drink something and to feed the birds. In that way, he saw the walls of Kastel and a tall tower of the Fehradija mosque, from which he could hear the priest calling prayers. He thought about his mother and brothers: "What are they doing? Are they well?"

# CHAPTER 2

## Bandits

Mooyo saw sturdy walls surrounding the Fehradija mosque with a tall minaret. There were also many fountains, which made the city appear very big and important for the Ottoman Empire. Mooyo was tired and thirsty from the long walk, so he got some water for himself and the birds, but before looking for a place to sleep the following night, he needed to relax. He sat on the stairs of one store, listening to the conversations of people walking by the store. Suddenly, a hand touched his shoulder. He turned his head.

"Hello stranger. Please leave the entrance to my store. I have heard that a big bandit is coming with his friends to rob us," said the owner. These bandits must have been the ones Mooyo saw between Una and Kamengrad. Mooyo ate his leftover meat. The government looked for bandits, killed them, placed them in the prison, or made them slaves. It did no good, for they often rode through the cities and villages, robbing people and riding back to the forest without any trace. Most of the time, they waited for caravans between the cities. They did not obey the laws of the government, for they only followed their own rules.

When Mooyo heard the words of the store owner, he was surprised that such things could happen in that big city, that someone could be brave enough to rob people and no one could stop them. At that moment, other workers were leaving the store and again warned him to leave the area.

"The bandits will take what they need, and after that, they will leave. I do not want to lose the whole store because of a few minor items," said the owner.

"I am tired from two days walking, and I must rest. I will not stand up and leave these stairs. You can go whenever it is safe for you. When you come back, I will pay you whatever you have lost," said Mooyo bravely.

"How can you pay me? Why, you are as poor as poor can be."

"Do you see this metal lock by your store door? It will protect you from bandits, and do not worry about my appearance. Clothes do not make the man rich any more than the sword makes a hero," replied Mooyo.

Finally, the owner and his sales people disappeared on their way. Mooyo wanted to stop the bandits even though he knew they could kill him like a small chicken and escape punishment.

After about ten minutes, the bandits arrived on horses. They were dressed in stolen silk and had big red hats on their heads, from which they had a golden rope tied on the end all the way to their shoulders. Mooyo had never seen such rich clothes. It looked like they were on parade for king, but they were very rude and drunk.

"Give us brand new raincoats, shoes, shirts, and pants," commanded the head bandit.

Mooyo stood close to the metal door. He walked into the store and quickly found all that the bandit demanded. It was his first time in that store, but he was sure it was much richer than even the bandit had imagined. He handed over the goods, still standing close to the metal lock. When the bandit distributed the clothes and shoes to his companions, Mooyo said to him, "Pay me for what you have taken."

"I do not pay for what I take. Don't you know that?" said the bandit, and all his friends started to laugh at Mooyo.

When Mooyo heard those words, as fast as a wink he took the metal lock from the door, struck the boss bandit with all his power, knocking him off his horse and onto the cobblestone street, where he died instantly. When his friends saw that, they galloped straight to the River Vrbas.

Mooyo jumped on the back of the dead bandit's horse and followed the thieves. As he approached, he struck one with the same door lock, and the bandit fell off his horse. By the time he came to the Crkvine spring, all the bandits were on the ground, some hurt more, some less, but happy to be alive. Mooyo rounded up the ones who could still walk and tied them with a rope. He put the wounded ones on horses, and he returned to the front of the store, where he found many people standing around the body of the dead bandit leader.

The owner and his clerk could not believe what the stranger had done to the bandits. Good news travels faster than a scared horse. The city spokesperson took the news to the mayor of Banja Luka, Mr. Pasa. The people wanted to know who that hero was, and other storeowners came to Mooyo with presents of fine clothes, money, weapons, food, and drinks. The table was set in front of where the dead bandit lay.

Mooyo had a good supper, with a variety of food and drinks. Finally, five soldiers and the highest officer from Mr. Pasa arrived. The people stepped back to make room on the table next to their hero. The riders were on very good horses and wore shiny clothes of silk, with golden buttons on their long suits and silver swords. Four soldiers from the group took the wounded bandits to the prison in the castle Kastel, while the people from both sides of city streets jeered and spat on them.

"Dear hero, his highness Mr. Pasa sent us to invite you to his castle, to be his guest for the good service you did for our city and for the Ottoman Empire," the officer said.

Another officer handed Mooyo a new uniform and added, "Please put on these new clothes, with this belt, sword, and two short guns because we cannot allow such a hero to wear ordinary clothes to his highness."

The owner took him to the store to put on his new uniform. Soon Mooyo stood in the doorway, looking like a real hero that would be remembered in this city for a long time.

Mooyo had followed his mother's advice, to be on the side of the weak, to fight only against bandits and robbers. In the moment, he thought, "I would be happier if my mother and brothers could see me now in front of all these happy people. How they would cheer and thank me. If Mustay-beg Lichki could see me now, he would offer me the hand of his girl."

He got on his new brown horse, lifted his hand in the air and spoke to the store owners and crowd. "Thank you all for the hospitality, welcome, and presents. If you ever have a problem with bandits again, send me a message, and I will come back and put these robbers in prison."

The people cheered, making way for him and the soldiers. Because of all that had happened in the past two hours, he had almost forgotten about the birds. They had been fed and cleaned by the town. All the presents and the birds were loaded on his horse.

Mooyo now rode on a horse the mayor Pasa had sent for him, and one of the soldiers was walking and leading that horse behind them. Mooyo could not believe what had happened in the past few hours, but he rode proudly on the horse over the cobblestoned streets of Banja Luka all the way to the stone castle.

"What will happen over there, when these people have shown such generosity and given me so many presents?" thought Mooyo.

The big door of the Kastel Castle opened, and servants and horsemen stood ready to take the horses to the barn. Two officers led Mooyo to the highest tower in the castle. Everything was as immaculate as in a fairy tale.

They reached the highest castle that was only shorter than the tower of the city mosque. The door opened, and a tall young man, led them to a big guest room, covered with a tapestries of different colors and designs, with long sofas on three sides of the room. All the sofas were covered with pillows. Mayor Pasa was sitting there with the city judge. As Mooyo entered, both of them stood up and greeted him with a friendly welcome. They offered him to sit on the pillows. He sat on one of the long pillows and sank in its softness and silky comfort.

"Welcome, hero," said Pasa, and Kadija nodded his head.

"I appreciate your invitation and kind greeting," replied Mooyo.

"Can you tell us who you are, where are you from, and why you came to our city?" asked the impatient Kadija.

"Your highness, I am from the area called Krajina, from the small city, Velika Kladusa. My mother sent me to Banja Luka to buy a cow for us. Licki Mustaj-beg exiled my family from Lika because I was in love with his daughter. Our uncle Kozlic Hurem-aga delivered us to Krajina, where we have made a new home. There I left my mother and two brothers who wait for my return. I am the oldest man in our family since my father died fighting for Licki Mustaj-beg somewhere in Principovina. We moved to Krajina to start a new life there." Mooyo finished his story and bowed his head.

As he spoke, beautiful servant girls set the table with a meal. They brought a pitcher with water, a plate to wash hands, and a towel to dry them. When the servants left, another came with tea and coffee, sweets, cookies, and cakes for the table.

After a moment, Pasa started to talk. "You can stay here for some days as our guest because I got an order from the king which I must follow. I will take you back there after you relax and enjoy, while I pack everything for your journey Krajina.

"We must protect and strengthen the border of the rivers Korana and Glina for our highness King and our kingdom," added Kadija with a worried expression.

"We will not talk about it right now. Let us eat and drink first. Please, help yourself," said Pasa.

They enjoyed the baked lamb, chickens, and turkey until they started to burp from so much food and drink. Mooyo remembered Halil, Omer, and his mother.

"If only they could join me here at this rich table."

When they finished the meal, the same servant girls cleaned the table and added more drinks. Every girl silently knew what to do, what to take, and what to bring on or off the table.

"Take the hero to sleep, and we will have more talk about the trip to Krajina in the morning. Please feel at home; do not be shy. Take anything you need. You are in charge of this hospitality and are welcome to this. It is not every day we have such a hero as you," Pasa said softly and sincerely to this young man.

Seiz walked with Mooyo to his guest room in which they had taken all the presents he had been given from stores and other business owners. Seiz got Mooyo's bed ready and took him to the bathtub. Mooyo was fascinated with Pasa's guest room. Everything smelled of lilac and lime-trees and was clean and white. The designs on the window curtains and rugs on the yellow hardwood floor were elaborate. A white sheep skin hung on the wall. It was used for praying. There were also many freshly cut flowers of different colors. To Mooyo, it felt like Heaven.

"Now, I will take you to the bathroom, and if you need something just call to me because I will be in front of the door to serve you," said Seiz with deep respect.

"Thank you very much, but do you know why they treat me like this?"

"I do not know anything, but his highness Pasa will tell you in the morning," answered Seiz.

Mooyo was worried about what he considered to be an overreaction. He didn't want to be part of something that could be wrong for his family. After undressing, he wrapped a towel around himself and entered a much bigger room with small and big swimming pools and a bathtub with steam and the scent of flowers rising from it. In the biggest bathtub, there were so many bubbles you could not see the water. He threw the towel off and entered the fragrant, bubbly water. He closed his eyes and relaxed in the warmth. When he opened his eyes, he thought he was dreaming. Around the tub were four beautiful girls wearing beautiful eastern style clothes. Their big breasts almost jumped from their vests. On their heads, they had silk scarves and over the faces woven pieces of handkerchiefs. He could only see their beautiful eyes. One girl added more hot water, another made more bubbles, a third one washed his head, and a fourth one washed his back. The hero made not a sound. The blood came to his face, but he enjoyed the experience. Still, he did not know if he was dreaming or not. How long he enjoyed the bathing he did not know. He was too shy to get out of the water and bubbles because his manhood was ready to explode in the warm water.

Eventually, he heard the sound of a hand clapping, and he opened his eyes. All the girls disappeared, and above him came Seiz with a big towel. "Did you enjoy the hot water and bathing in his highness' bathroom?" asked Seiz.

"I will never forget it," responded Mooyo as calmly as he could.

"For your act of bravery, there will be a special party tomorrow because all the people in Banja Luka have heard about you, and they are anxious to meet and thank you," said Seiz.

Mooyo followed him to his bedchamber, where he saw a drink in a silver pitcher and different dried fruits on wooden plates. On the wall were four candles in the candelabra.

"What is going on, and why do they treat me like his highness for that little thing I did, which I would do for anyone?" Mooyo finally asked.

In that moment, like a soft wind, on fast and silent feet, one of the girls from the bathroom, with a move of her hand turned the candles off and snuck gently next to him in the comfortable bed. Without a word, she started to caress him. He forgot his thoughts and only felt her hands, lips, and body. It was more than he could imagine in his dreams.

"These are only dreams," Mooyo thought before he drifted in and out of sleep under the body of that beautiful fairy. How long she was next to him and what happened there only she knew because Mooyo was melting in the well of her hot hips and drunk from her sweet lips. He fell relaxed and tired. He fell asleep and dreamt of real or imagined events.

# CHAPTER 3

## A Royal Morning

The roosters around the city of Banja Luka were singing their morning songs, and the Muslim priest prayed the first morning prayers. Mooyo opened his eyes and felt like he was born again. Seiz was nearby as a good servant.

"Good morning. Did you sleep well?" asked Seiz.

"I feel as light as a hawk feather, which is a sign I slept well and rested even better," said Mooyo happily.

"If you would like to refresh yourself in the bathroom, everything is ready there," added the servant.

Mooyo wished to wash himself after the events that happened the previous night in his bed. But this time, there were no women's hands, only warm, fragrant water, which gave him power and alertness. After bathing, he got dressed and was ready to perform his first morning prayers. Seiz joined him, and they prayed on the white lamb skin.

"Do you want coffee, tea, or something to eat?" asked Seiz when they had finished.

"Please, if I can have tea because something dried me during the night," answered Mooyo, but he regretted his words because the servant knew for sure who slept the last night with him.

Mooyo thought, "It is possible he brought her. I will be happy to know her name and to know whether it was a dream or not."

Just then, one girl set the small table, and another brought a pot and cup with tea and cookies.

"Enjoy the tea, and if you wish to lay down, feel free, like in your home," said Seiz, walking out the door with the girls. The pomegranate tea smelled and tasted delicious and the dried cookies, filled with nuts and raisins were so satisfying, that they brought back his power and red color in his face. When he remembered the girl from the night, he felt his manhood in his cotton underwear, and he wished to have her there next to him. After about one hour, Seiz returned with a sword, two short guns, a vest with silver buttons and a strange long-sleeved shirt woven with wire and buttons.

"This is a present from the store owners to wear in a fight because this shirt will protect you from swords and bullets."

Seiz put the gifts on the sofa and handed the short guns and belt to Mooyo.

"His highness invites you to his working rooms for lunch," said Seiz.

"All right, I am ready to go," said Mooyo following Seiz.

In the other high castle, they met Pasa and Kadija beside a wooden table big enough to seat 30. They were looking at a map of Europe. There was also a smaller map with the Balkan Peninsula and many different symbols. Mooyo did not understand the signs and maps, but he was curious. Kadija and Pasa were in good moods, with big grins on their faces and a warm welcome for him.

"Good morning and welcome to a new day, hero," said Kadija. He held a cup of black coffee. On a big plate were different food, fruits, and vegetables.

"Good morning, and Allah make you lucky," Mooyo said, embarrassed that he had not been first to greet his elders.

"Did you rest enough?" continued Pasa.

"Believe me, your highness, everything from yesterday was like a dream to me because you have truly treated me as a prince." With these words of thanks, Mooyo bowed at Pasa.

"Just sit and help yourself, and we will move to our work for we know you are in a hurry to get to Kladusa," added Pasa.

Mooyo was not hungry, but he knew that it would be rude to say no to food and drink, especially after Pasa offered it. The meal was long, but finally, they put their spoons down. Beside the curtains from the high door came girls walking like a dance. They cleaned everything so fast, and again they brought water in a pitcher and a big plate and towel for the three men to wash and dry their hands. Quietly they came, and quietly they disappeared.

"Now we will talk about my plans with you. I got an order from the King to protect our borders at any price because Germans attack us from one side and Venetians from the other side and many others from the East and West. As you can see on this small map, I think we can make a strong castle and in front of your region stop the attackers with our soldiers and weapons. We will put soldiers in the castle to scout our border and protect that entire region. If you see our enemy, you must attack them until we consolidate stronger formations to stop them," Pasa explained.

"Your highness, I do not have soldiers and castles. I have only my old mother and two young brothers," replied Mooyo.

"Today, I will send ten soldiers with my wise man to search the region around these rivers. We will find a place to build a fort and castle in your Krajina. Finding soldiers is a big problem, but Kadija and I were thinking how many prisoners we have to feed and watch, and how much money we must spend on them every day and night. Therefore, we have decided to make a military trial tomorrow. We will try all of the prisoners we have and we will threaten to hang them unless they agree to be under your command as soldiers to defend and protect your border. Everyone will get a piece of land and some forest on which they do not need to pay taxes, and their boys will be free of the requirement of military school in the Empire.

So, as of today, I am announcing that you are the commander of your region Krajina. For your faithful contribution to the King and Empire, you will get from me a thousand golden coins. How much and how you will pay the soldiers will be at your discretion. The weapons, ammunition, and other goods you will get when you are able to make a parade in front of your battalions. Of course, you will only give them weapons when you are sure they will not run away to be bandits in the forest again.

At first, you will get twenty cows, ten bulls, two hundred sheep, and enough grain for planting. You can give them the food, grain, goods, and weapons when you feel they have earned it. If you need any other help, any time, just send me a message. Every month, you will need to send me an update on how things are going in your region. Kadija and I believe that you can do it because we see in you a hero who will contribute to our Kingdom." Pasa finished his speech with a wave of his hand.

"We had a long discussion, and we think you can do it. For everything, you will be prized from our highness, the King," Kadija repeated.

Finally, Mooyo understood why they had treated him like a prince, for the little thing he had done. Should he take their offer or reject it? Knowing how his uncle left him with his family and what was in his region, the offer was not a bad thing because he needed to live there, and if someone attacked his home, he needed to defend it. His mother only asked him to come back with a cow, but he was offered so much more. Everything was there in front of him to make his decision. He realized it would be easier to defend himself and his family from a strong fort with many soldiers than to go somewhere to an unknown land and attack someone there. Krajina was his new home, and if someone tried to destroy it, he needed to protect it. Hundreds of thoughts swirled in his head, but when he added and subtracted everything, he made the decision to accept this offer and begin this new life.

"When the fort is built, I will call my uncle to be my guest," Mooyo thought.

"Thank you, your highness, for believing in me. I promise that I will secure my Krajina and keep its border safe and guarded twenty-four hours, but if stronger troops attack, I hope you will be there to help too," pledged Mooyo.

In that moment, Pasa and Kadija stood up smiling and shook hands with relief.

"Outside there are saddle horses waiting for us to see the prisoners in Banja Luka. You will be able to see how many soldiers we can have for your fort. I sent the idea to Sarajevo to their government to use the same idea about the court, and they will send more soldiers who wish to be free. In the beginning, you will use my advisor and twenty soldiers in case you have a problem with your new soldiers. If someone tries to escape, they must die where you catch them. You need to warn them," explained Pasa as they rode to the prisons on the other side of fort Kastel and above the river.

Right away, Mooyo had the opportunity to see the prisoners. He was sad when he saw the conditions in which they lived, and his heart went out to them. There were more than a hundred good, strong young men from which was possible to make a good formation, and another two hundred who could be good servants and guards.

"What do you think, knight? Is it possible to make good soldiers from these bandits in order to protect your region?" asked Kadija.

"That we will know a month or two after we offer them freedom from prison to be soldiers. As I see it, there are many strong men, and that is what we need," answered Mooyo. "Do you plan to have court today or tomorrow?"

"We will make it today after we clean them up," replied Pasa.

They rode away from the prison and down the cobblestone streets until they stopped in front of a large stone building from which they could smell charcoal. It was the blacksmith house where they make and fix weapons.

"From our Empire, we received directions for how to make powerful guns that can travel a long distance and damage thick fort walls. The blacksmiths are making them now, and when they finish, I will send at least two of that kind of gun to each fort," explained Pasa.

They checked all the plans and the mold for the new guns, and then they rode to the hills of Starcevica. Soldiers came out of the entrance of the small soldiers' station. They took care of the herd of horses and saluted Pasa.

"Do you want to choose a horse for yourself and one for each of your brothers?" asked Pasa.

"Your highness, I have already received so many presents, that I do not know how to thank you for all of them. I am scared you will think I am greedy, but I would be happy to have just one fast horse," said Mooyo blushing.

"You are now in the business with our dear Empire. Whatever you take, you take for protecting our Sultan and Empire, so do not be afraid to take whatever we offer to you," persuaded Pasa. "Young men, which one is the fastest horse on these meadows?"

"They are all very fast, but that white one that is grazing in the grass under that tree is always the first," answered one of the horsemen. Mooyo rode close to the white horse to get a closer look. He loved it immediately when the horse put his head very high to watch him without any fear. The other horses were strong and good looking, so he had a hard time choosing two for his brothers. Finally, he took the white one for himself and two similar ones for his brothers. The horsemen took them to the barn where they put saddles on them and took them to the fort.

They arrived at Kastel at noon. They ate more with plates piled with baked meat, bread, cooked vegetables and dried fruits. After lunch, they prayed, washed their hands, and together they walked to the city mosque for the mid-day prayers. The mosque was decorated with many ornaments just like a castle. The Muslim priest heard about the knight and personally came to shake his hand.

"It is pleasure to have this kind of hero in our company," said the priest, hugging Mooyo.

"I am not as big a hero as they think, but I will try to become worthy of their praise and honors," replied Mooyo.

"I hope that dear Allah will protect you in your life," said the priest.

Mooyo thanked him for his welcome and kind words, and with Pasa and Kadija he entered the place to wash their hands, legs, and face to prepare for midday prayers. Mooyo enjoyed the ritual, without minding how many people entered the biggest room of the mosque. The floor was covered with many rugs. Everyone came to Pasa, Kadija, and Mooyo to greet them until the priest gave the call for prayers.

After the prayers, young girls with handkerchiefs on their faces brought sweets and cold juice.

"Now we can go to the court room to see how many soldiers will decide to go to your Krajina and start their new lives as soldiers," said Pasa.

"You will sit in the court room, and when I finish reading the verdict, you can stand up, stand in front of us, make a bow, and plea for amnesty for all the prisoners who are willing to go with you to your Krajina and be your soldiers," Kadija explained.

"Do not promise anything to them until you take them to your land because some of them will try to run away during the first days if they see any possibility," added Pasa.

In the court room, the prisoners were sitting chained together in two rows. They sat quietly inside when Mooyo, Pasa, and Kadija entered.

Kadija read all prisoners' first and last names and then the sentences. He said, "In the name of his highness the King, all the men whose names I have read will be execute by hanging at the main market next Sunday, because of your rebellion against his highness the King and his Empire. Against this decision you cannot make any complaint."

The prisoners turned as white as linen, hanging their heads to the floor. Some of them became sweaty, and some of them started to sob softly. At that moment, Mooyo stood up, walked to the wooden table, and made a low bow.

"Your high and pleasant judge, is there any way to grant amnesty to these poor men because in my Krajina I need soldiers to protect the border, which is all the time attacked from the west, different enemies against our highness the Sultan and our Empire. We cannot protect my land if we kill all of them as you have said in your court decision. I believe that many of them would serve as valiant soldiers or servants if we could forgive them for their bad actions against our highness the Sultan and Empire," proclaimed Mooyo.

All the prisoners raised their heads to see their last hope for life and a better life.

"The decision was meant to be final, but we can change it to lifelong soldier or servant job, so that the prisoners can pay for their misbehavior," added Kadija looking to Pasa to see what he would say about the final decisions and his willingness to forgive. Nobody would have guessed that all of this was prearranged.

"Dear Knight, it is true that we need soldiers to defend our Empire, but these bandits will run away the moment you take the chains off their hands, and they will again attack and rob the caravans of goods. Again, we will need to waste our time catching them and setting up another court. However, if Kadija and you agree to this I will accept your decision. But, if any of them tries to escape, he will be hung without trial," said Pasa.

"Put your hand in the air if you agree to be a soldier for our Empire under the command of this hero named Mooyo Hrnjica from the region of Velika Kladusa, where you will under his command fight any enemy and protect every foot of our Empire.

Of course, all the prisoners threw their hands into the air as a sign that they agreed with this deal.

"Thus, from this day forward, you will be free, listen to my command, and other officers I introduce to you. I will feed you, give you uniforms, and the weapons you will receive in my Krajina when we arrive there," added Mooyo seriously.

The prisoners changed their expressions because this man had given them a second chance.

Everyone wanted to greet him, hug him, and bow to him, but the heavy chains around their hands and legs kept them in the middle of the courtroom. Pasa waved to one soldier who was next to him in a second. He whispered something. Mooyo heard and understood that Pasa wanted to make three small groups because when all of them were in one place without chains, they could protest or attack them. He wanted them in three different rooms with heavy soldiers on guard. With another wave, he called another soldier to tell him to take prisoners in small groups to the blacksmith who would remove their chains.

When the last two soldiers exited courtroom and the soldiers had closed the heavy wooden doors, Kadija spoke, "Excellent Pasa, excellent Knight. Our plan is going well."

"You were believable and strong. With this, we deserve a celebratory dinner tonight, and we will invite all the city's powerful men. I think that his highness the Sultan will be happy with the plan as we will secure this border of his enormous Empire," said Pasa, happier and relaxed.

When Mooyo heard those words "that border area" he realized that Pasa and Kadija prized other knights the same way, and that it was a well-made plan, so he was not the first nor the last who was honored in this way.

"Now that you have soldiers, you will need to wait until they build a fort, and you will be a well-known knight throughout our Empire and in the castle of our highness the Sultan. After I return from your Krajina, I will send notice to his highness about you and your family. From there, you will get the presents and recognition. Now, we can go to my sauna to relax and get a shave and haircut from my barber," said Pasa.

The young knight was still afraid to open his mouth because he was still scared they would change their minds.

The sauna had the aroma of fresh lime trees in bloom, and there was so much steam, they could barely see each other. From time to time, they heard someone added boiling water, but they did not see anyone. The little barber brought soap, a shaving knife, scissors and white towels, and started to shave their beards, and cut their hair. They enjoyed the steam that heated their bodies and relaxed their muscles.

The day ended with a dinner. This time, they were joined by many store owners, officers, and the main city Muslim priest. Around the big wooden table sat over twenty wooden chairs. On the other side of room, the musicians played fiddles and pipes. Girls served cold sour milk, water, apple juice, and everything the guests wished for. On the table, were many kinds of roasted meat, vegetables, bread, and soup, and cooked fruits.

The men talked about their business, caravans from East, and everyday life. After dinner, girls came with water and big plates and towels to wash their hands. When they were done, the priest called them to pray to God for all the food he gave them.

After praying, they moved to the sofas covered with many pillows. Many of them smoked the long pipes filled with strong tobacco. Girls served tea and coffee and disappeared behind the high door lit with small candles like Mooyo had seen before in the residency of Lichki Mustaj-beg. In the middle of the big room, the girls played in the circle, and the instrument players played faster. Everyone enjoyed the music and beautiful bodies of young girls whose faces were covered with woven cloth. They wore silk skirts and white blouses with red vests, silk handkerchiefs, and silver and golden coins. The different designs of the clothes made a beautiful mix of colors that took away all human worries. The celebration lasted deep into the night.

"Good night, and sleep well," said Pasa. "Tomorrow, we will travel to your Krajina, straight after breakfast."

"Good night to you, and thank you for all this hospitality. I will be happy to go back and see my mother and brothers. I already miss them," added Mooyo.

Seiz was there to take him to his bedroom. He undressed and made a move to turn off the candles. As he lay awake in bed, he considered the past events. It was another long day for him. He was sleeping when he felt the fairy from heaven, kissing his lips. Her hands and lips caressed his chest and body. He thought he was dreaming, so he enjoyed it without thought of anything else. How long it lasted, he did not know.

Like the previous morning, when he awoke, he was alone in the bed, thirsty and desirous to at least know the name of the fairy. If he could see her face, hair, the shape of her warm body, then one day he would ask Pasa for that girl. He took a shower for his prayers and the journey ahead. So many things had happened that he almost could not understand how it happened. Still, he must be brave and ready to make new soldiers from yesterday's bandits.

Pasa greeted him with pleasure, in the same room where they ate yesterday. He was dressed in white pants with a golden belt, and a white shirt with a red vest with golden buttons. On his head, he had a red hat with black tassels. He carried two short guns around his hips. He motioned him to sit next to him. On the table, were cooked and fried eggs, fragrant soup, bread cut into small pieces, milk, and a full wooden pot of dried fruit.

"I hope you relaxed and are well-rested for your journey to Krajina to build the castle for yourself," said Pasa, pointing to a seat for Mooyo.

"Thank you, your highness. The time I have spent here in your home has been like a dream for me," said Mooyo.

"Life is a big dream. Live and dream if you know how to dream. Life is short in this world, and you must start to cut your day in half to double it. Sit and eat, and we will see how we can combine our dreams with the dream of our highness the King and Kingdom," said Pasa.

In that way, Mooyo's trip to Banja Luka ended. He took with him bulls, cows, horses, one hundred and twenty soldiers as well as the title of commander of Bosnian Krajina. This voyage had changed his life and the life of his family.

# CHAPTER 4

## Mooyo Returns as a Knight

From Banja Luka to Kladusa the trip was much easier on the new horses. A scout and four soldiers were in front, and behind them were thirty well-armed soldiers, Pasa with Mooyo, a carriage with weapons, tools, an outdoor military kitchen, and everything else that Pasa thought they would need to build the new fort.

By noon, they were in Kamengrad, where our hero was well-known. At the fort, the commander welcomed them with all respect. They ate lunch there, prayed in the mosque, and then continued traveling to Kladusa. Mooyo was very happy because they told Pasa how he had helped them win the game of tug-of-war a few days before. He was so sure that he had chosen the right man for the commander job of that region.

By around five o'clock, all the soldiers, followers, and servants met at the Kosanica meadow, which from that day was known as Pasina Luka. There, they met the scouts and military engineers that had arrived several days before. They decided the best place to build the castle or castles to protect the region from attacks from the West. The soldiers were positioned on the hills to watch the region, the servants were setting up the tents, and Pasa, Mooyo, and his military engineers were searching for the location for the fort. On the map, they drew all the hills, streams, valleys, forests and rivers all the way from Petrova Gora to Pljesevica. Pasa was happy with their job, but he wanted to see the region in person.

"There are high hills, but we think that this one will be the best place for the fort because it will be secured by the surrounding hills, and every attack will be defeated on the other side of the river from the small bunkers. That means the fort will be secured from direct attacks because the river is a good obstacle for the enemy to cross," reported one of the engineers to Pasa.

"But why don't we build it on that hill which is higher and next to this one?" asked Pasa.

"In the case of a very strong enemy, big gun fire will always hit that hill, and the fort will be hard to reach, and for now we expect the enemy only from the West. In the case the fort cannot protect that hill and forest, there will be a chance to escape to another fort," said another engineer.

"Okay, tomorrow, we will start the buildings. Mooyo's fort can be done in four weeks. As I can see, you have enough stones around. Seven days from today, you will send me new maps of this region and news of how much of the fort is done," Pasa said to his engineers.

"With pleasure your highness," the engineers said.

"Dear Knight, my men are here for you to act as a battalion of soldiers which will stay here with you until you make your own unit and fort. With money, I promise you will be able to pay them what they deserve when the fort is under construction. Now, let's go to your mother and brothers because I'm sure they are worried about you," said Pasa.

"Thank you, your highness for not forgetting my family," said Mooyo.

In front of the tent, everyone was busy with something. The food already smelled from the big military kitchen, horses were grazing in the meadow, and others were pulling carriages. There were four soldiers with horses, the cow, and the bulls, and one smaller carriage covered with a dried horses' skin behind them on the hills above Kladusa. They took the shortest way over the meadows and small hills to be there quickly.

They found Mooyo's brothers and mother sitting around the wooden table having dinner. They stood up to see what kind of dignitary was heading to their new home. They could not believe what they saw, but they recognized Mooyo riding the tall white horse like a prince, in fine clothes, two short guns, and a long shiny sword. They greeted and hugged each other. Mooyo whispered in their ears that there was a person, with him, his highness, Pasa, from Banja Luka, his highest officers, and not to ask him about it yet. They invited them to sit around their table, and the brothers tied the horses in their new barn. Fatima and her two younger sons stood in shock for a few minutes at the remarkable change in Mooyo's appearance and the unexpected guests. Fatima bowed her head and then looked up reverently.

"Welcome, your highness. Welcome to our table to share dinner with us. It is a pleasure to have such an important man from our Kingdom," said Fatima.

"It is our pleasure to meet you, healthy and happy," said Pasa and sat on the bench around the table. The brothers came back to table and bowed. After that, they quickly brought water and towels for the guests to wash and dry their hands. Fatima served rabbit soup. Omer poured water over Pasa's hands, and Halil handed him the towel, so he could wipe his hands. The soldiers kept watch on two nearby hills even though no one was walking or traveling there besides some lost animals. After the soup, the old lady brought flat bread and two roasted wild turkeys.

"Welcome Pasa, you are lucky to come when a meal is on the table. Thank God, since we came to these hills, there has always something to eat. As you can see, we built this small home," Mooyo said, offering him pieces of roasted turkey.

"We have only lived in our new home for couple of days," explained Fatima, "If we had been here longer and had known you were coming, we would have prepared a richer feast for our special guests."

"This is all very nice, but tomorrow we will start to build you a castle, and you can give this house to some of your best behaved soldiers or anyone you choose. Then when I come to visit again, you can make a bigger feast," added Pasa, eating the turkey.

Mooyo's family sat speechless after hearing the strange news.

"Mooyo, after supper we will go back to my tent, and you can stay with your mother and brother here. In the morning, come with your brothers to organize your future soldiers. I will go back to Banja Luka tomorrow afternoon with some of my officers and soldiers. Everything else will stay here until the fort is completed. You will have a busy day tomorrow, with many jobs and responsibilities," said Pasa.

After supper and warm tea, Pasa and his soldiers rode back to Kladusa, and Mooyo stayed with his mother and brothers, horses, cow, bulls and carriage full of presents, and weapons that the people from Banja Luka had given him. His mother and brothers wished for a moment to be alone with him, so he could tell the story about all these goods and visit of his highness Pasa.

"Dear son, what is going on, and from where did these noble people come, especially Pasa? I gave you some gold and silver coins to buy a cow, and you came back with all this as if you found pots of gold. Please tell us what happened," said Fatima impatiently.

"My dear mother, I thought that we would not need anyone's help as long as we stayed together, believing in only God's help. Success comes as a reward for good and right actions. On my journey, I fought some bandits in Banja Luka in front of one rich store. I arrived at that store tired from my travels, and as I sat on the stairs to relax and eat the bread you had given me, the owners were running away from their stores leaving them open for robbers to take whatever they wanted. If they locked them, the thieves will break the doors, take what they wanted and burn the rest. The owners would lose everything.

They warned me to hide until they finished their looting. I was very tired and did not want to go away because I do not like when someone robs and takes what does not belong to him. Thus, I waited for them."

Mooyo told them what happened on his journey to Banja Luka and back, and that they needed to do work for Pasa and the Sultan to protect this region from Germans and Hungarians.

"Dear son, you have received such a great honor. We will all benefit from it. We will have a fort, a castle, and an army? Do you need to go again to be soldier?" asked his mother.

"My dear mother, if these Germans come to attack us, we will need to defend our new home and land. I thought about it before I decided to say yes to Pasa. It will be easier to protect us from a strong fort than from this little house. It will be easier to fight with strong weapons. Finally, it will be easier defend us with one hundred and twenty armed soldiers than just the three of us. To watch and protect this area, we will be paid, and it is better we are officers than soldiers for someone without heart and soul to send us in the battle to die for his recognitions, like Mustaj-beg Lichki sent our father to die for him.

We do not have land beside this, and we need to fight if someone tries to take it from us. Down there on the Kosanci meadow are one hundred and twenty bandits, who were prisoners in Banja Luka and got amnesty from me with the promise that they would be soldiers under my command. Everyone will get freedom for it, a piece of land and forest where we will together build homes. They will receive salaries, horses, and weapons, and for all that they need to be ready to defend this part of the Ottoman Empire.

I know that will be, for you and me a big responsibility, but if we are smart and stay together, everything will be okay. Pasa promised. he always help us with goods and men to protect this part of border. Tomorrow, they will start building the castle and fortifications above the stream and the meadows on the place the military engineers chose.

Mooyo pointed at the new horses. These are yours. In the carriage, you will find uniforms and weapons, and in the early morning we will go to the meadow to show them that they chose right man for that job. From tomorrow, these bandits and robbers will be transformed into soldiers. This is more than we could have dreamed of, dear mother and brothers," ended Mooyo, hugging his mother and brothers.

"Everything feels like a dream, but we will follow your decision, and I hope that God will help too. Soon we will be able to get your sister, Ajkuna, here too," said Fatima.

Mooyo's brothers were examining their horses ready to put them into the small barn they had built for the cow they were expecting their brother to bring from Banja Luka's market. After they put the horses in barn, they hurried to unload the carriage filled with goods they would need in their new castle.

There were different tools for farming, many pairs of short and long guns, saws, gun's powder, bullets, swords, and knives, and all the other presents from store owners from streets of Banja Luka. There were silk and other cloths for sewing, rugs, and so many finished suits and shoes that they could almost open their own store. Then Omer and Halil were surprised to see a cage with two small birds in it.

"Is it some special type of bird or turkey?" asked Halil, rubbing his stomach.

"These are little birds I saved from the cold and rushing water of the Una River during my first trip to Banja Luka. I did not want to leave them because they were too small to survive on their own. Maybe, they gave me luck for the events that happened. Who knows?" said Mooyo.

"I will take care of them until they grow up, and then I will let them go free," said Omer still surprised with everything that happened to them that evening.

Mooyo changed the subject. "How did you do during my trip to Banja Luka? Did anyone pass by our house or close to it?"

"Omer and Halil built the barn for the cow, hunted, and made a trap for wild animals which I cooked. Once four riders on nice horses passed us, but they did not stop. Halil was hunting, and he saw them from the hills."

That night was peaceful in their small but lovely house. Around were the sounds of crickets, which tried to put the small family to sleep. The brothers were fed and gave water to all the animals and birds, and after that they went to sleep.

When Omer woke up from his dream of riding his horse, Fatima was not in her bed.

His brothers were still asleep, so he quietly left the house to wash his face because of the superstition that you cannot see animals in a barn until you wash your face. He saw his mother doing the first morning prayers. She never woke them up, but so often, they woke up by themselves and joined her for prayers. The old woman prayed for health and luck for her boys since in them she saw all the world, gold, and other goods. She always made extra prayers for her husband too because she loved him so much. She never considered another marriage, for there was only him in her heart.

Omer gave water to the horses, cow, and bulls, and then he took them to the meadow that they had fenced in for their cow. There was a lot of grass for all of them, enough to be cut and dried for winter. Everything smelled of morning freshness, but the smell of warm tea from their fire completed that happy and beautiful morning. Mother set the cups around the table when Mooyo and Halil washed their faces. They came out dressed as if they were going to a wedding.

"Good morning, my brothers. You almost overslept this beautiful morning. I gave the water to the animals, and they are already in our pen," said Omer, who was proud to say what he did.

"It was hard to fall asleep last night," said Mooyo, trying to excuse himself. He missed the pretty fairy that came to make him sleep every night with her body moves and caresses that he would never forget. He still wished Pasa would give him that fairy more than most of those tools and weapons. She did not say her name because it must be secret, but when the building of this fort was done he would look for her.

"All three of us need to go to Kladusa, as Pasa said yesterday, to take care of the soldiers, servants, and other tools and goods that we need to build the fort. I will come home to sleep from time to time, and Halil and Omer will be here every night until they build rooms inside the fort for all of us. It is very important to look good like a real soldier in front of

Pasa, our future soldiers, and servants. Surely, it will help us to train those bandits. The first impression is always very important," said Mooyo to his brothers and mother.

"Does that mean that I need to dress up nicely and carry a weapon and sword?" Omer asked with an excited grin.

"Of course, go dress up like your brother, and I will be able to see all my sons on these big and nice horses' backs," said the old women, for it was part of the uniform of every man in Lika where they had lived previously. While Omer was getting dressed and finding the weapons, his other brothers were preparing the horses with saddles.

"What did you name your horse?" asked Halil.

"I named it Jogat, and he is the fastest and best horse from Pasa's pen, said the horseman in Banja Luka," said Mooyo.

"I will call my horse Malin because it is so calm and easy to put a saddle on its back," said Halil, tapping his horse's mane.

They hugged their mother and jumped on their horses like the three musketeers, who would surely die each for another. Their mother wiped tears of pride from her eyes. She was happy to see her three sons on horseback in their new clothes, with fancy weapons and ornaments on their uniforms, belts, and shoes.

"Watch and take care of each other. I hope that God will stay with you," said Fatima waving a white handkerchief. From a big wooden pail that Omer made of dried wood, she spilled the water behind them for good luck. She stood and watched them even when had disappeared behind the hills.

"How nice it would be if their father were alive to see them grown up and to give them some advice when they need it," she thought.

# CHAPTER 5

## Building a New Life

On the meadow near the stream, yesterday's bandits, cooks, officers, and servants were working like ants. Many carriages were loaded with stones and wood heading to the place they chose for the fort. The three brothers arrived on horseback in front of the biggest tent where the soldiers and servants had their horses, and one soldier led them to the big room in the tent where they found Pasa and his architects for the military structure. They stood up to shake hands with the three brothers, offering them a place to sit. Pasa shook their hands and let them sit next to him.

"We put everything on paper. For everything you need, my Velija will be with you until you complete the fort and until you make real soldiers from these bandits. When it is done, he will return to Banja Luka to inform me about everything you have done here. After lunch and the midday prayers, everyone will be in a parade in front of these tents to hear my words. Then I will appoint you first commander and protector of this region. From Banja Luka, I will send more cattle and grain to feed these people. While some of them are building the fort, organize others to plow the meadow to plant grain and vegetables. The region and its safety will be protected by my soldiers while I am here, but every day they will take some of your future soldiers to teach them how to watch the roadways and the region to Bihac following the river to the West and East to this big forest. Velija will teach your youngest brother how to keep track of soldiers, military goods, foods, weapons and tools as salary for soldiers and servants when you are sure they deserve it," he pointed to Omer and ended his advice.

When the sun rose above their heads, the men lined up for lunch. Pasa ate his lunch with Mooyo and his brothers in front of the plans and supplies. After lunch, every religious man made himself ready to pray the midday prayers. Everyone knew his job, and no one wanted to get in trouble, for they all knew that one mistake would land them back in chains. By two o'clock, all the soldiers and servants were in the parade line in front of Pasa's officers. Velija, Mooyo, and his brothers were in full uniform and weapons. One of the highest ranking officer's commanded "attention." They stood, and the officer commanded, "stay in your places," and Pasa talked to all the soldiers and servants declaring they recognize Mooyo Hrnjica as their highest commander.

The ceremony was short and clear. Pasa and ten soldiers headed back to Banja Luka. Mooyo and the main engineer went to the hill where the men were building the foundation for his fort and his home. Halil and some of the scouts and two bandits went to check the area of Krajine. The youngest brother went back to the tent to learn from Velija how to provide the men, food, clothes, shoes, and weapons. Velija was so organized, that Omer straight away liked his new job.

"Mooyo told Pasa in Banja Luka that you are the youngest of the brothers and that you are good in writing, reading, math, and art. It is better for him if you now take care of this responsibility because brothers will not hide something or take advantage of their privileges," explained Velija to Omer.

While they were going over the numbers, Mooyo was listening to the advice of the main engineer.

"After seven sunrises, you will be able to leave the small house and sleep here although the work will not be entirely done until about thirty sunrises. The stones are very good, and we have plenty of them. That means the walls around houses and castle will be too thick for big gun bullets to destroy. If you wish for any bigger room, just let me know, and I can adjust the plans," the main engineer said, showing the plans of the inside of fort. The men were working as if they had just woken up after a refreshing night's sleep. Nevertheless, they were scared of Pasa's soldiers, who controlled and watched them.

While checking the construction, Halil was riding with Pasa's scouts, who stopped from time to time and searched the other side of the riverbank. Everything was as calm and scenic as a fairytale. The quiet was filled with bird songs, bees buzzing, and the sounds of workers moving stones and building.

"Here we will have a break and give the horses water and food, but if someone wants to swim, the water is refreshing," said one of Pasa's officers. Even the river was cold; everyone swam and cleaned the dirt from his body.

Everything was going to plan. The walls grew higher and higher every day, and the buildings inside started to look like home. All the meadows around the area were plowed. Halil continued monitoring the region. Every bandit, now soldier was able to choose a place to build his home, and soon homes popped up like mushrooms after a spring rain. Omer learned everything from Velija, so he could easily go back to Banja Luka. Every day, they took about ten bandits from the construction site to practice military routines and begin their military education and exercise.

Amazingly, the men worked so hard that the construction was completed eight days early, which meant they needed to move Fatima from their small house by the Hura well. The move was bittersweet because she had grown accustomed to her peaceful and quiet home that her sons made with their own hands, almost from nothing. One bandit happily decided to move to their home and live in it. Omer and Velija moved from the tent to the big room with all the tools, weapons, money, that was in storage. There was a bedroom and living room for both of them. Velija was impressed with Omer's knowledge and efficiency in calculations. In his free time, Omer whittled faces in wood, making sculptures, so Velija saw a talented artist in him.

"Dear boy, where did you learn all that?" asked Velija.

"When we lived in Lika, I learned language and math with the daughter of Mustaj-beg Lichki because she had a private teacher. The carving I started by myself. The more I carved, the better I got at it. If I had better tools, it would go faster and much better, too. If you accept, I will carve your face on one piece of wood before you leave for Banja Luka," offered Omer.

"I agree. Continue carving and drawing, and I will show Pasa how good an artist you are," added Velija.

Days passed, and luckily there wasn't a single bandit who wanted to run away, which made their job easier. The soldiers continued to survey their work, as did Mooyo, Omer, and especially Halil. The workers were especially scared of him because that young, tall and muscled man was an expert with any kind of weapon or tool. If they tried to run away, their head would be cut off and hung on one of the sharp sticks made to dry the grass for cattle. Thus, they did their jobs and anything else that they were told to do. Their new homes were located on the hills around the fort, so they could hear the sounds of horns which signaled someone attacking the border. Many of them were now armed because they had earned the trust of their commanders.

After the first week, everyone received some money for their hard work, and no one felt he was a slave even though they were working for someone they had previously hated. Velija and Omer were happy to give them the first salary they earned from the money Pasa gave them. The men started working even harder because they saw that someone recognized their hard work. Their heads had been spared, and that man had cleaned them, given them drink, food, shoes, weapons, land, and loans. They were happy and thankful he showed up in the right moment. With him, they felt safe. During the military training, they saw how Mooyo and his brothers could handle any weapons. The men believed that there were no better knights from the blue sea to Vienna.

One day, good news came to Arnaut-Osman, who was the son of Hrnjica's older sister, and they came to the door of the new fort.

"We heard that a big Empire's army had come to these meadows, but we never thought you were with them," said nephew Arnaut-Osmane to Fatima and Omer.

"That is a long story, so come inside our castle, to sit and drink juice to our health and everything else, and we will talk about it," said Fatima with opened hands welcoming them.

Omer and the servants were home, but Mooyo was checking the West and Halil the East side of the border with the soldiers and former bandits.

On their way, they hunted deer, wild chickens, rabbits, or turkey, and when they came back, there was a feast. They gave the meat to the cooks to prepare a feast.

When Mooyo and Halil returned, their mother told them Arnaut-Osmane came to this part of this Empire. Arnaut-Osmane was a little angry at them for not telling him first, but he quickly changed his mood, and all agreed in the end that it was the God's will.

Mooyo began. "So, nephew if you want to be part of our forces, you are welcome. You will be an officer with a salary, weapons, and military supplies. For all that, with bandits and us, you need to help us protect this part of Empire."

Arnaut-Osmane replied, "I live off farming and hunting. Your offer is a good one because if someone attacks this region, they will attack me too, and I need to defend my home. I will be better protected with you than by myself."

"You chose wisely," said Mooyo, and they shook hands to the agreement.

"Add our cousin on the pay list, Omer. From tomorrow morning, he will bring his soldiers to the field," added Halil, smiling from ear to ear.

They talked until late evening, drinking the juice and plum brandy that their cousin had brought with him. Osman had lived in the region for a long time, and during the hunting season, he went all the way to the blue Adriatic Sea, so he knew that many forts were built on the Venetian side from the south and on the Hungarian side to the north. During the conversation, they decided that they would visit all the forts after they finished the construction and military training. They wanted to see how strong the forts were, how many soldiers they held, and what kinds of weapons they had.

"It is better to know who is in our neighborhood because good neighbors can be like brothers," added Arnaut-Osmane.

The Venetian Republic was becoming weaker because of new trade routes to the outside from Europe and the Mediterranean Sea. Every ship crossing the Mediterranean Sea with goods from Africa and Asia was taxed. Because of the new land discovered in America, all trade moved to the Atlantic Ocean, which was controlled by Spain, Portugal, England, and other Western European countries. Still, Venetians built forts to protect and maintain the border of their republic from the west. Germans and Hungarians stopped the Ottoman army in front of Viennese walls, and they started to build forts to the south in case the Ottomans attacked again. They knew that the Ottomans built their forts to protect their interests in the Balkans because they lost many battles, and they had some problems during the previous dynasty.

After thirty days, the fort for the Hrnjice family was finally complete. Every bandit now had a home, forest, land to plow and plant grains, weapons, and a salary for their hard work. Pasa sent them more horses, cattle, and four big cannons to place on the four sides of the fort.

The brothers Hrnjice invited Lichkog-Mustajbeg and Mooyo's best friend from childhood, Tale Lichanin, to visit and celebrate the end of the construction. The bandits were organized in military formations, and there was a parade in front of the fort. The main engineer handed the locks and the keys of main entrance door to the future commander and owner of the fort. From the walls, they fired each cannon. Everyone was ready to start the feast. On the tables were baked deer meat, lamb meat, turkey meat and bull meat.

Mustaj-beg Lichki came to the ceremony to show his support. Only by working together could they survive attacks from the West. As a gift, he came with some young cattle and four pairs of horses. They hugged each other as new partners. Now, they had a strong line of protection for the Ottoman border to the west. The brothers were happy and proud of themselves because for in only a month their life had turned around from banished homeless to commanders of a castle and fort. They were overjoyed with their new life, jobs, and responsibilities.

The first guest from Orashac was Tale Lichanin, the best friend of the Hrnjices. Since childhood, they had been ready to die for each other. That night, Mooyo felt happier and stronger having his right hand back at his side. He also liked his nephew Arnaut-Osman, who was the commander of thirty soldiers, but Tale was more responsible and loyal than anyone else. Even better, he brought their sister, Ajkuna, with him from Lika, so the whole family was reunited.

After two hours, Velija called them to the storage shed, where he thanked Omer, saying that he was the best bookkeeper ever. Omer handed him two wood carvings, one for him with his face, and the other for Pasa with Pasa's face. They shook hands, and Velija was ready to return to Banja Luka with some soldiers and news for Pasa that the region of Krajina would be secure. He personally believed it after living and watching how they worked hard, built, exercised, and how they watched and scouted the border. The only thing he did not like was the close relationship between the brothers and their soldiers and servants, but it was not his problem. The servants and soldiers sat together with Hrnjices at the same table and ate meals, and nobody was treated like a servant, even if they had a job they needed to do.

When they accompanied Velija, they went back to the storage area to finalize the plan for protecting the border.

Arnaut-Osman checked what was going on in the south and Lichanin Tale to the west because their views of their neighbors from their posts were clear. They still needed to know how many soldiers were in each fort, how well they were armed, and how strong they were. Meanwhile, they continued exercising with their new soldiers, watching and scouting the border, and growing as much food as possible for winter. They would meet again in Tale's house in two weeks.

"When it's time to work, we will work. When it's time to celebrate, we will celebrate," they called to Mooyo.

The party lasted three days and nights. They ate, drank, danced, and stayed awake too. Mooyo's men were living in their homes, but they knew when they needed to go on duty to watch the border.

The cattle were still together because there weren't enough for every new soldier to get one, but when their number rose, they would share, so each could have his own cow, bull, and some sheep. The soldiers who lived far from the fort got a horse. If there was danger, they could arrive at the fort quickly. Everyone knew that the noise of two small guns meant alarm, and they needed to hurry to the fort. This part of the Balkans was coming alive again since the time when many citizens had died fighting against the Ottomans.

This location was better than the old one, but the citizens needed to live well. If they were loyal to the occupation laws, they could avoid the taxes and other steps to get the land.

The former bandits started to marry, and there were many parties and weddings. Whenever there was a party, there was a dance, play, and horse and athlete races for the bread, cake, sheep, or calves. Everything depended on who the groom was and how wealthy he was. They lived the life of knights all for one, and one for everyone. They helped each other on the fields, hunted, cut wood for winter, cut the grass and collected the hay, and built barns for those who had a cow, sheep or horses.

This harmonious and happy life was there for the people who desired peace. Everyone felt the warmth of their homes and a new connection to that area. The bandits' past lives were forgotten. The land and forests provided food. They needed only peace and respect from their neighbors.

By the first winter, the barns were full of hay, dried wood, boxes of flour, store houses full of grain, attics full of dried meat, and the underground cellars full of fruit and vegetables all from their own labor. Some had wives or girlfriends from before, so they could now invite them to this part of the Turkish Empire.

Hungarians did not attack them from the west, but the scouts saw soldiers watching the border from the other side of Glina and Korana. At least, from the east, everything was as good and peaceful as it could be.

# CHAPTER 6

## Friendship and Coexistence Cannot Last Forever

There was peace between the Una and Glina rivers. The good news of the Hrnjice brothers spread from Zagreb to the Adriatic Sea, from Mostar to Gorski Kotar. The peace on the Ottoman – Venetian border was destroyed only by occasional bandits, who appeared from from the highest forest hills, where they hid and terrorized the villages, cities, or caravans and stole whatever they needed. They did not take only cattle and food; they often took young girls or boys, too. Mooyo's soldiers had to keep watch and be ready to protect the people of Krajina. Fortunately, the main travel routes of these devils didn't cross their area, so they were usually protected.

Mooyo and his soldiers often went to Zadar, Split, Obilic, Janok, Udbine, Skradin, Mostar, and other small cities and villages making new friends and building the reputation of Krajisnik. Their wish was to live in peace with their neighbors. The relationship with other people on the Balkan Peninsula was enhanced by common language, the need to exchange goods, and desire to coexist with those with different occupations.

Often Mooyo went to Senj, a small city on the Adriatic coast, where Captain Senjanin-Ivan resided. They ate and drank together and compared military skills. Everyone respected each other. Mooyo was loved, and he became a special guest in every pub or coffee shop from the sea of Kotor and beyond.

Once, during the Senjska Alka, Captain Senjanin-Ivan invited the Krajisniks to compete in a fighting game with his competitors. It was a new game for the Krajisniks, and they participated by taking a round chain with a long wooden stick. They showed that they were skilled fighters and players. After Alka, Captain Ivan invited all the competitors to a party in his fort. There they ate, drank, danced, and partied for two full days and nights. Mooyo and Ivan became blood brothers.

"Dear brother Mooyo, I am giving you my sword and my faith in case you or your family and friends get imprisoned by any Catholic knight. My people and I will get you out."

"Dear brother, Captain Ivan, I am giving you my word. If you or your family and friends get imprisoned by any Ottoman, my family and friends will free you, too," Mooyo said, hugging Ivan and giving him strong faith (ahd-u eman).

"Your fate is mine, and my fate is again yours."

Using a sharp knife, they pricked their thumbs and pressed them together. In that way, they became brothers, a Muslim with a Catholic. Those kinds of brothers are rarely found in Muslim or Catholic books, but those agreements were so often made in that region. It was very hard to say good-bye, but they needed to go back to their everyday lives and send the note to Banja Luka about the safety of the border. Thus, Mooyo's horse rode fast as lightning, and the news of the new friendship traveled far.

The peace on the Ottoman-Venetian and Hungarian border lasted for a long time, but the Ottoman troops needed to defeat the bandits on the high hills and forests. New bandits were everywhere, even on the area between Una and Glina. Robbery, arson, and kidnapping of girls or boys had become a big problem for Mooyo and his soldiers. They had to comb the forest and hills to protect the citizens from these new terrors.

Spring was almost over. The grass was green, the forest was dressed in leaves, orchards bloomed, and the meadows were full of fragrant flowers of every color. Young lambs played in lush hills.

One early morning, Halil and thirty-four Krajisniks went to scout the area. They rode all the way to Kunara Mountain. They let the horses drink from the stream and sat on the grass to take a break. They took out their food and ate their lunch. Everything around them was so quiet that they could hear the buzz of bees on the first spring flowers. That location was the end of their area, so they were not in a hurry. The hot sun, cold beer and long riding on the horses over the hills and meadows made them sleepy.

They set one man to stand guard while they napped before returning to the fort. They did not know that from the bushes the bandit Mijat and sixty other bandits in his company watched them.

The bandits waited until the Krajisnici were in a deep sleep. Then Mijat quietly crawled on his knees and elbows to the sleepy sentry, covered his mouth, and stabbed him with a knife, killing him. Luckily, young Halil woke up before they could cut off his head. He ran and hid behind some high rocks. They used their long rifles and shot behind him. They wounded him many times, but he fired back and killed four bandits, and being without shields, the bandits and Mijat ran back to the forest because they did not want to lose more friends. Halil was very skilled with his rifle, and they were not able to get to him. However, Halil was so wounded that they thought he would soon bleed to death from his injuries. He was in a lot of pain, but he tried to stay awake and calm.

At that moment, a gray falcon landed on his hand. It was one of Mooyo's birds from the River Una, which Omer trained to be with one scout all the time. Halil tore a piece of his shirt and on it made a note for his brother Mooyo. He tied the cloth to the falcon's leg, and the falcon flew toward Glina. Halil stayed behind the cold rocks, close to the Ramo well, hidden under a green pine tree. He was able to tie his wounds with pieces of his shirt, to stop the blood as much as he could. His head felt heavy, but he knew he must not fall asleep.

It was already dark when the gray falcon landed on the window of the castle. The falcon scratched at the window of Mooyo's room, but he was asleep and could not hear the bird. As always, he woke up Fatima and she ran to open the window for the gray falcon. She untied the cloth and started to cry and called her oldest son.

"Wake up, Mooyo. Get on your fast feet. Halil is dead in the mountain Kunara with thirty-four friends."

Mooyo found his two short rifles and through the still opened window shot them as an alarm. In front of the fort, his aunt Kovacevic Ramo came. Mooyo's horse was saddled, and they galloped to Kunara Mountain. They rode to Ramo's well because they knew that all travelers and bandits drank there. When they arrived, all the grass around the well was pressed down and sprayed with blood. In the grass, they found the dead bodies of the scouts. Mooyo and Ramo turned over each to find Halil's body, but they did not find it.

Then Mooyo said to Ramo, "Let's try to find tracks of a horse or man because the bandits must have taken Halil with them to the mountains."

They followed the tracks, and on one flat area in the woods Mooyo saw about fifty bandits and their commander, Mijat. Mooyo could not see Halil with them, so he attacked them. The bandits didn't see and hear him in time because they were busy baking a lamb. Some of them grabbed their rifles and shot at him, but he killed thirty of them, and the rest ran up the mountain.

Mijat tried to escape with them, but Mooyo's fast horse got him, and he fell on the grass under the horse's legs. Mooyo was wounded by bullets, but he stopped the horse, took a metal stick and hit the bandit, demanding, "Where is Halil?"

"Halil ran behind the cold stones," the bandit replied. "I do not know if he is dead or alive because darkness came. He shot and killed four of my friends, and I didn't want to lose any more of them."

Mooyo tied the bandit's hands to the saddle of his horse.

"My aunt, get on horseback and check behind every stone and cliff to see where Halil is and if he is still alive."

Ramo rode a short way when from under the pine tree, Halil called, "Mijate, leave me alone to die in the peace," Halil grabbed his rifle, thinking that Mijat was coming back to finish him. He almost shot his aunt.

"Halil, my dear child, you are safe if you can survive those wounds," shouted Ramo.

"I will survive my wounds, but I cannot get over my friends and my best friends Rajkovic Becir who died by the well. There I lost my wings and my hands," sobbed Halil.

At that moment, Mooyo came to them, and they washed his wounds with brandy, putting some special herbs on them. Then they tied them with a fresh cloth. They put Halil on Ramo's horse, so he could ride to their castle, and he commanded Mijat to dig graves for the thirty-four Krajisniks and cover them with dirt, stones, and branches. After Mijat buried them, Mooyo tied him and took him to prison. After that, he knew there would be no peace for him and his Krajina because if a bandit like Mijat had sixty friends with him, how many other bandits would there be?

When Halil got home, Fatima ran to get three barbers to take care of his wounds properly, so he would not get infections.

Halil felt much better after two weeks, but Mooyo kept him at the fort for a month. They sent a note to Tale Lichanine, Lichki Mustay-beg and nephew Osman to relay what had happened on Kunara Mountain. They set up a better sentry and watched not to lose more men than they already had in a small moment of carelessness.

# CHAPTER 7

## High Alert

Peace was broken, and Krajina was on high alert. Every day, one troop of soldiers scouted the left side of the fort all the way to Primorje and on the right side to Kunara Mountain. They learned a lesson after losing so many soldiers. Nevertheless, they continued to do business at the farmers markets in Split, Zadar and Senj. During one of the trips to Zadar, Arnaut-Osman and thirty friends were attacked in the Modrovica Valley. Brehuljic-Simun from Primorje with his troop of soldiers waited to ambush them. They were being paid by the Hungarians to bring down the Krajisniks and their allies. Osman lost twenty soldiers and was put into prison by Ban of Zadar. Brehuljic-Simun cut off the heads of the brothers Musagici and the head of Dizdarevic Meho. Orlan-bajraktare was wounded but alive and just like Halil, sent word of his injuries and the suffering with a gray falcon.

When Mooyo got the news, he jumped on the back on his Jogin and rode like an arrow to Kunara Mountain, where he could find Osman and the young Krajisniks. From Kunara, he rode to Tihonja and straight to Jadikovac Valley. While he was looking for his friends, he heard someone sobbing behind a pile of stones. Mooyo jumped off his horse and discovered the wounded Orlan-bajraktare.

"God's man, Orlan-bajraktare what happened to you, Osman, and our other friends?"

"Dear brother, Mooyo, when we returned from Zadar's farmers market, we were ambushed by Brehuljic-Simun and his many soldiers. Brehuljic-Simun killed many Krajisniks. He beheaded two brothers Musagice and

51

Mehu Dizdarevica and tried to capture Osman, and take him to Zadar, but they could not tie his hands or kill him," replied Orlan.

"Listen well, Orlan-Bajraktare. I will put you on Jogina, and it will take you to Kunara Mountain where young Krajisniks are waiting for me on a clover meadow. Tell them what happened here and wait for me no more than three days. If I do not return, that means I am in prison too," Mooyo told him, and they parted. Mooyo rode toward the stoned city of Zadar, and Orlan rode toward Kunara Mountain.

On his way to Zadar, Mooyo met herdsmen watching Zadar's cows.

"God help you, dear brother. Did your cow stay here today?" asked Mooyo, acting like a young Hungarian.

"God help you, man. My cattle were brave and calm until they banished a prisoner called Osman by the city gate because no one could tie his hands. Ban is offering a reward to whomever can tie his hands," said herdsman.

When Mooyo understand his words, he killed the herdsman, took his clothes and put them on. Then he chased the cattle to Zadar's gate, where he saw many citizens from Zadar talking about what to do with Osman because they could not tie his hands and put him in prison.

The herdsman went to the mayor to kiss his hand and please him. "Give me the strongest rope you have, and I will tie Arnaut-Osmana."

The young mayor replied, "Go away, you herdsman of Zadar. He will eat you alive before you can capture him."

Again, the herdsman pleaded to the mayor for the strongest rope. "Give me the strongest rope and let God and my luck help me."

The mayor gave him a rope for tying ships to the dock, and the herdsman walked toward Osman. Osman hit him so hard that he almost broke his bones. At that moment, Mooyo, dressed like a herdsman said in Turkish, "Calm down, calm down Arnaut-Osman. I am Mooyo, and I know you are a better fighter than I am, but you do not have my advantage. We will fight all the way to the horses, and we will jump on them and run through the gate to the green meadows."

When Arnaut-Osman heard those words, he smiled and nodded. They fought until they reached the gate and jumped on the already saddled horses and galloped through the meadows. Behind them, the soldiers from Zadar city rose. By noon, the Zadrans' could still see them, but shortly after, they could follow only their tracks. In that way, they came to Kunara, where they met many young Krajisniks ready to attack the city of Zadar to free them if they had not escaped in time.

They finally rested because the soldiers from Zadar had given up or lost their track. Thus, Mooyo made the decision to go to the castle of Brehuljic-Simun and avenge the brothers Musagice, Dizdarevic Mehu, and the seventeen other Krajisniks. One hundred young soldiers joined him to avenge their friends.

This time Mooyo made a plan. When they got close to Primorje, he told them to do attack after they scouted the area and the castle. They did as he instructed. On the edge of the meadow, he saw a tall pine tree. He rode his Jogat to the pine tree, tied it around one branch and climbed to the top of the tree. He took a spyglass from his belt, and through it he was watched the captain of the castle of Simun. The castle was high and surrounded by two tall fences. At that moment, twelve soldiers exited through a big door in the fence. Mooyo saw carriages drawn by four black horses. Captain Simun's love was in one of the carriage. They were heading through the meadows to a garden beside a small stream. They all stopped, and from the carriage stepped out Simun's beautiful wife. When Mooyo saw her face, both of his hands were shaking so much that his spyglass fell. He picked it up and put it under his shirt, jumped on his horse and hurried to the bushes where he left his brother and friends. Mooyo was awestruck by the beauty of Simun's wife, and he told them from his horse what he saw. They jumped on their horses and galloped through the meadow to the garden. When the Hungarians' saw Mooyo, they turned their guns on him. He was far away in front of his friends because of his fast horse and wish to get to the woman first.

"Stop right there, Mooyo from Kladusa! If you do not stop, you will die here!" yelled the Hungarians in unison.

Mooyo did not care about their warning. He galloped straight to them. The Hungarians shot their rifles. Just then, the young Krajisniks attacked and killed twelve Hungarians. Simun's wife jumped onto a carriage horse and she kicked the horse to gallop back to the castle.

Jogat was faster than her four mares, so he ran in front of them and turned them back to the garden from where his other friends came. From the carriage, Mooyo took Simun's wife and put her on his horse behind his back. They collected weapons and horses from the dead Hungarians and galloped back to the mountain.

On the mountain, Mooyo handed his horse to Simun's wife to walk it around the place where they were going to rest and drink some beer. There

Mooyo saw that he had lost the small guns from his saddle. He had carried them with him since he got them.

"Oh no, where did I lose my guns?"

The woman answered. "How much they praise you. Mooyo is the best hero in the world, but he is sad because he lost his two guns. Do not be sad about the guns. If you take me to Kladusa alive, I have in my pockets many golden coins with which I will buy you much better guns."

"I have many different guns, but those were special to me," he said. "You will stay here on the mountain. Put the sentry all around and watch for bandits. I am going back to find my guns," he said, jumping on his horse and riding back down the mountain.

He returned to the tall green pine tree, where he spied Simun's castle. There, in the grass, he found his two guns and got the idea of going to the castle and setting it on fire as revenge for their killing the Krajisniks. He rode through the double fences and hid his horse behind the castle. He entered the first door and was in the living room where old Brehuljic was sitting. When he saw Mooyo, he took his sword from the wall and attacked the foreigner.

"How did you come to this white castle? What devil brought you here? Did you come to rob the castle or to lose your head in it?"

Mooyo took his sword from his belt, and they started to fight in the large room. In one swing, he hit the old man on his leg, and the old man fell through the window, falling on the cobbled-stones in the yard. He died when he hit his head on the stones.

Mooyo sat in the old man's chair and finished his cold beer, but through the broken window, he saw a cloud of dust rising high in the sky. From that cloud, close to the castle came a young man on a black horse. The man was dressed in silk and shiny gold. When Mooyo saw his long mustache, he realized that he was Brehuljic Simun. Mooyo became nervous because he had heard that Simun was a strong and skillful knight.

On his way to the castle, Simun saw dead soldiers in the garden. When he opened the gate to the castle, he found his father's body by the castle wall. It was as quiet as midnight. He took three men's heads from his saddle bag, and threw them in the yard. His father was still warm, so Simun realized that the man who had killed his soldiers and father and taken his love could not be far from the castle. He jumped on horseback and galloped like lightning to the mountain.

Mooyo became worried about Simun going to the mountain and killing his brother and other friends. From the fireplace, he took some fire and set it on the wooden floor. He ran down to the yard, collecting the heads of his fellow Krajisniks. He jumped on his horse and galloped to the mountains after Captain Simun. Mad and sorrowful, Simun galloped to the first row of young pine trees. When he turned his head toward his castle and saw smoke and flames rising from his roof, he realized that he had left someone in his home that was burning. He turned his horse and rode back home as fast as possible. Soon, he saw a man on horseback, and when they came close to each other, they started the fight like two lions.

"Bastard, from Kladusa, Mooyo, it was easy to take the feathers from the birds, but you need to fight with an eagle." He was so happy he found the man who had made a mess of his home and family and to get revenge for his soldiers, father, love, and castle.

When Mooyo hit Simun, the fire touched the ground and burned the grass. When Simun hit Mooyo, the fire touched the ground and burned the grass. They both broke their swords, and threw the handles in the grass. Then, they fell on each other on the burning grass. They fought with their hands for two hours, until blood and white foam oozed out of their noses and lips. Mooyo dreamed of calling his brother for help.

"Where are you Halil? Please help your brother if you are somewhere."

Simun was exhausted and scared that another brother would be coming to help, so he looked around. Suddenly, Mooyo jumped on him, and with his broken sword beheaded him. After that, Mooyo tied Simun's horse to the saddle of his horse, jumped on his horse, and rode to the well in the garden where he washed his face and hands. When he caught his breath, he jumped on his horse and rode up to the mountain. Far away in the sea, he could still smell the smoke from Simun's burning castle.

He had avenged the Krajisniks, but he was unhappy because he thought how long he needed to revenge his soldiers, family, and his home. He knew for sure these knights were the ones that had ruined their peace and happiness.

On the mountain, he met the wounded Orlan-Bajraktare, his brother and cousin Arnaut-Osman, the Krajisniks, and Simun's wife. When she saw Simun's horse, tied to his saddle, she said, "Look. It's Mooyo the bandit from Kladusa. He stole my husband's horse."

Mooyo put his hand in the saddlebag, pulled out Simun's head, and handed it to her. When she saw the head, she started to cry. Halil gave her a long hug, trying to comfort her. They went to Krajina where Mooyo married Simun's widow. He made the wedding party after two weeks because by then the young lady felt safe and happy in the hands of the young knight, forgetting her past, beliefs, and looking for a better future in the new castle. However, his mother wasn't happy with his decision. Only Ajkuna was excited.

The groom was very lucky and happy, but in his head was still the question of why men who spoke the same language, lived in the same region, and had almost the same customs so often killed each other?

When Mooyo married and settled down, his brothers started to think about their futures. One morning, Omer, dressed in his best clothes and decided to go to Lika, where he left his childhood sweetheart. Mooyo did not like it, but he wouldn't stand in his way.

The areo on the other side of river bank was very safe, so they let him go there with two friends. They left happily, but they never came back alive. Only the gray falcon returned, which was sad news for the brothers and their mother. How could they lose such a warm and generous man who was loved by everyone in the city?

The other brothers took thirty soldiers and jumped on their fastest horses following the path to Lika. When they came to the Korjenica spring, a bandit named Stojan and his crew attacked them. The young Krajisniks defeated them with their swords and rifles. Some bandits and Stojan were killed immediately, and the other bandits threw their weapons to the ground and raised their hands in surrender. The surviving bandits told the story of how they ambushed the young boys, killed them, and took their horses, weapons, clothes, food, and coins. Then, they showed them the place where the Krajisniks found Omer and his friends lying dead. They forced the bandits to carry their bodies back to Kladusa, where they buried them properly. Mooyo and Halil cried in despair.

The Krajisniks were overwhelmed with sorrow and fear. Such frequent attacks from bandits seemed impossible to stop. In addition, there had been no rain for two months, so most streams and rivers were nearly dried up, and the crops were dying. Pasa from Banja Luka asked Mooyo to collect taxes in goods or coins from the citizens, but they did not have enough food for themselves. Mooyo knew very well what conditions the citizens of Krajina were in, so he sent a letter with his man to Banja Luka in which he stated that his people were on the verge of starvation due to the summer drought, and that they could not take from them what they did not have for themselves.

Pasa didn't like his letter because he needed to send taxes to the Sultan, so he felt as if Mooyo had refused his command and forgotten all he had given to him. In his eyes, it was a betrayal.

Thus Pasa wrote a slanderous letter to the Sultan against Mooyo. He claimed Mooyo took taxes from one storeowner to the sum of forty thousand grosha, and he didn't send the money to the government. After that, a verdict came to the Mehmed-Pasa Vucho to kill Mooyo and five Krajisniks who refused to follow the central command. How much conditions had changed for Mooyo and his people.

Mooyo, Halil, Osman, and Tale Lichanin realized that they needed to fight the Ottoman Empire if they wanted to keep their heads on their shoulders. They thought that the Ottomans would help them, but if the Krajisniks could not comply with an unreasonable request, the Ottomans would turn on them and kill them. To make the Krajisniks scared, Mehmed-Pasa Vucho sent them a copy of the Sultan's verdict with Mehmed-aga, and he asked them to follow the government's command.

To scare Mehmed-aga and his soldiers, the Krajisniks shot their biggest cannon from the top of the fort wall, which turned Pasa back. After much contemplation, Mooyo decided to change his lookout and his name, shave the mustache, stop cutting his hair, and paint his white horse many colors. Even with the disguise, Mooyo rarely left the safety of his region.

Meanwhile, his wife gave him his first baby son, whom he named for his fallen brother, Omer. No one in the world was happier at the birth of a son than Mooyo. From the knight that was always on the go from Kotar to the Adriatic Sea, he became the best family man.

However, due to the Sultan's order, the brothers spent many days digging tunnels from the fort to the nearest forest. If a much stronger enemy attacked them, they could safely escape to the mountains.

# CHAPTER 8

## Onward to Obilic

Despite the hard, dry summer, the Krajisniks survived the winter and entered the spring. Finally, peace returned to their region. However, Mooyo missed his friends and brother, Captain Senjanin-Ivan, so he decided to visit him. He took his wife and son, and in the fort he left his infantry. Captain Ivan was very happy to see his dear guest, so he made a special party. However, the next morning a man arrived covered in dried blood. It was Kovacevic Murat-Beg, wounded and close to death. When they washed his face, he opened his eyes and mouth.

"Where were you Mooyo when we needed you? When we needed you, you were not there. The enemy burned your castle to ashes, killed your dear mother and kidnapped your sister."

Mooyo put his head in his hands and wept for his dear mother. Finally, he looked up.

"Do you know which enemy it was, how many soldiers were there, and who their commander was?" asked Mooyo.

"There were about fifteen hundred soldiers. One commander who was on a white horse had a long black mustache and was dressed in silk and gold. The other was on a black horse and had a thin mustache, a wide forehead, and a golden medal on his chest."

"Oh, my dear Murat-Beze, that was Jankovic-Stojane and Milan Cesedzija from Obilic city."

"Oh my dear brother, I need to go to Obilic and free our sister from them," said Halil without hesitation.

---

"Slow down, my brother. We can go to Obilic and lose our heads there because they are expecting us. On the road to Obilic, they have surely set many ambushes. Listen to me. I will write a note for you to take to my brother priest Ridjanine in Garista. Tell him who you are and why you have come to him, and he will help you reach Obilic and free our sister. We must use our brains not our anger and muscles," said Mooyo. On a piece of cloth, he wrote a short letter to his trusted friend and gave it to Halil.

"You will ride on my horse. Because of the disguise, no one will know in Obilic will recognize it as mine. But, even on my horse, you will need to ride about two days to Garista, where in the middle of village, there is a castle with seven floors, covered in a yellow metal. Feel free to say everything to my friend. He will help you free our sister. I am going back to our fort to collect soldiers, and go to the forest where we will wait for five days. If you do not show up, the soldiers and I will attack Obilic. I don't care who will die or survive because burning our home and enslaving our sister and killing our mother is unbearable."

They said their good-byes and parted. Captain Ivan shared their pain with his brothers. He loaded a carriage with goods that they would need to restore their burned home. Mooyo went home with his wife, son, the wounded Murat, and other friends. Beside their fort, they found Tale Lichanin, Osman-Arnaut, and many other Krajisniks, already rebuilding what their enemies had burned. Mooyo told them where and how he sent his brother. He also told them his plan to organize Krajishniks to attack Obilic.

"Dear friends, it was the only way I could stop Halil when he heard what happened here. He wanted to go to Obilic right away when the news came to us.

That same day, after fixing the roof, they met in front of the fort. At the fort, they left carpenters and roofers to work and set soldiers to watch the area while three thousand prepared to go to Obilic. They buried his mother, and three thousands men prayed for her soul with the promise that they would avenge her death. She was an innocent victim of this useless violence.

In Garista village, the orthodox priest Ridjanine saw the rider and waited for him with his rifle, but when Halil told him who he was, the priest welcomed him as a dear guest.

"Thank God for this day. I can see Mooyo's younger brother, Halil."

With his opened hands, he directed him to his yellow castle to meet his daughter, whom Mooyo had saved once from bandits. Once, bandits had robbed the priest's home and taken his daughter with them as a slave. Mooyo had freed her and returned her to her father. After that, the three of them had become like family. She took care of Halil's horse with pleasure.

"How is my brother Mooyo-Aga?"

"Mooyo was well in our Kladusa until someone ruined our peace," said Halil and quickly told her all that had happened there.

"I believe it because my house has been struck by many soldiers."

Then his daughter, Ruzica, set the table with drinks and food, and they talked about everything. Halil showed him Mooyo's letter, and the priest understood what must be done. Halil went to sleep, and in the morning, the priest brought clothes for Halil to disguise himself as a Hungarian soldier. While they were having breakfast, the young Ruzica made a bundle with food and drinks for their journey to Obilic. They rode all the way to the meadows in front of Obilic.

"In front of us is Obilic. I cannot go any farther with you because Milan Cesedzija can be suspicious and cut off my head. There are seven guards at the city gate. They will ask you the password. If you don't give the correct one, they will not let you enter. The priest handed him a paper with the password.

"You must enter the city before darkness, and in the middle of city you will see a bar. Get off your horses and go inside the bar. Ask for the waitress, Luca. She is like a sister to Mooyo and me. Feel free to tell her who you are and why you have come. She will help you free your sister."

The priest wished Halil and his men good luck. Halil went to Obilic, and the priest returned to Garishta. Everything happened as the priest had told him. After giving the password, they let him enter the city, and from there, it was easy to find the bar. Luca looked closely at Mooyo's disguised horse. After examining it, tears came to her eyes. She recognized the horse but did not realize it was Mooyo's brother.

"Young captain, did you buy that horse for money, or did you get it in a duel?"

Halil played a joke on the young waitress.

"I got this horse in the duel, in the mountains. I cut off Mooyo's head."

When she heard these words, she began crying. Halil asked her, "Do you like the knight Mooyo, more than me?"

"Oh, dear God, I like Mooyo more than three hundred young captains. Mooyo is my God brother."

Halil's heart went out to the sad and loyal waitress. "Oh Lucija, in truth, dear lady, I am Mooyo's brother, Halil. It was a cruel trick I played on you, and I am terribly sorry."

When Luca heard this, she left the horse and ran to hug young Halil.

"Of course, Mooyo told me about you. Thank God for this day that I can see you with my own eyes," said Luca, still holding Halil in her embrace.

"Go inside while I feed your horse, and you can tell me everything that has happened with you."

She took the horse to the barn, and Halil entered the bar where a few men were sitting around a wooden counter. When Luca returned, she took him to the second floor, with drink and food. There, Halil told her the news.

"Mooyo and Priest Ridjanine sent me to you for help freeing our sister."

"I'll do whatever I can."

Because Halil came to her dressed as a young Hungarian captain, she thought of disguising him as a young girl.

"Oh, Halil, dear brother, you are more beautiful than any girl. You are white, but I will make you whiter. You are ruddy! I will make you ruddier. Then, I will take you to the sister of Milan Cesedzija, as if you were engaged with Mandusic Vuk whom they fear greatly."

"I am in your hands, dear sister. Do what you think it is the best," Halil agreed.

Thus, Luca dressed Halil as a young and poor bride of Mandusic Vuk. They walked to the city. On their way, young citizens asked Lucija, "From where comes that beautiful young girl?"

Lying sweetly, she said, "This is my cousin from the village. She is going to marry soon, but she doesn't have any attire. That is why I am taking her around our city. If you can offer any goods for her, I will appreciate it."

In this way, they got many presents and some money until finally they came to Milan's gates. There were four gates, and on every gate were four alert watchmen.

"Do not be afraid, when you see Milan Cesedzija because he can discover our mission and join our plan," advised Lucija.

At last, they met Milan, who was suspicious of the girl, but when Lucija told him who was engaged to her, Milan shivered, choked, put his hand in his pocket, and handed the girl thirty silver coins.

"Take her up to the white castle, to my sister Rosandra. She will give her some goodies too."

The waitress took the girl up to the white castle to the room of Milan's beautiful sister. They entered the room, and Rosandra welcomed them.

"God has given us a good, young waitress."

Lucija kissed her hand. Halil looked over the wide and beautiful room. He saw his sister Ajka sitting on a soft pillow, leaning with her hands on a window with tears in her eyes and face. His heart raced, but he tried to stay calm.

"From where comes this beautiful girl?" asked Rosandra.

"This is my cousin from the village. She is engaged, but she doesn't have any of her bridal attire, so I brought her to you to see if you could give her something."

At that moment, Rosandra looked at Halil, and in her heart she thought, "This is not the forehead of a girl."

She took a picture from her pocket, and studied it and Halil. She was not fooled, for when she saw him, she immediately recognized him.

"You know what, waitress Luca? You can go back to your bar and sell wine. Leave this girl for a day or two, and then come back for her. The two of us need to talk with Milan's fiancee because she is still very sad, and she hasn't decided to marry my brother yet. Possibly, we will make her happy and persuade to marry him." Rosandro led Luca to the door.

At midnight, everyone in the white castle fell asleep. Then, Rosa spoke to Halil.

"Oh, Halil, why do you hide here in this room, when you don't have toil or trouble?"

Halil told her, "Most beautiful Rosandro, call me Turkish, but I am not without trouble."

"Stay well, Mooyo's Halil. You think I do not know you? I spent much money getting your picture a long time ago. Please tell me the truth."

"Oh, Rosandro, I pledge to you like God, do not tell on me. Instead, help me free my sister."

Rosandra nodded and promised Halil, "Oh, Halil, my heart is yours. I will help you free your sister if you promise to God you will take me with you."

Halil looked at her soft skin and kind, brown eyes. "I swear to God I will not leave you," he promised.

That day had been long for Halil and Luca and even longer for Mooyo and the young Krajisniks waiting anxiously in the hills above Obilic. When darkness came, everyone walked around the city. Milan Cesedzija walked with his captains, too. The walk ended in the bar the next morning.

"Oh, Halil, the holder of my heart, it is time for us to leave now," said Rosa, kissing and hugging Halil.

The girls got dressed, and then Rosa ran down to the gate and commanded her servants to saddle three horses for her. The servants were surprised at her sudden departure, and they asked, "Where are you going, dear miss?"

"I will take this young Turk for a ride to our new white church to raise her spirits because she is so melancholy,"

The servants believed her story and hurried to saddle the horses. She took Milan's black horse and hurried with Halil and young Ajkuna. The three jumped on the horses. Ajkuna still didn't know that the third girl was her disguised brother, Halil. They came to Luca's bar.

Halil rushed to Luca and told her, "Dear waitress, please give me a fast horse and my weapons to return quickly to my Krajina."

Luca went to the barn and returned with Mooyo's horse and her dark mare. She filled a sack with things she needed to carry with her. They rode to the city gates and over the meadows to the hills and mountains above Obilic.

Meanwhile, Milan came home from a bar to find the castle empty. He ran to the barn, but the horses were missing. Milan realized what had happened, and how his suspicion was right. He gave the command to the big gunner to fire the cannons and sound the alarm to chase Halil and the girls. People rushed to Milan's castle.

"What happened tonight, dear master?"

He told them the story. "Tonight my slaves and sister escaped."

Milan jumped on a small horse, and they galloped over meadows, while his soldiers rode over hills to chase Halil and the girls. Halil and the girls heard the cannons, and they realized that Milan and his soldiers were behind them. They galloped as fast as they could to reach Krushevac Mountain.

By sunrise, they were on the mountain, from which Mooyo through his monocle spied Halil, the girls, and the chasers.

Mooyo commanded his army, "Dear brothers hiding in ambush. Don't call Halil. We will let him pass through our line, and then burn his pursuers. I will try to shoot Milan Cesedzija, and you, brothers revenge Krajishniks and the fort."

In a short time Halil and the girls arrived, followed by Milan and many soldiers. When Milan came close to the Krajisniks, Mooyo shot him in his forehead. Soon, the waiting Krajishniks attacked the other soldiers and there was a big battle. When the soldiers from Obilic realized that Milan was dead, they ran back to Obilic. Many lay dead on the mountain although the Krajishniks had very few wounded. They took horses and weapons from the dead soldiers from Obilic and followed Halil to the lakes. From there they rode back to Krajina, proud they had fought back bravely.

They restored the fort and castle, and Halil married Milan's sister, which pleased them both. From then on, they never left the fort unguarded because their enemy, allied with foreign friends, always tried to attack them. Many of them tried to kill Mooyo and destroy that fort and control all Krajina.

For many enemies, Mooyo's horse was the main problem because although his Jogat could not win races, he had saved him from numerous dangerous situations.

# CHAPTER 9

## Another Plot against Mooyo

One time, in the castle of Jankovic-Stojane on Kotar Mountain, four friends met and talked about Mooyo's horse. They were Captain Gavran, Captain Janichic, Captain Stojan, and a bandit named Paun. They were drinking, eating, and talking about countries, cities, horses, and knights. During their conversation, they mentioned Krajina, Mooyo, and his good horse.

"Listen to me, my three friends. We surrounded and ran many times behind Mooyo, but he has a good horse that always takes him above our soldiers circle. If we can find a knight who is able to steal his horse, and bring it to us in Kotar, we can easily clip his wings. I will give that knight two bags of gold and silver coins. I will build him a castle next to mine, but bigger and more beautiful. I will buy him the finest furniture and everything he needs, and on top of that, I will give him my sister in marriage. If we can only find that hero," said Jankovic-Stojane.

When Paun heard it, he said, "Here sits the hero born of my mother. I will go to Mooyo in Kladusa. I will serve him for a year, and then I will steal his horse and possibly kill him. I will return with the horse and his head for the price you are offering. When I leave you, you must write a letter and send it by pony to Mooyo. In the letter, say I killed forty of your soldiers and two officers. Then write if he ties me and brings me to Kotar, you are ready to make a friendship with him." Thus, the bandit made a plan to steal Mooyo's horse.

With that promise, all three captains shook hands. The bandit asked for a promise from them that if he did the job, he would get the promised rewards. Stojan's servant brought paper and ink, on which Stojan wrote the promises that whoever steals Mooyo's horse and brings it to Kotar would receive: two bags of money and a castle equipped with everything needed. On top of it, he will give him his sister as a wife. He signed the paper, and the other two captains signed it as well. Finally, they called for a judge and handed him the paper, to save it until Mooyo's horse was brought to them.

"Listen to me captains, I swear on my cross and faith, that I am going straight to the Krajina, and I swear I will not hide from the Turks," said the bandit Paun, standing up from the table.

"Listen to us Paun. Be smart, and do not die a fool. Do not lose your head for nothing and shame us. We stand behind our promises. We will send the letter after you get there. We will wait here for your return with Mooyo's horse."

The captains stayed there drinking wine, and the bandit left them because he wanted to prepare for his journey. They wished him good luck.

Paun entered the border of the Ottoman Empire. On the border, the lookouts stopped him with their rifles ready to shoot.

"Where are you going bandit, Paun?"

"I am no longer a bandit, I hung my rifle on the wall, and I will never use it again. Being a bandit was very painful for me. When I had lunch, I didn't have supper. I am mailman now, for those who pay me, I take their mail. I am going to Kladusa to take this letter from Janko-captain to Mooyo."

The soldiers could not believe his words, but they let him go because he was a good liar. Thus, he rode on his horse all the way to Krajina and Mooyo's white castle. Mooyo and Halil were sitting and at first did not recognize him. They were sure that it was a mailman from faraway. Halil took Mooyo's monocle and immediately recognized the rider.

"On horseback is the bandit Paun. He has come here to die. I will cut off his head, for he has caused much trouble in our area."

"Oh, Halil, my only brother, is that a brave solution? We don't cut our enemies' heads when they come in peace as a guest," advised the older brother to his younger one. Just then, the rider came to the front door of their fort.

"Give the command to the servants to hold his horse, and you can follow him up to my room, to discover the reason he came to our doorstep," said Mooyo to Halil, who listened and followed his wish.

The servants and Halil welcomed Paun, and he greeted them respectfully, asking to talk with Mooyo. The servants took the bandit's horse to the barn, and Halil and Paun walked up the stoned stairs to Mooyo's room. There, Mooyo met them. They greeted each other. They invited him to sit on the sofa, and the servants brought a pipe and coffee. In Krajina, they welcomed their guests, whether friends or enemies in that way. When the guest relaxed, Mooyo tried to assertain why he came there.

"Welcome to our home, but I am surprised you found the bravery to come to Kladusa."

"Dear master, Mooyo-aga, I have heavy problems, and it is one of the reasons I came to you. When I tell you my problems, if you do not understand me, cut off my head. On the other hand, if you understand me, spare my head."

"We never cut the heads of our kind guests, but tell us what problem has brought you here?"

"I swear to God, I served Captain Janchic for fourteen years. I secured ways on the mountain with a hundred soldiers, but for that job, I was almost not paid as much as my soldiers. One day, it was enough, so I jumped on my horse and went to Kotar to ask for the money they had promised for our job. Janko wanted to delay payment until the New Year. We fought, and he called his security to tie me and put in prison. I took my sword and cut many soldiers and his brother Captain Milan. I ran to my horse and escaped to mountain Kotar. If I go to another master or captain I know that one will give my head to Janichic, so I decided to come to Kladusu. In that way, I came here, and you can do whatever you decide," said Paun.

Mooyo was duped, but Halil and the servant Radojica Mali did not believe his story. However, they could not say anything against the decision of an older man.

From that day, Paun was a lookout in that region. While fighting with other bandits, Hungarians and others, Paun was a well-skilled and loyal soldier. The news spread everywhere.

One morning, they saw a new mailman on horse, with a letter on a wooden stick. Halil waited for him at the gate and paid him for the piece of paper. He took it to Mooyo in their castle. The letter had come from Kotar, asking Mooyo to deliver them Paun because all the commanders from that region were looking for him. In exchange for Paun's head, they wanted to make peace with the Krajishniks. Mooyo now believed Paun even more, but it did not convince Halil or Radojica Mali. They told him how the bandit would cause them huge damage, but Mooyo did not pay attention to their pleas. He took Paun with him around Krajina and even to parties. Paun's plan was going well.

One night, Mooyo decided to go to a party with other well-known knights, and he called Paun to join him. Paun said he had a headache, so he stayed in the fort. Mooyo went to the party with Radojica Mali. Halil was with his love Rosandra in their room, but he didn't trust Paun, so he put his horse in a special locked barn. When it was very dark outside, Paun ran to the room where they secured weapons. He took what he could carry and walked barefooted to the barn with Mooyo's horse. With a knife, he cut the horse's blanket, and tied it over the horse's hooves. In that way, Halil could not hear the clatter of the horse's hooves over the stones. When he was done with it, he jumped on Jogat's back and rode in the direction of Kotar. After that, Mooyo and Radojica returned from the party to find the gate of the fort wide open.

"Why is this gate open?" asked Mooyo and Radojicu.

Radojica ran to the barn, but Mooyo's horse was not there.

He quickly ran back and said, "Dear master your horse is not in the barn."

He breathlessly ran up to the room with the weapons, but Halil's weapons were missing, and the bandit was not in his room.

"Dear master, Halil's weapons are missing, and Paun is not in his room," said Radojica.

Mooyo called his servant. "Run, Rade, and jump on Halil's horse. I will give you my weapons to follow Paun to Kotar. We will follow you shortly in Kotar," commanded Mooyo.

Rade quickly jumped on horseback, grabbed Mooyo's weapons, and followed the bandit to Kotar. Mooyo sounded the alarm for help from other Krajishniks.

"Halil, send whoever comes to our fort to Kotar because Paun has robbed us terribly," he said, jumping on Paun's horse.

By then, more than a hundred horsemen with weapons were already waiting in front of the fort, and they all galloped behind the servant Rade. He knew the shortest way to Kotar. When he rode over Jadar Mountain, he came to the meadows. In front of him, he saw a horseman trotting unaware that someone was behind him. Mooyo looked through the monocle as Rade chased the bandit. At the end of the meadows was the fort of Captain Janichic. The guards saw Paun, and they opened the fort gate for him. When Rade saw Radojica Mali, he stopped Halil's horse and took out the long pipe rifle, aimed and shot Paun. The bandit fell off the horse, and the horse stood by his dead rider.

The young Krajishniks watched the events. When the horseman fell off the horse, they hurried to the fort. The Kotorans jumped onto their horses and chased behind the Radojica, who jumped off Halil's horse, took his guns, cut off Paun's head, and jumped on Mooyo's horse. He finally galloped toward Red Cliffs. Rade fled over the meadows and behind him galloped three hundred Kotorans with Captain Janchic in the lead on a giant black horse.

Janko fled like crazy in front of his Kotorans and called Radojicu, "Bastard, bandit Radojica, I will chase you until I cut you even if I lose my head, too."

When they saw the young Krajishniks, they made an ambush for the chasers on Red Cliffs and waited until Radojica crossed their ambush line. When he passed through, he went behind Captain Janichic and three hundred Kotorans in the range of their guns. The fire landed on the chasers. The fight lasted nearly two hours, leaving more than half the Kotorans and Captain Janichic dead on the mountain. When they saw their dead leader, they fled back to the fort of Captain Janichic. Mooyo kissed Radojicu on his eyes. The Krajishniks collected weapons from the dead Kotorans, took their horses, and happily rode back to Krajina.

"Dear Rade, what were you planning to do if Paun had passed through the gate?" asked some Krajishniks.

"In the name of God and my faith, I would have chased him even unto death. I would have ridden on Malin through the gate into the fort as well," Radojica boasted to Mooyo and young Krajishniks.

Mooyo promised Radovan, "In your Glamoch, I will build you a white castle because you saved my Jogat."

After that, they were happy and satisfied that they had squashed the plan of the three captains and one bandit. With a song on their lips, they returned to their Krajina. Mooyo kept his promises and Radojici Malom built a castle in the middle of the Glamoch meadows. When the castle was done, they became brothers forever.

# CHAPTER 10

## A Well-Deserved Rest

Unfortunately, because of the empire's unfair disagreement with Mooyo, he spent most of his time in Krajina although sometimes, he disguised himself and visited his friends and blood brothers, who were still loyal. Often, he discussed the unfair taxes from the Ottoman Empire with his friend Captain Ivan, Priest Ridjanine, and other blood brothers and allies. The years passed quickly, and he watched his son grow into a young man who needed adventures of his own.

Over the years, foreign invaders had grown more powerful, and all the knights and people from the Balkans were so disunited because of small squabbles and disagreements about rank in the army, that Mooyo and his friends did not know how to unite them despite their common language. In addition, they continued to be disgusted by the Ottoman occupation. As foreigners brought different religions to them, they had to adjust and serve the foreign invaders.

Mooyo got news from his blood brother and friend, Captain Ivan, that wealthy men wondered if something had happened to Mooyo, so they sent spies to report whether he was alive or dead and take him to Pasa, who would then send his head to the Empire in Constantinople. He knew that he needed to do something because his enemies were still trying to kill him.

"It works in that way, my friend. When they need you, they dress you in gold, but when you are no longer useful, they cut off your head. I will have the same problem someday my friend, but we need to be smart to keep our heads on our shoulders," said Captain Ivan.

"Do not worry. I will find some way to keep them away from my head," Mooyo said, trying to hide his worry.

"If I can help you in any way, you and your family can count on me," said Ivan, shaking Mooyo's hand.

There, they parted. Mooyo no longer used his old pathway to go back to Krajina, but instead traveled a secret path through the forest. He wanted to leave Krajina. He could no longer trust people. He trusted only his brother and friend Tale Lichanin. When he stopped by a lake where his horse drank water, he got the idea of faking his death in town. He knew the people who spread gossip in Krajina. They would pass the news all around the region and beyond. When he got back to his castle, he told Halil the story from Captain Ivan and about his plan to hide from the public. Mooyo bought a small house in Kamengrad using the name Mustafa Kozlic and moved there with his wife and son. After that, he returned to fake his death. His friend Meho Katarica had died in a fight with a bandit named Jovan. He devised a fake story about how Katarica had killed Mooyo with a golden bullet from a long pipe rifle because the townspeople believed regular bullets could not kill him. Katarica allegedly found Mooyo with his wife, and killed him by the village Pozvizd. In order to make the story more believable, they said Halil found and killed Meho Katarica, to avenge his older brother. Everyone believed his story, and Mooyo could live quietly for a while.

Mooyo raised his son, teaching him about everything that life and survival requires. Although he missed horse races and the places he used to visit before, all his hopes and dreams were placed on that young man. There, in the main street, Omer became a man. Mooyo opened a store, where people from Kamengrad could buy silk, and other necessities. Mooyo invited his friend Captain Ivan, who had a business in Senj too.

However, eventually, his longing for his castle above the stream of Glina corroded the knight, pushing him to jump on his horse and visit the hills above Kladusa. He longingly watched the fort where he could not live anymore. Often, he brought his son Omer, to teach him that the fort and castle were once built for him as a reward for his heroism. Halil and Mooyo showed him the tunnels, which they had dug, so only they knew how to get in and out of the fort undetected.

They wished for better days when they could return to their fort and castle and live happily, but the next years were worse and even more cruels.

Burning with desire to return to his home, Mooyo aged quicker. When he could not get rid of his longing for his castle, he decided to move to a small place named Pecigrad. Soon, he got sick, and during the night, Halil took him to their castle, where they treated him without success. He died looking at the small city, meadows, and hills surrounding his castle, with only one unfulfilled wish: to unify the Balkans into one kingdom, without any foreign invaders or occupiers. They buried the knight on the hill above the fort, so he could rest in peace watching over the fort and the village that was built for him and his men.

All his wishes he transferred to his son, Omer, but in mind and soul, Omer was a good businessman. He owned stores in Kammengrad, Bihac, and Pecigrad. From his father, he had inherited a good character and had many friends and associates wherever he went. This helped his business grow very well. Every coin he earned, multiplied at least ten times, so he became a very wealthy storeowner. Yet, he didn't spend much and never showed off his wealth. He was lucky that his wife shared his humble character. In truth, she was an excellent housewife and mother to his sons, who, like his father, thought about business and coexistence with all neighbors and good people. The values he had learned from his father, he passed down to his kids, and they grew quickly.

In order to escape the "tribute in blood" whereby all young men had to serve the empire as soldiers, he put aside enough gold coins to bribe local judges and government officials, so that his children would not be put in the books until they had grown. He hated that the Ottomans took boys from their regions to train them in military schools in a new language without knowing their real father, mother, and other relatives. When his uncle Halil and his best friend Tale Lichanin had died in a battle near Banja Luka, Omer became depressed for a long time, but like his father, he needed to go forward despite the loss of loved ones.

Because Halil had no male heirs, Omer ordered one of his sons to live in the castle to keep it strong. Omer paid all the servants and soldiers with money he earned in his stores. But, even though he was good in his soul, helping other Krajishniks, with credit and zero interest, when they needed to pay taxes and they did not have enough for themselves, great misfortune befell Omer. Two of his sons were in a caravan full of goods on the way from Bilece to Krajina. Somewhere halfway to their destination, they got ambushed by a group of bandits, who killed the salesmen, soldiers, servants, and horses. They stole the goods from the caravan. From that day, Omer mourned his two sons, fearing that he could not survive such grief, and he carried that sorrow to his grave.

Omer's remaining son, Hasan, took responsibility for the fort and all the stores. In order to avoid his brothers' fate, he spent much money on soldiers and servants to guard the region on all sides. With luck and hard work, the stores made so much money that he could buy everything he needed. At the fort, he installed new cannons and other modern weapons, and in one tunnel, he hid many gold and silver coins and precious jewels. He knew that he could defend himself from any possible enemy with his skilled soldiers and modern weapons.

His sons, like his father, were spared the "tribute in blood" with his money, but he trained them in every kind of military skills. In addition, they had tutors who taught them business, geography, and history.

Of course, Hassan also taught them their family history especially about his grandfather Mooyo. The citizens still sang songs about Mooyo's adventures and great heroism during special parties and occasions. The boys were very proud of their heritage and their last name. The honor built a strong connection to the fort and the whole region of Krajina, despite the fact that they were still under Ottoman occupation. They carried their hero and idol, the knight Mooyo Hrnjica, in their hearts. They wanted to follow his model. They made all the walls around the castle stronger, and wherever they could, they used iron in the castle. One more tunnel was dug all the way to the riverbank from the east side. All the soldiers and servants knew about that exit because they worked on it. The four brothers know the other exits.

Beside the stores and profits from them, the brothers were intense cattle ranchers, from sheep to horses. From the meat and dairy products, they earned much money.

All their workers and servants were trained how to use weapons in case they were called to protect them from enemy attack. They felt strong and safe in Krajina, and they enjoyed life and freedom just as long ago when their grandfather came to that part of Bosnia.

# CHAPTER 11

## Changes for the Worse

Life in Krajina was like a fairy tale. The citizens, from the poorest to the wealthiest, the people lived in peace and prosperity. The bandits from that region disappeared or moved away from Una and Glina. The brothers Hase, Rekan, Serif and Hasib wished only for health and peace because they had everything else. But their peace did not depend on only them, but from the very powerful empire, and its wish to control the Balkan Peninsula. Eventually, the Russians defeated the Ottomans, and the French defeated the Austrians. The English had their interest in some regions, too. The apparent peace under the Ottomans was exchanged with a new occupation from Austro-Hungarians. The Krajishniks were ready to fight against the new occupier because the forts across the river Glina were strong, and they were not easy prey for the new occupiers.

They tried to cross the river, but they lost many soldiers. However, the Austro-Hungarian commanders found a way to sidestep Krajina and cross over other east and south villages and cities all the way to the border with Serbia. The Bosnians fought bravely, but fort, after fort, were crushed under the boots of Austro-Hungarian soldiers. They would have crossed even farther had the Russians not stopped them.

When the brothers Kozlic heard the news that the rest of Bosnia was under new occupation and that their fort might soon be destroyed, they moved everything important from it and into their homes near their stores in the village. They moved older people, children, and women, and they fought with the much stronger enemy, which attacked from the south and east. The fort was almost fifty percent destroyed from cannon fire, but the Krajishniks didn't give up, and the enemy soldiers could not enter the fort. Hasan and his son, Hasib were killed by the enemy's cannons, but the other three brothers and some remaining soldiers decided to use a tunnel and leave the fort at nightfall to head to Keserovici, and from there ride by the riverbank to the nearest hills where many of them owned homes and land. They took many weapons and ammunition to bury around their homes. In the fort, they left only cannons and dead friends they could not to carry through the small tunnel. The next day, when the enemy soldiers came to the fort, they could not believe that there was no man alive. From the surrounding hills, the young Krajishniks watched them through spyglasses.

The fort was so destroyed that they could not put many soldiers in it, believing that it would cost too much to rebuild it. Everything had become eerily quiet. The new government made police stations in Pecigrad and Cazin. The brothers did go close to the police stations, for one brother had decided to move above Vranova Greda, but the other two brothers stayed under the hill of Hrabljenovac using aliases, in case the new government were looking for them.

The new government was just like the old one. It collected taxes, but people were happier because there was no longer a "tribute in blood" for the Krajishniks. The brothers recognized that the new king was better than the old one, and they lived life in peace staying far away from their own castle. They still managed their stores and raised cattle on their land from Pecigrad to rivers Korana and Glina.

They eventually realized that it was easier to live in a small home than a castle because there they were not the targets of envy and didn't have to constantly fear someone taking their home away. They lived like other Krajishniks, working and enjoying life. They were happy that they could see the ruins of their castle every morning from nearby hills. They could watch their servants taking care of cattle on their meadows, cutting and drying the grass for winter, planting and harvesting grains, and picking fruit from their orchards. Still, in their souls, they yearned for the stone tower walls they had owned before.

They lived like this until a big new war. Again, the citizens needed to die for foreign occupants. The clever brothers paid money and gold to avoid the war's evil trenches. Because of their money, they survived. They had no desire to die a bitter death for occupiers who would only make new taxes on their land and from their sweat.

Luckily, the front lines of the war were far from their homes, and luckier still, their occupiers lost the war, and they became part of a new state, the Kingdom of Serbs, Croats, and Slovenians. They were not interested in the new name or the new government as much as their freedom from foreign occupiers. They were happy the Austro-Hungarians had lost the war because they had destroyed their castle and the peace they had enjoyed there. They learned about the new king, who was one of them, spoke the same language, and came from the same place. For that reason, they loved him more than the foreigners who had controlled their land in the past.

The brothers and their families continued to live as small storeowners and farmers guarding the secret of their real heritage.

Some years were good with a lot of grain, fruits and vegetables, but others were very dry, hard, and very long. After the war, some people became very poor, but together they survived everything.

Just when they relaxed after World War I and were starting to enjoy their new lives, they heard the news about the Germans, who had invaded some countries in Europe. They sat and thought of moving somewhere far from all these wars, but they loved their home and the land where the graves of their parents grandparents were buried, so they pushed those thoughts away.

Life was not peaceful for long because Hitler, Mussolini, and some domestic traitors invaded the entire Balkan country in just twelve days. The Krajishniks and Krajina became part of the NDH in 1941. The brothers and some of their good friends worried about what would happen to them in that new nationalist state. Most of the citizens in between the Una and Glina rivers were Muslim. Hitler knew what card to play there. "Divide and conquer" was always a successful strategy for any occupier in the Balkans, so he allowed nationalists who waited for him with the flowers and "Nazi" salute to form a new nationalist country under his boots. Of course, he helped them with weapons and war supplies, and used them as part of his army to kill their neighbors.

The Krajishniks dug up and cleaned their buried weapons. They placed watchmen at the main entrances to the villages and cities from Una to Glina. They chose Huska to be their commander. He got his military training from the Kingdom of the SHS army, and everyone thought he was the best man for that position. His army grew every day because their strategy was not to attack anybody unless they attacked them first. Every army could travel over their region if they traveled in peace. The Germans did not feel threatened, so they gave them weapons and other supplies they needed, thinking they would use them to fight Tito's partisans. However, Huska had good communication and collaboration with the partisans too because they never attacked each other.

The citizens continued their lives and jobs on their farms, as if there was no war at all. Meanwhile, five thousand Krajishniks were ready to fight and protect their region against any enemy any moment day or night. In that way, the people escaped massacre from the Germans and especially the domestic national enemy throughout the war. Unfortunately, when the German army grew weaker, Tito's partisans grew in number and power. Finally, Huska was pressed to put his military structure under of the command of the partisans.

He was negotiating with the partisans when the Germans got information from their spy about talks between Huska and Tito's partisans.

To stop them, the Germans promised a command position with all military structure to an envious Krajishnik, who was their spy, and he ambushed Huska and killed him. The man, who saved thousands of Krajishniks and his soldiers decided to ally with Tito's partisans.

During all this unrest, the castle became overgrown with weeds, trees, and wines because no one had time, energy, or money to rebuild it. Two Kozlic brothers were killed at the end of the fight with renegade soldiers from a different nationalist army. The third brother escaped the war hiding in pits they had dug before the war in a forest surrounding the village. In addition to Huska's soldiers, he commanded watchmen on the hills above the villages. During the daytime, children had the job of watching the main paths while they were watching the cattle on the hills and meadows. Whenever children spied unknown men with weapons, they would blow trumpets made of chestnut bark. That was the alarm for all men older than ten years to hurry into the pit or Medin's cave. Unfortunately, the pits and caves were not heated for fear the enemy would discover them. Therefore, Hase became very sick and shortly after the war, he died of pneumonia.

His sons stayed, for a short time, as successors of his estates. When the Second World War finally ended, new communist laws took possession of their land, forests, and some houses and stores because the government thought that they owned much more property than they needed. They never said a word about the castle because it was just a shadow from the past, and of course it belonged to the new government, that never spent a coin to renovate it or put it back into use.

The brothers continued to work in agriculture and livestock. Huse had many friends from Krajina to the Adriatic Sea. When he needed money or salt, he would cut the oak trees in the forest of the new country.

"Before they took it from me, it was my forest, and I felt I had the right to cut the trees and sell them," Huse explained to his wife, who was scared of his actions. Sometimes, he needed to steal trees and cut them during the night.

The Krajishniks were punished because they didn't collaborate with the partisans quickly enough, so every day became harder and harder. The new state created a tax called "redemption" for the citizens who didn't have enough grain to feed their hungry families. The government workers taxed people as much as they wanted and in their own ways. They often took the last cow from farmers' barns. In that way, once they took a bull from Huse's barn to the taxation office in Pecigrad. However, the bull untied himself during the night, and in the early morning returned to Lulashev's hill above Huse's valley.

"Hurry up, give me knife to sharpen, and kids get him in the barn quickly," ordered Huse to his family. When he said "the knife," they knew what would happen to the bull. They were afraid because they knew that the bull belonged to the taxation office now, but they needed to listen to their elder. The children brought the bull, and Huse and Husein started their job. In Dip Valley, where they could not be seen, even by their neighbors, they killed the bull, and dried the meat in the smokehouse for plums, pears and apples. They were scared to dry it in the house attic because they knew that government officials could come looking for the bull or meat. Luckily, they didn't, so they had plenty of meat for next two months.

"It was not their luck to eat what we raised with hard work," said Huse to Husein, laughing and thinking that this was God's justice.

The Krajishnik's property was pillaged every day from government officials, and they could not protest. Worse yet, when there were two very dry summers in 1948 and 1949, the taxation became unbearable. Those years brought hunger to the citizens in Krajina. The people ground the corn together with cornhusks and chestnuts to feed their hungry families, yet the government still demanded taxes from them.

The people from Krajina decided to protest against Tito's government and the terrible taxation. It happened on May sixth, 1950 when the Krajishniks from Cazin, Kladusa, and Slunj protested against Tito's "redeem" taxation. Seven hundred and twenty Krajishniks protested against the new communist country.

In response to the protest, the army of the Folk Republic of Yugoslavia and government officials acted with aggression against the protestors. They quickly divided them. Many were killed on the spot while others were sentenced to death by firing squad, or sentenced to many years in prison and hard labor for the government. One hundred families with about seven hundred members were forced to move to a camp in Srbac, which was a camp for disobedient Krajishniks.

Huse and Husein didn't take part in the protest because they thought if Huska was not able to escape with his five thousand well-armed soldiers, this small number of protestors could not do anything against an army with over one million soldiers. However, they managed to safeguard the property of their evicted neighbors, and they helped them with food, clothes and

---

other essentials during their camp life in Srbac. After the protest, the entire region sank into poverty and misery. The government didn't care about them and didn't sponsor any factories, schools, or hospitals for the people.

They were punished for the protest for many years. The men went to other states to find jobs. Many of them died from ordinary diseases. Eventually, Huse and Husein died of lung disease and alcoholism. Their inability to fight against the communist injustice led them to drink homemade plum or pear brandy. They were disheartened because they could no longer fight the system, which took so much from them and their people. From a wealthy family, they became common people, without any better future for their kids.

The same kind of depression took over their kids as well, and they too escaped in alcohol. By the end of the sixties and beginning of the seventies, Huse's sons were searching for bread in West Germany. Husein's sons found jobs in Slovenia, like many other suffering Krajishniks.

Workers from Germany were able to go home once or twice a year, and those from Slovenia once a month. The people joked about Bosnians working in Slovenia; when a male child is born in Bosnia, they face him toward the west telling him "there is your bread," and a child born in Slovenia is faced South-East telling, "there is your daddy." People made derogatory jokes about Bosnians, how they are dumb and strong. It goes together, that if you are dumb, you need to be strong.

One day, in Krajina a Krajishnik was born, who wanted to stop the tradition of working and making a living only in Slovenia, Croatia, Austria, Germany, Switzerland, and Canada, or America. As an excellent student, from a wealthier family, he graduated from college in economics. He had a dream for his Krajishniks to stop earning their living as laborers and servants in other countries. He wanted an end to the punishment of living in misery and poverty. Thus, he organized agricultural cooperatives and used his knowledge and a tractor to plow the land. He built a company with only one tractor and by 1980 he had thousands of tractors, trucks, and busses. From one hall, he built a hundred other halls and factories. From one product, he assembled about three hundred new ones. From a single asphalt road, all others roads got built, and from a single water source, all people got running water in their new homes. From one lighted town, all villages and homes got electricity. From a few old school buildings, all schools got new school buildings, and people moved into apartments. The Krajishniks started to return to their native land and work there, sleeping every night in their own homes with their families. The joy and happiness on peoples' faces returned with their new lives. In addition to jobs and wages in the company, everyone who owned land was able to rise and sell his own product to the companies Agrokomerc, Sanitex and Grupex all around the former Yugoslavia, Europe, Canada, and countries around the Middle East. Many new buildings and homes were built in the cities, suburbs, and villages.

The fort and castle were rebuilt for the first time since the Austro-Hungarians destroyed it with their cannons. Houses and apartments were built around the fort for businessmen.

No one was happier than the Kozlic family even though they lived far away from their castle, and they could not ask for that property that was built for their ancestors. It now belonged to the city and country like a historic monument. They were happy that someone had renovated it and brought health and happiness to their Krajishniks. They constructed a monument to their great-grand grandfather, but the communists never allowed it to be erected in the city, in the fort, or on the hill above the castle. Nevertheless, the picture of Mooyo Hrnjica and his horse were printed on paper bags.

How long could the Krajishniks enjoy the company, prosperity, and satisfaction? In Krajina and Krajishnici, it could never last long.

A new variety of communist secret police, assisted by nationalism, created the Agrokomerc trial for allegedly misreporting livestock production. The Krajina's biggest patriot, and the man who started the company declared the country's "enemy number one." They put him and his closest management in a prison in Bihac, and there started three years of show trials. This caused the companies to decline, and the prosperity of the Krajishniks was halted once again. Production decreased. The company got a bad reputation from their allies because all newspapers, television stations, and radios smeared the Krajishniks as thieves who robbed Yugoslavia.

The president and his cabinet escaped a three-year trial free and clear, but the company suffered enormous damage, and it was difficult to put it back on its feet. Still, the Krajishniks were proud that they took off their bad reputation.

The biggest son from Krajina got the name "Daddy" after he tried to bring back the reputation of the company he founded. He sought help from foreign and domestic investors to increase the production to the previous level, and in that way, he went to nationalist party, which was aided by the West. They were creating the European Union as a prototype for American and Asian economies.

After the death of Tito, a socialist country could not exist anymore on the Balkan Peninsula. It was stuck between NATO and Russia. It had to be destroyed no matter the cost or loss of life. Once again, the Bosnians including the Krajishniks believed in "golden spoons," which the party leaders quickly propagated. Each promised new wealth and prosperity for whoever followed them.

Thus began the carnage from Slovenia to Croatia, Bosnia and all the way to Kosovo.

# PART II

---

# Escaping One Evil and
# Finding a New One

August 21, 1994

A long column of refugees: men, women, and children carrying bundles of belongings on foot, tractors, and horse and carriages snaked its way toward the small city of Vojnic. It was under control of the military Djurashin II, who was fighting against the recently declared Republic of Croatia, which they not recognize as Orthodox. Thousands of people were fleeing the war in the former Yugoslavia. They left their homes to escape danger and the new ideology. Every fool with a rifle now represented the law and could make decisions to make his life better. Nothing could stop this irrational war, which put innocent, honest working people in the crossfire.

They were heading to Europe and the promised East Germany because before they left their hometowns, they heard a rumor that refugees would be welcome there. For many Krajishniks, the word Germany meant good jobs because many of them worked there in the 1970s, returning with German marks, which they could exchange for local currency. Many families got wealthy because of the good exchange rate. Mooyo, the descendent of the long-deceased Mooyo the first, heard the misinformation from a policeman named Braco when they were still in their city. People told fantasies to the distraught people, who were sick of the long war. Most of them believed the stories and passed them on to everyone they met.

---

Mooyo did not care where he went, whether Germany or Albania, just somewhere without war, just to stop the uncertainty. Still, he worried as he walked in the caravan of people fleeing their homeland. He wondered how far his son and wife were, turning his head forward and back to find anyone he knew. He didn't know how long he had been walking when a tractor pulling a carriage full of people crossed him. His wife called to him from the carriage, waking him from his thoughts. Their son was sitting on her lap. Again Mooyo felt happy and strong, even though he was going into the unknown. They were going farther away from the evil war.

They traveled to Vilin Tochak, which is in front of Vojnic. There the column stopped. People sat in the shade of trees. They found water and watermelons, and many of them had packed some food. The first people in the caravan were in cars, carriages, or tractor trailers.

Mooyo had escaped in his packed Zastava 101 car, but he abandoned it in a traffic jam, so he hopped on the carriage. They slept in the caravan above the Glina River that night.

"Whatever our future holds, we are alive and healthy, so we will survive somehow!" thought Mooyo.

To get to Vojnic, the caravan headed in the direction of Slunj after some hours of waiting. Most people did not know where they were going, nor did they care; it was not important at that time. They just followed the caravan of people out of the danger zone. They believed they were headed to something better than they had left behind.

Mooyo sat with one arm around his three-year-old son. His wife was able to take one bag with clothes mostly for their son. They came to Batnoga, in front of the halls where Agrokomerc, the company from their city, bred young chickens. The people stopped there and started to crowd into the halls, happy to have a roof over their heads. Mooyo's wife's cousin gave them a horse blanket, and they found a small spot to rest. Next to him was his friend from high school, with his mother, wife and one son, his son's friend. Next to his friend was the city judge from before the war. By the door were many members of his family; uncles, aunts, and one other family member from their neighborhood.

The quiet and empty halls came alive for a few hours. From somewhere, they got chocolate, and they drank water from a nearby stream. They got information about the store where they could buy more food. The lines in the store were almost a kilometer long.

When Mooyo arrived, there was no more bread, but they bought some salami and canned food because their mouths and bellies were sick from the chocolate they had eaten over the past two days. They had some German marks. Mooyo's wife carried it tied around her hips because it was less likely for someone to check her. His friend bought a small loaf of three-day-old bread for ten marks from an Orthodox lady, they shared the cost and split the bread, so everyone got a slice, and for their sons, they saved three slices to last until they would have the chance to get more.

The next day, when Mooyo was not able to buy bread in the store, he bought a bag of flour. His wife's cousin cooked some flat bread, so they finally had something fresh to eat. There were other friends and cousins, but everyone was worried about how to feed their own family members and save something for the next day. On the fourth day, the military members from UNHCR provided water for the people from big military tanks because many people got sick from drinking water from the stream. They even brought plastic gallon jugs, so people could keep some water. Out of a sheet of metal from an old chimney, people made dishes, plates, cups from which they drank and ate, and by a farm, they built an outdoor stove, from which came smoke and the smell of different kinds of bread. For a few days, the place acted as a refugee camp. The Red Cross came and built tents, military doctors helped sick people, people sent written massages searching for family member, and Mooyo sent a message looking for his father and mother because he didn't know where they were.

The UNHCR started to distribute bread, supplies, groceries, plastic, and blankets, so the refugees felt a little bit better. In front of the halls, they built toilets and bathhouses where people could clean them. Mooyo tried to look over the hills, but the forest blocked his view of his birthplace and the home of his ancestors. He got upset one day when he was walking with his son in front of the halls, and in the distance, they heard a rooster's song. There was no light in the halls that early.

His son couldn't speak many words yet, but looking ahead over hills, he said to him, "Let's go to Majka, Daddy. Those are her roosters singing by those homes."

His heart broke at that moment, but what was there to do? Going back meant going to prison, where they would beat him. Otherwise, it meant going to the front line of battle and kill or be killed. He knew why he left, and he would not return until there was peace again.

There was a rumor of a few thousand people who went to Turanj in front of the suburb of Karlovac, but they were stopped by police and armies from the newly Croatia. After that story, came news about reuniting family members, which meant that if someone's family was staying at a camp in Turanj, and they were in Batnoga, the government would give them a chance to travel and live in that refugee camp or vice versa. Mooyo asked for details. Some young men had visited Turanj while going over hills and meadows on foot, but Mooyo could not use the same path, knowing how many land mines were now buried in the ground. The only place that he visited was a hornbeam forest, where he cut hornbeam trees to bake different kinds of Bosnian bread because the bread delivered by UNHCR was enough for everyone.

For a while, he got up the courage to work illegally with his friend, Smuk and his friends for some Orthodox whom Smuk had met during their journey to Batnoga. They promised him that nothing would happen to him even though they had to walk through a big forest called Gredar. There, they dug up potatoes, picked corn, and for their efforts got food and water. They were also allowed to take some potatoes, onions, beans, cheese, and milk with them. Mooyo felt so bad, but he knew that he and his family needed to survive because they were already getting sick from the different kind of bread. One night, when he came back from picking corn, he found a letter that the Red Cross brought from his mother and father in Turanj near Karlovac. There were many words covered with a black marker, but he could still understand that they were well and healthy living in a home just above Slunjska Brda. They invited him to join them.

"We need to see how to get to Turanj tomorrow," he said to his wife.

But how could they make it happen? It was the main question. In the morning, he didn't go to work for the Orthodox because he was looking for a way to Turanj. The night before, the judge from the hall disappeared during the night because somebody helped him escape to Croatia or Serbia, but no one knew the details. He heard from some people that his cousin helped the judge leave, so Mooyo tried to find him, too. He found him, but his answer was no because it was too dangerous.

Mooyo didn't give up. He continued looking and asking around. The Red Cross was working on the list to possibility reunite family members.

Looking for another way to get to Turanj, he met Bacu, a man from his neighborhood. Bacu did not live in the camp because he knew an Orthodox man who had worked with him in Italy a long time ago, and the man offered him his home near the camp. Bacu said that the Orthodox always had a solution for everything, but Mooyo did not trust him. Still, he told him he had a man who would take him and his family from Batnoga to Turanj for one hundred-fifty marks.

Mooyo and his family needed to illegally escape camp and walk to the house where Bacu was staying. He needed to wait until Bacu set a day with a soldier named Tambura, and until he could find another person to travel with them because Tambura actually charged three hundred German marks for the trip. He was lucky because his cousin wanted to go to Turanj with her kids, and from Turanj to Italy where her husband lived and worked.

Every day, Bacu went to the store where he could drink some beer and find people willing to leave the camp. Mooyo told him how he found the other people for the trip, so he could finally arrange the day for them to leave.

At the camp, life existed of bread and some other groceries, but when the first rains came, the roofs of the halls started to leak, and by morning, the smell of humidity and staleness was everywhere. The people, again, lived without any hope. There were some meetings because life there was equal to zero, and they needed to go somewhere. The Orthodox picked corn, and the people cut all the wood around the camp, so life got more and more miserable.

Some days, he thought of going back to his home over the hills and forest, even if he could step on a land mine or they killed him there. For him, it didn't matter. He was sorry for all the struggling the people lived through and being at the mad, wet, mercy of drunken soldiers of SAO, who could treat them whatever they wanted, without any justice for their actions. Everything was going up and down in his stomach. There was more and more misery and mistrust every day and everywhere.

Fortunately, one muddy evening, Baco's wife came with the news that they needed to go to their home early in the morning, and from there Tambura would take them to Turanj. The woman with the news brought a little sunshine and hope.

The night was long because he wondered what would happen to him and his family on the way to Turanj. The same soldier might assume that they have a bunch of money, and easily take them somewhere in the woods, rob them, and in the end, kill them. It was a risk, but there was no other hope.

In the morning, while the other eight hundred-sixty people were still sleeping, they crept out of the hall with their cousins, walked through the bushes, and made it all the way to Baco's temporary home. On their way, they saw the ruins of homes where before war Catholic people had lived. There were only walls and chimneys without wood on the roofs, without windows or doors. Everything was overgrown with weeds, bushes, and trees as if no one had lived there for many years.

"Dear God, are we going to see our homes like thise one day?" He thought when they walked in the foggy dawn.

Everything was possible because when they were still living in their homes, the soldiers came and took away their cars and batteries, saying they were using them for the military. They could not protest because they could get beaten or worse.

The little home by the road was still sleepy and quiet, with curtains on the windows, so there was life there. The grass was freshly cut, laundry hung on the line, and logs were piled beside the door. A woman opened the door, and after such a long time, they smelled a real home. It was heaven after their life in the smelly hall with eight hundred-sixty war weary people. They said good-bye to their cousins and helpers and entered the living room. Baco's wife made them coffee, which helped them focus on the new day and their anxieties and fears of land mines and vindictive soldiers or police catching them. They talked about many things that could happen on their journey.

They had to wait another day for Tambura who didn't show up, so by late evening, they decided to walk back to the camp. This time, they walked back on a curvy road, with many potholes, weeds, and overgrown bushes on both sides of the road. They left their bags there. Until they arrived at the store, they didn't see anyone, but near the store was a control point with drunk soldiers, policemen, and many refugees that no one paid attention to.

They asked Baco if Tambura had received news of the trip to come at the first tent in the camp because some of Mooyo's wife's cousins lived there. In the hall, they didn't talk about their attempt to escape even though some of the people assumed they tried. They waited for news about the trip. That same night a message arrived from Baco about how they should be there the next morning because this time for sure the guy would come to take them. That night, Mooyo had a nightmare about leaving the camp and walking in mud and what could happen to them on the way from Batnoga to Turanj.

Early in the morning, just like before, they walked around the military check point and they arrived at the small house. Once again, they said good-bye to their escorts, and in the living room, they had coffee listening the excuses from Baco and his wife about why the guy hadn't come the day before.

"Baco, it is not very important, but try to tell him to drive us to Turanj in the safest way possible," said Mooyo even though he was having trouble following Baco's words due to his nerves.

"Do not worry; he is our man. He lived in Crnaja, near Shturlic, and I have known him a very long time. I would not have told you about him if I did not know him well," said Baco.

After about thirty minutes, the soldier arrived in a Zastava 101, just like the one Mooyo left on the congested caravan. In the city people were so frightened by the shooting, that many of them just left their vehicles on the streets despite how hard they had tried to take the vehicles with them. Tambura was a tall and skinny man of about forty. He didn't seem dishonest or distrustful, so Mooyo relaxed a bit. After loading their refugee bags, he sat in the front seat while the women and children sat in the back seats. They were packed tightly, but they had no choice.

The ride began on a narrow road near Vojnic. All the roads were overgrown with weeds and bushes as nobody had cleaned or managed them in the last three years. The car reaked of tobacco, alcohol, and gas, but it was not as important as getting to Turanj and Mooyo's parents. He wanted to live together as they asked in the letter he received from the Red Cross. Turanj was in a suburb of Karlovac. They passed empty homes. Some houses were nice looking, but others had overgrown weeds and bushes. The unkempt houses belonged to the Catholic people who had been expelled before the war.

The ride was so long that they felt as if they were going to Munich.

While riding along the curvy, obscured road, three cars came in their direction. The first and the last one looked like pre-war police cars. In the middle was a military colored car. The driver of the first car pointed at a stop sign for Tambura.

"What will happen now?" asked one of the passengers fearfully.

Out of the car came an SAO policemen and another officer dressed like the old JNA, but with different badges.

Tambura got out and talked with the man who was in the police car. The travelers could not hear the conversation. At the end of the conversation, one policeman got behind Tambura's steering wheel, and Tambura got in their car. They turned back on the narrow road. The travelers didn't know what was going on, but they were still driving in the direction of Vojnic. They had cramps in their stomachs and faces as white as ghosts. They were too scared to ask what would happen to them?

After a while, they arrived at a police station in Vojnic. The policeman told them to get out of the car with all their belongings. Another policeman came from the building and talked with their driver. Shortly, he told them to go inside the police station. There, he told them to sit on a bench and wait.

When the policeman was gone, Mooyo told his wife, "Whatever happens, don't take our child from your arms. If they ask you, tell them the truth, who we are, where we are from, where we want to go, and always stay with the truth."

After an eternal thirty minutes, they called Mooyo to the office where he met the officer, who asked him his personal information; who he was, what his job was, where he wanted to go, and why he paid Tambura in advance to drive them? In the beginning, the man was nice, but after a while he became agitated, yelled, and tried to convince Mooyo to agree that he paid Tambura in advance for the ride.

Luckily, Mooyo was carrying his SFRJ passport, personal card, and the letter he received from his parents from the Red Cross that he showed to officer. He repeated that he agreed to pay Tambura one hundred and fifty marks for the ride once they reached Turanj. The questions were repeated a hundred times, and he remembered movie interrogations. Fortunately, the examiner didn't beat him, and it lasted only until two o'clock in the afternoon. He kept to his story, showing the letter he received from his parents in Turanj, how they were refugees in a home, where they had a decent living condition. That was the reason he wanted to go there from the chicken hall where he lived with eight hundred-sixty other people.

He told the officer how his life was so difficult there and how he got sick from the water the UNHCR transported in tanks from the Korana River. He told him how he was worried for the health of his three-year-old child, who was his only child. There were questions about what he did during the war, what his position was in the old JNA army, and other questions, but he always told the same answers. After about two o'clock, the officer left Mooyo to go to the hallway to his wife, son, and cousins, and he never returned.

In the hallway, he found his wife, son, and cousin with her sons. They were able to talk, and he asked them if they were interrogated, too. They said that no one examined them. They were all hungry, but they needed to be strong. About fifteen minutes later, a policeman from next shift arrived, and the new policeman came and talked with them. He knew they were refugees from Kladusha. He was a very nice man in his forties. When they relaxed a bit, they asked him if Mooyo's wife could go and buy some food for their hungry son. He said yes and told her to hurry back. Fata came back with some bananas and dried cookies for all of them.

Eventually, they called Mooyo to the same office with another JNA officer who examined him about the same things as the previous one. Mooyo repeated the same story. The examination lasted until four o'clock in the afternoon, luckily without beating or maltreatment. After a while, they told them that a UN truck would take them back to Batnoga and the hall full of humidity, bad odors, and uncertainty. White UN trucks arrived in front of the police station. From somewhere, they brought many other people, refugees, who were also captured on their way to Turanj or Batnoga and who would also be returned to their old camps.

Mooyo looked at Fata and his head sank. They begged the policeman to put them in a truck heading to Turanj, but it was futile. Everyone had to return to own designated camp. They were bumping up and down in the UN trucks on the way from Vojnic to Batnoga over damaged and narrow roads, thankful that at least they had not ended up in prison or in a place where someone would rob or beat them.

The adventure from Batnoga to Turanj was done for Mooyo and his family, but not forever because he knew they had to go somewhere far from the madness and stench of the camp. They got back at dusk, so not many people saw them getting off the UN truck. First, they stopped by Mooyo's brother-in-law, who lived with other men in a tent at the entrance to the camp. They told them what happened during the day, enjoying the smell of bean soup, which they ate happily because they were so hungry.

They snuck back in the hall to escape the questions from other people. They did not want to be in trouble because they left the camp illegally. Mooyo's night was full of nightmares about the police interrogation and worries about what to do next.

In the morning, there was dew, condensation, and smog above their heads. Everything smelled old and moldy. He decided not to go home during the war. The soldiers made the justice by the rifles. His hope was that the Red Cross could help him move from there to Turanj. It was long to wait, but the hope was there because he didn't want to try unsafe transport again.

The days became very long and boring, with very little hope for the trip to Turanj. During one foggy, rainy day, news finally came that the next day the A/C trucks in charge of the Red Cross would be coming to take people to Turanj, to reunite family members. They were afraid to get too excited about the news, but a glimmer of hope was there. Around eight o'clock, the trucks came by the Red Cross tent. Mooyo was given his brother-in-law's name, and his wife and son their own names. They packed everything that was possible to carry with them and waited for their names to be read, so they could climb into the truck. They first called Mooyo's brother-in-law's name, and Mooyo was able to go in the trailer before his son and wife. He was loaded with all their belongings because he told Fata to only worry about their son. There was no place to sit in the trailer, so people were standing and holding onto each other. From the trailer, he was not able to see or hear Fata and his son climb in the other trailer. He lived in hope, but he would not know for sure until they reached Turanj. The distance was not long, but the soldiers at military checkpoints held them until it was very dark. Something was going on outside, but they didn't know what. The soldiers sounded mad and drunk, and someone was shooting from a machine gun several times, but they did not know where. Luckily, no one shot at the trailers because if that happened, there would be blood up to their knees.

Finally, the officials from the Red Cross got permission for the people to leave the trailers and look for their relatives, but it was already very dark. Mooyo was not able to find his wife and son, but he did locate his brother and teacher, Amor. They started to walk down Turanj looking for a sign for the tire shop where Mooyo's cousin was staying. Loaded like mules, they walked down almost to the Korana River where they saw a small building with a sign "Tire Shop." It was the place where many refugees slept. Fortunately, they found someone inside who was still awake. He came to the door sleepy but eager to help and see them. After talking for a while, he told them that his parents were staying way up in the hills of Turanj, and during the darkness it was not safe to go there because of the UNHCR check points and the Serbian military.

"Duljo will take you to my other brother-in-law, where you can sleep until morning, and then someone will take you there," said his cousin, Turcin.

They agreed because it was a very long, scary, and uncertain day especially for Mooyo, and he still didn't know if his wife and son had arrived in Batnoga. The cousin gave them some bread and cans of lunchmeat that he had in reserve. Later they learned that he distributed the food for refugees for UNHCR at that station. They wished each other good night and went into a small building. On their way, they saw many homes destroyed by the fighting between the HVO Croatian army and the SAO Serbian army.

They entered a small room of about twelve square meters, with beds made of planks and a wood stove that lit the room, so they did not need other light. They ate the bread and lunch meat, and went to sleep. The beds were comfortable compared with their beds on the concrete in Batnoga.

Mooyo was so worried about his wife and son that it was hard for him to fall asleep, until the fatigue of the day overcame him. The night was over quickly, and conversations and noises from the streets awakened them at eight o'clock. When they were ready, his cousin's brother-in-law walked with them to the hills of Turanj. On their way, they met many refugees, some they knew. They passed by one UNHCR checkpoint and another until they got to a checkpoint of the SAO Krajina police. On both sides of the street, they saw some nice, and some destroyed houses. Later, they learned that the destroyed homes belonged to Catholics who left there before 1991 and moved over the Mreznica River to Karlovac because the area was controlled by the SAO military.

Duljo took them to a four-story house by the checkpoint of the Orthodox military SAO Krajine, which was in front of a coffee shop. When they opened the door, Mooyo finally saw his parents. They hugged and kissed each other like never before, but they were surprised not to see their grandchild and daughter-in-law, which would have made the family reunion complete. Mooyo's mother and father shared the house with a many other refugees, but they had a private room, a bath, and cold running water inside. There was no electricity, but they were able to heat water on the stove and take a bath like civilized people. After many questions and answers, his dad headed to the checkpoint to find a policeman who could transport his daughter-in-law and grandson to them because his dad had known that man since they arrived there.

Mooyo's dad returned quickly because he easily found a man who would locate the missing people during the day. The same guy had already gotten another women and two kids, and he just needed a letter for Mooyo's wife to believe to him. Mooyo wrote the letter and explained to his dad where the policeman needed to go and show the letter. The policeman had to go to the first tent at the entrance of the camp, where Mooyo's brother-in-law was staying. His dad paid the man.

His mother and father had fresh milk, cheese, beans, and a whole chicken, which they got from an Orthodox family, whom they helped on their farms. The family gave them what they could in return.

"Please, my mother, bake the chicken for us," pleaded his brother to their mother.

"Sorry, not until my grandson arrives," replied their mother. She loved her first grandson almost more than life. While they were waiting, she made a nice soup with parts of the chicken, and on another plate, she roasted some vegetables and other parts of the chicken because she was expecting her grandson and daughter-in-law soon.

At last, a white "Fico" car came in the front of the house where there were some horses and carriages. A policeman got out of the car with Mooyo's wife, son, and another lady with two kids. There started hugging, kissing, and crying happy tears. Mooyo's older sister lived and worked with her husband and kids in Austria, and the younger one was with her family in Batnoga at her husband's side.

They ate supper together, all happy to be under one roof. In the end, they knew that a simple life with health and family is the most valuable gift of all. Through their conversations, they learned how their parents left their family home with five cows walking behind them over the hills and valleys all the way to Poljana to a cousin on their father's side, and from there through Dugo Selo to Turanj. There they met Milan and his wife. They went to work with them, and for it they got all the dishes, fruit, vegetables, and other things they needed.

Milan was his father's favorite, for they both liked to drink, and Milan always carried bottles of brandy or wine with him. They all slept that night, but Mooyo was nervous being so close to drunken soldiers and policemen and having the check point so near the house, even though his father told him nothing would happen because he knew them. Mooyo knew that drunk and armed soldiers could change their minds like the weather. He explained to them how he wished to be behind the UNHCR checkpoints, where he felt much safer.

During the night, they heard occasional gunshots, but mostly it was quiet, so they slept in the room on the mat that Mooyo had carried in the trailer with the convoy from Batnoga. His wife told him how she and their son were left there, how she returned to the hall, and there was nothing of theirs left because people took everything. She told him how one old, poor man offered some food for their son. Then the convoy left for Turanj without them. Many other people were left even though they were on the Red Cross roster. The members of the Red Cross promised that they would make another convoy for the rest of the assigned people.

That fall morning in 1994, the sunrise was beautiful, but after a while, fog moved in. The people in front of the house were fed because they successfully escaped Bosnia from Dugo Selo. For breakfast, they had eggs and soup. In Batnoga, some Orthodox ladies were walking through the camp trying to sell eggs for five marks each. There were some good people like Zdjelar C. from Rudnik, who brought some groceries to Mooyo's family because he knew him from peacetime. In his truck, he carried wood which he sold him to the people all over his neighborhood.

That day, Mooyo's parents took them to meet their Orthodox friends. Milan and Stana had a home on the path to the Mreznica River, and their only daughter married a Catholic man across the road. When they got to their friends' house, they had brandy, coffee, and lots of conversation.

After the visit, Mooyo and his wife wanted to search for her younger brother who had written them that he had a room for them by the river, between two UNHCR check points on the border line between the HVO and the SAO Krajina.

That beautiful day, they walked down to the river to find him. On their way, they met different people they knew from their old neighborhood, talked with them for a moment and went to the tire shop where Turchin distributed humanitarian supplies for refugees. Some people had goods such as clothes, shoes, and some groceries on the side of the road. Turchin had some sweet goodies for their son. Because Turchin distributed the supplies for the refugees, they asked him whether Fata's brother was on his list. Fortunately, he was a distributer for bread and other supplies to one part of the camp, so he was easy to find.

They walked on a narrow road littered with pieces of wood, bricks, destroyed furniture, cardboard, and bread. There was more than enough bread for the refugees because they distributed it every day. Mooyo felt sorry when he saw so much discarded bread on the streets around the houses. He remembered for the rest of his life the first days in camp Batnoga with no bread and only chocolate because someone was able to leave their city with a truck loaded with it from Agrokomerc. It was the only food for them the first three days except for what they brought with them. Mooyo had abandoned his car loaded with food, clothes, and other groceries on the congested road in Hukica Brdo.

They asked people they met about Fata's brother. People pointed to a small brick house. It looked like someone just built it before the war. It was in good condition since it was so close to river. In the front of the house was a little barn made of concrete blocks. They climbed up the concrete stairs and knocked on the door. Fata's brother came out surprised. His brother-in-law was very skinny, with many broken teeth because the soldiers found him home during the invasion of his village. They took him to Buzim, where he passed through "Buzimski Dresh," where they took prisoners who were suspected of working for the opposite side. The prisoners were tortured by people on the both sides the road. They beat them. In the prisons, executioners were the leaders of hate and fear.

The room Fata's brother saved for them was the same size they had with Mooyo's parents. The mattress was on bricks on one side of the room, and on the other side, there was a stove and a table made of planks.

Mooyo and his wife and son moved into that small room. There was no toilet or bathroom in the house; instead they used a barn, which had drainage lines. The food, roof on the heads, bed on the four bricks, and stove they got from UNHCR. They needed only to find wood for stove. Wood was vital for heat and cooking. Mooyo and his brother-in-law hacked the hornbeam trees in the small forest. Mooyo's father borrowed a horse and carriage from his friend. He bought a new handsaw, and they were ready for the upcoming winter. When they brought the wood, Mooyo collected all the discarded bread around the houses on his street, from his house to the tire shop. He didn't walk in the ruins. He picked up only what he could reach from the road. He collected two full paper bags of bread, which his father took back to Milan's house. Milan thanked him for the bread which he used to feed the cow, horse and chickens. Mooyo thanked him for borrowing the horse to move his wood to his refugee house.

Almost every day, Mooyo visited his parents on top of the hill of Turanj.

On his walks up and down, he met many familiar faces from his past, cousins and friends from school and work colleagues. There, he found his cousin Senad and school friend, Rasim, who owned a stand on the side of the street selling utensils and brandy. On another day, he found a school friend who had lived with him in the camp at Batnoga, and the three of them talked about their situation there and the possibility of moving further. Seno told him that every night, people escaped over the river, and some of them walked all the way to Slovenia. He knew the people and the place where people crossed the river Mreznica to go to Karlovac on a small plastic raft if they were lucky enough not to be caught by the Croatian police. They paid twenty marks per person for the ride in the boat. Everything was risky because there were people who stepped on land mines and lost their legs on the road. The lucky ones got referrals to go to the hospital in Karlovac. The people used every possible opportunity to get to Croatia, and from Croatia to cousins and friends in countries in

Western Europe. Mooyo's brother and his cousin Zenga were building a room in the attic in their parents' house.

The fall days in Turanj were nice and sunny, but everyone knew that winter was on its way. One day, Mooyo and his father visited Milan. They talked about how much bread people were throwing away because the UNHCR distributed too much. They made a plan for Mooyo to collect the extra bread for Milan, and he would give him fresh milk, cheese, and vegetables. They built him a dolly to deliver the bread to farmers in exchange for the fresh produce and dairy products. For his family, he earned many dairy products, and the good, sensible Stana would kill the chicken and keep it for his son, too. In that way, the rest of the fall days passed in Turanj, controlled by UNHCR. Some of the refugees disappeared if they had someone across the border where would open their doors for them. The Croatian police asked for a gigantic sum of money to take a person from the camp to somewhere in Croatia.

Mooyo tried to get a referral, and he crossed the checkpoints, but there were too many policemen to leave the city.

He had a number of friends from childhood who lived near his father and received pensions from Germany in Zagreb. Two escaped illegally from the war to a place where they could not be mobilized again. He made contact with his aunt in Slovenia who told him if he left the camp, they would have the place for him. The big question was how to get out of the camp over two swollen rivers and bridges while police on both sides watched.

His aunt told him that she knew a man who could take him from Croatia to Slovenia for four hundred marks. He didn't have enough money to pay the policeman for the ride to Karlovac City and the river crossings during the night. It was a big risk especially for their child. All he could think of was how to escape camp with the smallest risk.

During the next couple of days, news came of how men living the camps in Batnoga and Turanj fought with guns for their city and homes because they didn't want to host thousands of refugees. Mooyo talked with his family to see what they thought about it. His brother decided to go back with his cousin and school friend, Zenga. They tried to convince him to wait, but he didn't listen even though he never trained to be a soldier. Their mother cried, and their father was worried.

One sunny morning in the end of October 1994, Mooyo loaded his dolly with old bread and pushed it all the way to Milan and Stana. From somewhere came two Orthodox policemen to ask them for diesel fuel. They asked him who he was and why he was there. Milan tried to explain to them how he brought the old bread for his cattle. They were very unpleasant to him, yelling that he should be there fighting for his home, and how people were dying for their cities while he was taking a walk. After they got the fuel and drinks from Milan, they left. Milan told him not to worry, for they were drunken fools and would not do anything to him. It was the last time Mooyo visited Milan's home. He stopped by his parents to tell them what happened, and how he would not cross the UNHCR check point again.

From that day on, he never crossed the UNHCR checkpoint or went too close to the Orthodox check point. Different news came to them every day. The people were upset, quiet, and they looked coldly at the rest of the men in the camp because they weren't fighting to free their city and villages. Mooyo met Seno, who lived in the attic of one of the destroyed buildings close to the river. They talked and planned their escape from the camp.

During those days, the UNHCR military stopped one car at the checkpoint. They discovered machine guns and ammunition because the car possibly came back from the place where they trained men with weapons. That was a warning that someone with power was pushing the rest of the men to fight.

Mooyo called his aunt in Vrhnika, a small city twenty kilometers from Ljubljana in Slovenia. She told him, "Just leave camp and go anywhere in Croatia. From there, a man will take you here for four hundred marks."

What about his wife and son? The water in the river was very high from the fall rains. They didn't have enough money to pay the Croatian police to take them out of the camp, but he couldn't abandon his family. The days and nights were full of worries. One man finally brought three hundred marks from Fata's aunt in Croatia. They had some other money that Fata carried on her hips, but it was still not enough to pay the police. His parents came to visit almost every day. They could hear explosions in the distance.

One day, they got news that Halil had wounded his arm, and that he was in a hospital in Knin. His parents became worried and sad. Everyone worried for their sons, fathers, and husbands who fought for their homes.

After that sad news about his brother, Mooyo told his wife, "I must go back, but I first need to buy rain shoes."

When Mooyo woke up, it was foggy. He went from seller to seller to find rain boots because his shoes would fall apart with the first rain and mud.

While shopping for boots, he met some commanders and their drivers because they left their city. He knew some of them, so he greeted them.

They asked him, "When are you going back? We need every man to fight for our city?"

Because so many townspeople had fled their city and villages, everything had fallen into ruin. Because of them, men and youths were losing their lives, and there was a big chance to die or be pushed out of their homes once again. He told the men, "After I find good shoes, I will join you guys."

However, by the time he told them good-bye, he firmly decided not to go back. He would not buy the shoes or fight. He would try at any cost to cross the rivers. He walked back to Rasim's store, where he met his school friend Suad and the brother of another school friend who died in a battle before they left their region. He offered them positions in the store to convince them to go back. They shared a brandy, and everyone went his own way.

On his way back to his room, Mooyo met Bakir, a man who found a way to go to the hospital in Karlovac and back. He delivered letters and money for refugees from their relatives outside camp. One of his sons was ill, and he had permission to go to the hospital every other day.

Mooyo still had the problem of finding a way to take his wife and son to Karlovac. He knew how to cross the swollen river in a rubber boat, but he was scared of his son falling into the cold water. He had two brothers living in Zagreb who told Mooyo that the transport from Karlovac to Zagreb would not be a problem. Mooyo told him about his aunt in Slovenia, and the man whom his aunt had told him would take people from Zagreb to Ljubljana for four hundred marks. Bakir promised to drive him to Zagreb if he took his son over the river. However, three hundred marks were only enough for one person. The land mines were between the Mreznica River and Croatian's border. The sentry on the border often shot at anything suspicious in the dark.

"Okay. I will talk with my family, and we will stay in touch," he said to Bakir.

Mooyo walked slowly to his little room. On his way, people glared at him, but he paid no attention. In the room, he told his wife why he didn't buy the rain shoes, and that he met Bakir.

"When I arrive, I will call for you and our son. Crossing the rivers is a very big risk, and walking between the military camps at night is another risk. You know that we do not have enough money to pay for an illegal ride from Croatia to Slovenia. And the most important thing is that you and our son cannot be taken by the military," Mooyo explained to his wife.

"Whatever you decide, I will agree to, but remember that when you decide to go, there is the possibility that something bad can happen to you, and we have this child who needs us," Fata said.

She knew what it meant to him to stay longer there, where people didn't like him. At the camp, there were people who could come during the night and take him and do something worse than only take him to war again. His parents visited them that day, and he told them his plan to go over the river. His parents were very sad, but they encouraged him to go because Halil was already wounded although they didn't know how bad his injuries were. These were painful and difficult decisions, but there was no the other choice.

Mooyo met Bakir again to discuss the plan and the night they would try to cross the rivers. The days became long, and the nights full of dread. He watched his three-year-old son, and in his soul, he cried and his heart bled because he needed to leave him and go to the unknown. Luckily, darkness came early, and they put him to sleep. He felt that if his son were awake, he would not be able to leave him and cross the river. He gave Fata the phone numbers of the people whom they should be first to settle down with in Croatia and later in Slovenia.

Bakir came on time with his wife, boys, his neighbor, and her son. They were hoping to go to Germany where her husband worked for many years. Mooyo kissed his sleeping son, promised his wife that when he settled down somewhere, he would find a way to bring them. He suggested she stay with his parents after he left.

The night was so dark that it was not possible to see your fingers in front of your eyes. They walked through the ruins, bushes, and weeds to the river, where they found more than fifty men, women, and children waiting to cross in a small raft. Over the river was an electric cable tied to willow trees on both sides. People used it to hold themselves up in the raft.

The ride cost twenty marks, which Mooyo paid. He split the four hundred marks with his wife, and hid the rest in his coat epaulettes.

After they crossed the river, they walked in the darkness in groups of ten, shying from the lights of inhabited homes. When they came to the main road, they had to run across when it was clear of cars. So far, everything was going well, but in front of them was the bridge, which they had to cross if they could see it in such darkness.

They walked through a cemetery and beside abandoned houses on the other side of the hill. In front of the factory stood the bridge leading to Karlovac. Despite those conditions, they finally found the bridge, but they saw the light of police who were guarding the bridge. They believed that the policemen would leave the bridge in the morning, and then they would be able to cross the river and reach the city. The minutes were like years. It was freezing, and the morning dew was falling like ice pellets. The people were quietly lying in a junkyard, staring at the bridge.

After endless hours of waiting, more police cars came, and many well-armed policemen, and HVO soldiers got out of the cars. They walked to the junkyard with their machine guns, from which came ultra-red rays, revealing the refugees hiding close to the factory. They called them to come out with their hands above their heads, telling them how they were surrounded on all sides. Policemen and soldiers came closer and closer to where Mooyo was hiding with two women and two boys. They yelled at them, but the high ranking officer told them not to harm them, for he knew who they were. They asked about weapons, even though they knew that they could not be armed. They didn't put handcuffs on them, but they put them in police cars and took them away.

The order came to Mooyo, so he realized that he would once again cross the two rivers back to the refugee camp in Turanj. They told them to get out in front of the police checkpoint in front of the bridge. They took one refugee into a small examination room.

When they called for Mooyo, it was about three o'clock in the morning. He was so exhausted he had to fight to keep his eyes open. They asked similar questions to the ones in Vojnic. "Who are you? Where are you from? What is your occupation? Where were you trying to go?" He didn't hide anything. He told them he was heading for Germany. They laughed at his answer. There were two men in the small office, one in a Croatian police uniform and the other in plain clothes.

"Just let me go to the city, and it will be my worry how I can reach Germany," said Mooyo.

"Possibly you could get there because you know the geography," they grinned at him and finally let him leave. Other policemen told him to return to the UNHCR check point and go back to Turanj.

At dawn, Mooyo knocked on his door. His wife was surprised drowsy, but she teased, "you got to Germany fast and came back even faster."

"It doesn't matter. At least I tried, and I will try again," he said, taking off his clothes. He climbed into the warm bed next to his son because he was still cold from laying in the junkyard. He fell asleep tired, cold, and bitterly disappointed.

Morning came. The wind carried multi-colored leaves. Mooyo woke up because his son was jumping all over him. Although he was happy to see him, he didn't know what to do next. Bakir knocked on their door during the breakfast.

"They caught you so fast, but it is good you got very close to the bridge," comforted Bakir.

"There were too many people in one place. There must have been over fifty men, women, and children," said Mooyo.

"If you want to try again tonight, I have a man with a mobile phone, and a cousin in Karlovac, who will come to Jugoturbina with his car to take you to his apartment. Of course, you need to pay him for the ride, but it will be not much," explained Bakir.

"That is excellent because the bridge was watched so carefully, that only birds could fly across," added Mooyo.

"Then, tonight we will come at first dark and again cross in the small boat."

Bakir left them because he needed to talk with the other man who would join them.

Luckily, his parents didn't visit them that day, which was easier because his mother would cry again and his father would be sad. He spent the day with his son and wife in the room because he didn't want to be in front of angry and disappointed people.

Before dark, they put their son to sleep, and he and his wife waited for two women, two kids, and one new man, whom Mooyo didn't know. Bakir knocked at their door. This time, Mooyo took a hat with him to keep his head warm. He kissed his wife and sleepy son and went again with the same small group.

They crossed the river in one raft because they planned to walk together to the other river and bridge. This time, they didn't pay for the ride in the raft because Bakir knew the man, and he told him how they had paid the previous night, but they were caught on their way. This night was clear and cold. From the hills, they heard a burst of automatic weapons. They ran over the road when it was clear. They climbed to the top of the cemetery hill to avoid the houses where people lived. If the citizens heard or saw them, they would call the police, who would find them. Then they went down the hill toward the Jugoturbina factory in front of the bridge over the Dobra River.

The sky was full of stars, which meant it would be colder and frostier than the night before. They walked through the junkyard to the river near the bridge, and they hid in the bushes because there was a police car on the bridge. Mejrin told them that they would stay there until the police left, and then he would call his cousin to take them to the city.

They huddled very close to each other to keep warm. Mooyo's long coat protected him from the frost. They waited until dawn, half asleep and half frozen.

It was daybreak when the police car finally left the bridge. From the other side of the river, they saw trains, which meant there must be a train station. Mejrin tried to call someone, but the person didn't answer. The minutes became hours and hours like years.

Finally, at around seven o'clock in the morning, the man answered the call, and Mejrin told him their location. They crept under the bridge. Luckily, they didn't see any other refugees, so there was only their group of six. A yellow Zastava 101 stopped in front of the bridge. The mobile phone rang, which was the signal it was safe to come out from hiding. After the two women and two boys got in, there was no place for Mooyo or Mejrin in the car.

"You two wait for me here, and I will return quickly," said the driver. He started driving over the bridge. The men waited for an hour, but the car didn't come back, and Mejrin became nervous.

"Let's sneak across the bridge ourselves before someone comes back to guard it. We will hide in these train cars, until that monkey comes to get us if he was not caught by the police and put in prison. Even if they caught him, we will escape on our own. I have another cousin I can call if this one fails," said Mejrin.

They straightened their clothes, wiped mud off their shoes, took off their hats, and firmly headed across the bridge in the direction of the train cars. There was a lot of trash and graffiti. There were also many bushes, which meant that the train cars had been there for a long time. Their hope was the mobile phone, with which they could call someone else to get them if their driver was caught with the first refugees in his car.

At least some of their obstacles were overcome, and they were in the free part of the new Republic of Croatia.

# CHAPTER 12

## The Republic of Croatia

November 1994

Mejrin and Mooyo waited in the train car because the man who took the women and children never answered the call. Mejrin became nervous and pale. The battery in his phone was almost empty by nine o'clock in the morning when his phone finally rang.

"Where are you man?" he asked. Mooyo couldn't hear the man's response. Mejrin finally closed his phone, which was almost dead. His face looked calm.

"When I leave the train car, you need to follow me slowly if you don't see a policeman or man in uniform," said Mejrin.

After two minutes, Mooyo jumped out of the train car, and from a corner, he studied the street in front of the bridge. People were walking quickly, possibly hurrying to their jobs. There were no men in uniform, and it was safer to walk out to join Majrin in the direction of the yellow car. Quickly, he joined Mejrin. The car stopped, and they both got in.

"When I got home with these people, my wife was awake, asking to drink coffee with them. I sat on an armchair and immediately fell asleep. She didn't know I needed to come back to get you," the man apologized.

"The battery ran out, how many times I called you. I was scared to death the police had caught you, and you all ended up in prison. Then they would come to get us, too," explained Mejrin.

Mooyo was not interested in other people's business because he was so happy he had crossed the second barrier, and he was in the car on the road to Karlovac. Soon, they arrived at an empty parking lot in front of a two-story building. From there, the driver took them to the second floor and his small apartment where they met the other refugees sitting around the table sipping coffee. They were happier when they saw them because the two women knew Mooyo better than the other guys. The driver's wife brought more coffee and sandwiches for them because it was already ten o'clock.

They enjoyed the coffee and sandwiches. During their conversation, Mooyo realized that those men knew each other well, and that they were waiting from someone to arrive from Austria to take Mejrin to Zagreb. Bakir's wife had the phone numbers of two brothers-in-law that lived somewhere in the suburbs of Zagreb.

After a while, the driver offered them beer made in Karlovac. The taste was a little bit different possibly he hadn't had it in such a long time. They sat there until twelve o'clock, and Mooyo used the time to ask if he could clean his shoes and clothes in their restroom. He checked his coat and pants for dirt from walking and lying in the junkyard the previous night. Everything could be cleaned, and he switched his pants for the other pair he had under the dirty one.

Eventually, Mejrin's cousin from Austria arrived. Then the driver, Mejrin, and the man from Austria went to the bedroom and talked in private for a long time. Mooyo's only thought was getting to Zagreb as soon as possible.

After a while, the man from Austria offered to drive them to Bakir's brother's place in the suburbs in Zagreb because he was driving there anyway. Mooyo asked how much he owed the driver for the ride from Jugoturbina, and he said that every adult should pay at least one hundred marks. He went to get money from his coat epaulet for the short ride, drinks, and food the driver gave him. He was thankful for the ride even though he only had another hundred marks in his coat, to get somewhere safe. He thought he would get there because his cousin in Zagreb owed him some money, and with that money, he would be able to travel farther.

By two o'clock, they were sitting in a wide Opel Record with Austrian license plates driving to Bakir's brother.

With the new driver, they didn't talk much, but he never stopped talking, cursing, and spitting about all the people from their city. He was from another city that forced them out because they did not want to fight with other neighbors and citizens with a different faith. The passengers sat silently praying to be safe and not caught by the police. The driver could stop in front of a police station or anywhere and call the police on them. Luckily, it didn't happen because of the business that Bakir had with him, Mejrin, and the other driver. The ride on the highway from Karlovac to Zagreb wasn't long, and they arrived at a small one story house, where Bakir's youngest brother lived with his wife. The driver unloaded them and hurried somewhere else. Mooyo asked him how much they owed him for the ride, and he answered that they did not owe him anything because he was driving that way anyway.

The homeowners opened the door politely, but Mooyo was nervous. He was still afraid that the last driver would call the police on them because of how much hate he showed against them during the drive. The housewife gave them coffee, and she hurried to make the lunch for them. There were no phones in the house, and Mooyo asked the man if he could walk for him to the phone cabin and call his cousin to come to this address and take him from there like he agreed. For lunch, they ate baked potatoes and pieces of chicken. The food tasted delicious because they were so hungry. It was already dark when his cousin finally showed up at the door.

"I will be happier if we call a taxi because I do not look presentable, and I would be too conspicuous for the police if we meet them at the train station or in a train," Mooyo said.

Again, Bakir's brother had to go to the phone cabin to call a taxi for them, but he was happy to help and show his hospitality. The taxi arrived quickly, and Mooyo said good-bye to all the people there, giving them his aunt's phone number in Slovenia if they needed transportation there. They wished each other good luck, and he left the house with his cousin.

Bucko sat in the front seat, and Mooyo sat in the back. The ride was very long as Bucko lived with his retired father close to downtown Zagreb, renting the apartment of Bucko's wife's cousin, where they lived like refugees. He left Bosnia like a patient escaping with fake medical papers. Everyone was trying to find a safe place far from the war. His dad made them a nice supper, and they ate, and asked everything they wanted to know about what was going on in camp or in their city. Bucko's wife, mother, and daughter were attacked that August morning when there was a fight over their city, and more than sixty percent of people escaped to peace. They had a fancy, big home because his dad had been a ground mine worker his whole life in Germany, working, saving, and building that home.

Mooyo updated them about his family, their family in Batnoga and Turanj, and about his plan to go to his aunt in Slovenia. Mooyo took a shower. He felt clean and sleepy after his adventures the previous night and day. It was nice to leaflets again in a clean bed in a large, warm room. He woke up early but stayed in bed until he heard someone awake. With their morning coffee, they talked about their cousin and Bucko's grandmother, who was in the refugee camp in Batnoga, too. When his cousin woke up, he joined them. Mooyo wished to call his aunt as soon as possible, so she could send the man to take him to Vrhnika, a small city about twenty miles from Ljubljana, where Mooyo had visited her almost every summer during his childhood.

His father had worked in Ljubljana for many years, and during summer breaks, he would take him to his sister to stay for almost a month, where he explored every single place in the city and its surroundings. He made a lot of friends with domestic and foreign children whose parents were all over the Balkan. Mooyo enjoyed these summers because his uncle worked the night shift and owned a bike that he could ride during the day. There was water in that place where they spent many days catching big fish with a net. With the bike, he visited surrounding farms and orchards. His aunt would come back home from her first shift with a delicious cake for him almost every day. He would never forget those days.

"I would be happy if you call my aunt, so she can send a man to take me to her," Mooyo told Bucko.

"Here is the phone. Give me the number, and we will call her," said Bucko.

"I think you need to do it from phone cabin because it is possible they are spying on this conversation," Mooyo suggested. "I don't want you to have a problem with the police because of me, and I don't care to be caught and taken somewhere in the midst of battle."

Bucko agreed to use the callbox, and his dad asked him to buy a newspaper when he got outside. Mooyo gave him the number. Bucko's dad made himself busy in the kitchen making lunch and listening to the news about fighting in Bosnia and Herzegovina. There was so much war propaganda and dishonesty, always criticizing the other side. All the news had to be taken with a grain of salt. Otherwise, you would believe the nationalistic warmongers happy for this war to last forever. They got rich selling and reselling war materials, food, clothes and shoes, gas, and everything else they could bring to the war fields, that people and army needed. A fifty kilos bag of flour was two hundred marks one liter of gas was thirty-five marks half mixed with water. Humanitarian supplies were like a drop of water in the hot summer. Still, they had survived the last two years without electricity or running water because water pumps could only work with electricity. Thus, people used spring or well water.

Bucko returned after about two hours with news from Mooyo's aunt. She said she would call them after she contacted the man who would sneak him over the Croatian-Slovenian border.

After lunch, Bucko's dad went outside for a walk, and they could talk about the business only they understood.

"I left camp with two hundred marks, and I paid one hundred to the first driver from Jugoturbina to Karlovac," Mooyo started. "I thought maybe you could pay me back some of the money you owe me."

Bucko looked thoughtful and asked him to cut his son's hair the first time and become his godfather. However, he refused to do it and give him the money.

Mooyo hadn't expected that answer because they had grown up together, played soccer, kissed girls from the neighborhood, and gone into business together. What had changed? It must be the war.

Bucko bowed his head and blushed. "Mooyo, I'm so sorry, but I don't have the money either because we must pay for this apartment and food for the two of us. I can only give you one thousand Austrian schillings. That is all, and even this is too much at the moment. I know that you put money into my business, but there is just no money now. I believe better times will come when all this is over, and I will pay you back right away," explained Bucko.

"I understand. Hopefully, my aunt can pay the man," he agreed. After all that, he still had only two hundred marks in his pocket. They sat and talked until the phone interrupted them. Bucko answered the call and handed the receiver to Mooyo, saying it was his aunt. She was thrilled to hear his voice after such a long time, but Mooyo noticed that something in her voice sounded wrong. She told him that the man who takes people over the border asked for a thousand marks for to take one person from Zagreb to Ljubljana.

Mooyo's breath stuck in the chest.

"Dear aunt, you know that I do not have that kind of money. It cost a lot to get this far. Can you call my other uncles in Slovenia and my sister in

Austria to lend me money to get out of here? I promise to pay back every single mark," pleaded Mooyo.

"All right, I will call your uncle in Nova Gorica right away because he can quickly bring money to me, but your sister and my brother are far away, and I know how you wish to be here as soon as possible. Sit there and don't worry. I will find the money and call you again to let you know when the man will come to get you," said his aunt hopefully.

After the phone call, Mooyo was depressed, but Bucko comforted him how he had lost money and his car trying to take his wife and daughter from Bosnia to Croatia. The people took money, but they didn't get them out. He remembered how a music teacher from school took his new car, a Jugo 45, for the cross-border transfer.

Bucko's dad was a good cook, but Mooyo felt bad taking someone's food, and he hoped that his aunt would soon send someone to take him away.

The night was long and full of worries. What if he paid that incredible amount of money, got caught, and was forced to return to Turanj? It would all be for nothing. He wasn't sure what the next day would bring. He wondered where his wife and son were and how his wounded brother was doing. How about his tearful mother and grieving father? He knew that his aunt would find the money because his mother had four brothers living and working there before the war started. Many Bosnians worked in construction or other factory jobs in Slovenia. Mooyo's dad worked in that field too, but he was laid off when the war started, and they closed the borders. Sleep finally found him late at night.

The noise from the streets of Zagreb woke him up even though everything was covered with a thick fall fog. The morning was still fresh with the smell of coffee Bucko's dad had made. They drank coffee while Bucko was sleeping. His dad told him he was going shopping in the city that day. Mooyo asked him to buy him a small bag, warm pajamas, and two pairs of warm socks in case he got caught and ended somewhere in a cold prison cell. Mooyo gave him one hundred marks to buy it in kuna, the new Croatian money. The man left him in the apartment. He read the rest of the newspaper from yesterday, and listened to war propaganda from different stations.

Bucko's father returned with a small bag, warm pajamas, and two pairs of warm socks. He knew he was moving west where the winters were cold, long, and snowy.

Mooyo put his passport, personal ID, and his original diploma from college in the bag although none of those documents could ensure his legal crossing. Still, they had his personal information and pictures, and everyone could recognize them because they were the same from Triglav to Djerdap. He wondered whether his wife and parents were wondering about his whereabouts and whether he was put in prison, stepped on a land mine, drowned in one of the two rivers of Karlovac, or been shot by soldiers guarding the Mreznica River. He left his aunt's phone number with his wife, but he didn't know if they called her? He watched the silent phone until nine p.m.

Finally, it rang. Bucko answered and handed the phone to Mooyo. It was his aunt calling from Vrhnika. She said that his uncle would bring the money to her tomorrow night.

"Did anyone call from Turanj?" he asked.

"Your wife called. I told her not to worry, that you made it to Zagreb, and I told her to take care of your son and herself, and we would find a way to bring them here too," explained his aunt.

"When is the guy coming?"

"Possibly, he will come tomorrow. I gave him the phone number to call you when they come to Zagreb," his aunt explained before hanging up.

Mooyo thought that it would be easier to breathe the air of that small, foreign country of Croatia. It was one of six Republics in the ex-Yugoslavia in which Mooyo was born, graduated from school and still felt at home. When other European countries broke the borders between each other, these small regions put more and more emphasis around their nationalities even though they spoke the same language and were very integrated. They resembled each other. The only difference was their faith, and it did not matter to them until these nationalists instigated this war and brought suffering to all people regardless of which religion or country they belonged. He knew for sure that he was now a foreigner because he needed more than a passport to cross.

Maybe tomorrow he could leave and go somewhere where he could again to be free and happy to walk on the streets, which until yesterday were part of him and his whole country. He saw the suffering and casualties of so many good and happy people. For fifty years, the people of the Balkans tried to heal and overcome the small differences of their religions, but now it was falling apart.

They killed each other during World War II when the foreign occupants happily robbed them. He believed that behind all this suffering were another foreign occupants, an invader who happily robbed him once again because he would sell weapons and anything else they needed for the war to these weaklings. When the war ends, they will owe him. Yet, they will take everything they have to build for the next fifty years. There was not a powerful person alive who would listen to this idea because in this region, people believed the slogan "divide and conquer." When you trust foreigners more than your own neighbor, there is no help for the country.

He remembered his happy years before the war. The memories were fading now with the past three terrible years of wartime. It was crazy that a man needed a bagful of money to escape an area where people live happy lives, sleep, wake up, go to work, and start every new day with joy. He was unhappy with the war in Cetingrad, across the border from Croatia and Bosnia, where Orthodoxes and Catholics fought on the day his son was born. It started like that, but he believed that after rain sunshine would come to his life, and he would have much happier days than those he had ever lived during the war. Mooyo hoped to God that his son would not remember these days because he was still young.

During the night, he woke up after a dream about the Croatian police catching him, putting him in prison from which he would not see daylight for a long time. Like other mornings, he and Bucko's dad had coffee together because Bucko always slept late. He and his dad lived there spending the retirement money his dad earned in Germany working in a coal mine. They could be happy because they lived on their own money, and it was the reason that Mooyo didn't want to lean on them.

At around ten o'clock, the phone rang. Bucko answered it and talked with someone for ten minutes.

"Okay. We will be there at one o'clock. Do not worry," Bucko said, hanging up.

"Godfather, make yourself ready to go, for on the main train station will be the man to take you to Slovenia."

"Why are we meeting at the main train station which is always full of police, who can be suspicious and ask me for my documents?" asked Mooyo.

"Do not worry. You never threw stones at God, so everything will be fine. Try to walk and look like before the war when you walked there freely and safely," encouraged Bucko.

"I really need to get to my aunt's. I will see what I can do over there. Can I get a refugee permit to stay and find a job because before the war, there were always jobs in Slovenia, and I could earn enough money to bring the rest of my family," added Mooyo.

They ate lunch together, and he was ready for the road. He put on his shoes and coat and put everything else in the small bag. They sat on a metro and rode to the main train station. In the subway, they didn't talk, but when they got out of the train station, Bucko told him to stay there, where were so many people were waiting for the subway. He needed to find the red Reno Five in the parking lot behind the main station, and he would come back to get him.

Luckily, there was not a single policeman around. During wartime, police would stop people without any reason and ask for their documents. Mooyo followed his friend, keeping an eye on the parking lot. After ten minutes, he waved at him from the other side of the tracks motioning him to cross. Together they walked to the parking lot where a little red car with Slovenian license plates was parked.

"I am going back, and I wish you good luck. Slowly walk to the red car and get in. There are two other people, possibly refugees in the car, and they will ride to Slovenia with the same man," said Bucko.

"Thank you for everything. I hope that better days will come, and I will be able to pay you back in some way," said Mooyo tearfully, shaking Bucko's hand.

"It was nothing. If I were in your position, I know that you would help me the same," said Bucko, heading back to the train station.

In the car was a young girl Mooyo knew from his neighborhood. He didn't know her real name, but because of her huge breasts everyone called her Samantha Fox. The other young man he didn't know, but he greeted them and sat in the back seat of the small car. Samantha was happier when she saw him. They didn't talk much because the windows of the car were open. Soon the driver arrived with another man that Mooyo knew named Pajo from Todorovo. He had visited him with his brothers-in-law during the war to take a bath and clean their clothes.

In the car, they greeted each other when the driver started the car and drove it on the busy city street. The three of them were crowded in the back seat, so they could not move. They traveled to the nearby highway, and for a short time, they were on Zagreb Ljubljana highway. The driver talked on a walkie-talkie, and from his conversation, they understood that there was another car with refugees wishing to cross the border and get to Slovenia and then to God knows where.

Their dreams carried them as far as possible from evil, torture, humiliation, death, and other abominations. The driver was driving too fast, and on his radio, he got news that they had to get off the highway, as there was a police car behind them. The driver turned off his radio. He held the steering wheel with both hands.

They took the first exit off the highway and arrived at a small city with very narrow streets, but the nameless driver skillfully managed a fast left and right on the streets. They left the small city on the Croatian–Slovenian border and turned onto a narrow road covered with white gravel by a fenced cemetery. They saw scattered houses on the other side of the cemetery. The driver again turned on his radio and asked for Shtefek, who gave him news that he was in Dezela, which the Slovenians called their new country, Slovenia.

Suddenly, the refugees understood that they had crossed the border. They had made it at last! After all their suffering and struggles, there was a universal exhale. They looked at each other's faces and smiled. Even though they still had a long way to go to reach their final destinations, the worst was over. Mooyo could scarcely believe that this time it finally worked. He was free.

They had to ride on a narrow road with many curves, over hills and valleys, a small forest, and cultivated meadows with vines swollen with ripened grapes. Mooyo controlled his excitement because the three adults were so crowded in the back seat, they could barely breathe. At last, the car stopped in front of one house not far away from the road. It was a very nice little cottage with a small vineyard and garden. The driver spoke Croatian with a slight Slovenian accent.

"You can get out of the car now with no worries. Go to the porch when I park the car in the garage and wait until another car comes to take you ahead," said the nameless driver.

# CHAPTER 13

## The Republic of Slovenia

December 1994

The four Bosnian refugees sat on the beautiful porch of Slovenia. The late fall sunshine made its way west, just like these four people. Clouds floated freely across the sky, and chilly air and sunshine covered every border. The refugees huddled timidly as shadows that someone might wipe away. The driver disappeared into the elegant cottage. They were hungry and thirsty, but they didn't know if the hunger came from the tense car ride or the fear that the police would catch them.

There were no other houses nearby, so they could finally talk freely with each other. Pajo recognized Mooyo, and he told him he was going to his sister's in Ljubljana. Samantha told them that she was going to her sister in Austria. They asked each other about friends and cousins they left in different places when another car with a Slovenian license plate arrived and stopped in front of the cottage. Their driver didn't get outside, so they assumed that the new driver was someone who often visited this cottage.

He waved to them and then went into the house. After about fifteen minutes, their first driver and the other man came to them and shook everyone's hands. He didn't tell them his name, but he said, "Welcome to Slovenia."

"They almost caught us on the highway, but luckily I did not have any person without documents with me. We had time to get off the highway and cross the border before they checked me," said the Slovenian.

---

"They cannot catch me because that car has a honed cylinder head. It can drive faster than the speedometer, " said the first driver.

The second driver turned to face the refugees. "You will ride farther with me to Ljubljana, but we will wait until the traffic is gone from the highway, and we will drive slowly."

The two men disappeared into the cottage while the refugees sat on the porch with hope that the new driver would take them to their relatives. They wanted to go quickly and be free from the Bosnian war, where everyone fought against everyone, thinking and helping their nationalist leaders to make some new big or small country under their control. The war-hungry leaders pushed their pawns, invested money, provided weapons and well-trained soldiers no matter the price. How many soldiers and civilians would die to make a great Croatia or Serbia?

The Slovenians wanted to make a small independent country without any plan to extend their borders, so Mooyo didn't condemn them for his suffering even though they started the war. Still, in this place, he was now a foreigner even though his father and many other cousins had built that Republic over many years. He remembered the sad Sundays when the bus or busses with Slovenian license plates came in front of a small store and school, where men of different ages waited with their bags of clean clothes, baked chicken, and flat bread to take with them to Ljubljana or Nova Gorica to earn money to feed and clothe their families. The workers stayed there for a week, two weeks, or a whole month, and Friday evenings, they would return home with the money they had earned. Mooyo watched these workers, and he promised himself that he would go to school as many years as possible to never ever have to pack his bag and go to Slovenia to earn his bread.

That memory came to his mind as he sat on the cottage porch, but now here he was in Slovenia to save his head. That moment he thought how "never say never", because you never know what the future will bring. He never would have guessed that something like this could happen to him.

Someone was talking, but Mooyo was far away.

Suddenly, the new driver told them to go with him. The first driver didn't come out to say goodbye when they left the porch.

Mooyo realized that it was an organized chain for transferring people, which involved many drivers and maybe police from both sides of the border. Fortunately, that car was larger and more comfortable. Samantha sat up front. The driver smoked, and he offered cigars to Samantha. The three men in the back seat suffocated from the smoke. The new driver drove the speed limit, so the travelers felt much safer. They had the feeling that there was no border to cross in front of them, and their cousins were waiting to see them.

Most of them hadn't seen their relatives since October 1991 when the fighting began in Croatia and Martic's SAO Krajina. The fighting sprang up all around the border, and many roads isolated cities and towns. During wartime, the news came to their city that the place between the river Una and Glina would become part of Croatia, which meant the citizens would become "Croatian flowers," like long ago. That meants they could bloom until someone cut them (in translation, it means to work for them for a piece of bread until their backs broke).

Mooyo thought about it while others smoked or slept in the car. When they woke up, they could see the lights of Ljubljana. He remembered all those lights from when he visited his aunt with his dad during a summer break long ago. He was always fascinated with those lights because they signaled the end of his trip in his father's car where there were always at least two or three men taking them from their city to work. His father had promised to take them if they paid for gas.

His cousins on his father's side lived at the entrance to the city. It was a short drive through the city full of lights, and they could see people in front of shop windows decorated for Christmas and New Year's. After several turns, they arrived at a narrow street and faced a building with four stores. The driver skillfully parked his car between other cars on the side of the street and turned the car off, so the travelers assumed they had arrived at the pick-up place.

They followed the driver up a spotless staircase to the second floor. Behind a big wooden door with a peephole waited a man in his early forties. He welcomed them and invited them into the apartment. They sat in the kitchen around a wooden table with six chairs. The nice decorations on the wood reminded Mooyo of the plain pieces of wood he and his uncle collected from the dump to heat their apartment during winter when his aunt lived close to the river Ljubljanica beside the old brick company.

"How was your trip?" asked the host to the driver.

"From our "meje" it wasn't bad, but they almost caught us on the highway near Brezice," said the driver.

"Who could have caught you? It would not have been the first time you escaped the police patrol," said the host. His name was Hoky, the man his aunt told him had a business taking people from Croatia to Slovenia for four hundred marks, but he quickly increased the price to a thousand marks.

The new driver and Hoky finished their business in the guest room, and when they were done, the driver disappeared with the money Hoky paid him for the transport of the refugees. He called the refugees' relatives and asked them to bring the money.

Everything was done quickly and efficiently. Mooyo could tell that the apartment was a link in the chain for illegally transporting people across the border. Mooyo waited for his aunt, worrying that she would not arrive. Hoky told him that he was driving to Vrhnika. Someone came to pay and take Samantha. Mooyo was not able to see her because all the business of paying and picking up people was done in another room. When someone came to take her, Hoky came into the kitchen asking him if he had a hundred marks with him for change. Mooyo took one hundred marks from his coat, and gave it to him. In his other pocket, he had the remaining hundred marks he got from Bucko in Zagreb. When Samantha left, they walked out to Hoky's car and drove to Vrhnika.

In the dark night, the city was full of street's lights, so Mooyo recognized some well-known places, streets, and bus stations. Everything reminded him of the past when he felt that the city was a second home, when he peacefully took the bus to Vrhnika, looked at the store windows, and walked to the bus station or train station and other precious places. Just before the war started, he drove his father from their city to Vrhnika and visited his aunt one last time. With him were his wife and his younger brother, Halil. They woke up early that Sunday and arrived around ten o'clock. They stayed until four o'clock, took his father to Ljubljana where he had place to live on Vic, in the workers' buildings, and the three of them drove back to their city. Sometimes, Mooyo slept in his father's work building if they arrived there late because of traffic. There, they could sleep, take a shower, use the kitchen, or do anything else they needed. He remembered his father's building because it was across the street from a gum factory. If the workers from the factory didn't throw him some gum, he used to call from the street, "Man, throw me some gum, man gum," until someone opened the window and threw him some gum wrapped in a paper towel. They looked like cigars, but they were sweet and lovely treats for kids. Sometimes his father's coworkers would give him gum, too, and he collected them to take back to Bosnia. Sometimes, he would collect more than a hundred pieces of gum.

While daydreaming about summers past, he almost forgot that this was not his country anymore. Suddenly, he saw the sign "Welcome to Vrhnika." His aunt had an apartment, and from the window he was able to see the main entrance to the factory where she worked. In the parking lot in front of number fourteen, Hoky parked his car. The parking lot was empty, and they walked up the familiar stairway to the door.

His aunt kissed and hugged him. She saw him there safe from the mud, freezing cold, tears, blood, injustice, lawlessness, and all the other abominations of war.

Mooyo greeted his aunt, and they talked about people that were still in the camp at Turanj or Batnoga or still in Bosnia. They had coffee and beer, even though he was very hungry.

Hoky was in a hurry, so he could not wait until Mooyo's aunt found the money for the ride. As soon as he got the money, he left. Mooyo felt happier when he saw Kazo, the son of his aunt's brother-in-law. Mooyo bought his first car, a Zastava 128 from him because they wanted to sell it. It was a Yugoslavian car, made in Kragujevac in the Red Flag factory with many parts from Italy.

The table was full of drinks and food. During the meal, he thought about his son, wife, brother, mother, and father. Did they have something to eat that day? That thought cast a small shadow on his success crossing over the border. Of course, he was nine hundred marks in debt because his aunt borrowed money from his uncle in Nova Gorica. Another uncle donated the last hundred marks. He believed God would help him pay it back as quickly as possible. If the war ever ended, there would be a job for him there, and he would work and live life as before. He knew the day would come, but he needed to be patient.

In that way, Mooyo started his days and nights in Slovenia, a country even smaller than the Republic of Croatia. It has only about two million citizens, who live on twenty thousand square kilometers. Slovenia borders Croatia, Austria, Italy, Hungary, and the Adriatic Sea.

He spent time with Kazo while his aunt and uncle worked and their son was in school. There was a television with many international channels, so they could always find something interesting to watch.

His aunt liked to watch some Spanish and Italian series with subtitles under the pictures, which he had to read to her because she was a slow reader. The stories showed people living happy, peaceful lives. When the shows were over, they returned to their humble workers' life. Mooyo shared a room with Kazo, who had two uncles in the city. Kazo told him that there was another cousin living with his own brother. They all had to have refugee permits, with which they would be legal foreigners, so they started to ask people how they could get them.

On the weekend, Mooyo's uncle and another cousin came to visit him. They talked about many events from their city and refugee camps. Everyone was worried about their families and friends still in camps in Batnoga or Turanj. They both had jobs and sent them money whenever they could. He told them that their families were in camp Batnoga. He didn't know if they were still there. He knew that most men went back with weapons to free their city and some villages, and that some people went back to their homes if they were far enough from the front lines.

Soon snow covered everything because Slovenia is surrounded by mountains and very close to the Alps, but the apartment was warm because the building where his aunt lived was almost new and had a modern furnace. The only problem was that his aunt didn't have a phone, so they used the phone in his uncle's cousin's apartment on the next floor. Mooyo finally spoke with his wife and son. She told him that they were all well, including Halil.

Just before New Year's, Mooyo's uncle, Hasan, and godfather, Semo, came to Vrhnika from Austria. Semo's wife was somewhere hiding in Karlovac, and he needed to illegally get her to Austria, but she needed a place in Slovenia to stay for a while. He had already taken his two sons there.

The biggest problem was getting a permit to live legally in Slovenia. They tried everywhere to get it but without success. Again, they went to the guy who took them there because someone told them that he could get permission to stay for a hundred marks. One night, Hoky came to their apartment to get their personal IDs, and they promised him when he returned with the permits, they would pay him. Without the permits, it was dangerous to step outside the apartment.

Mooyo stayed inside all the time, but Kazo visited his cousins and friends all around the city. His father visited him often from Austria with many supplies for his brother and sister-in-law. One weekend, Mooyo's uncle from Germany and his sister from Austria arrived with some clothes for him and some groceries for his aunt. He felt much better that he was not hurting his aunt's family's budget. Everyone gave him some money before they left, so he had a couple hundred marks.

One weekend, his father's good friend visited with his wife. He still hadn't received his refugee ID. The other two boys living illegally like Mooyo had heard a story that the police checked Hoky, found their old IDs, but they let him go because they didn't have any proof that he was doing something illegal. All three of them got so scared that the police would catch them and send them back to the Bosnian fighting during the worst winter time.

Kazo and Refik decided to go to the police station and report them selves before the police came to their cousin's apartment to get them. Mooyo refused to go with them, no matter what. However, the same day, a police car drove to the building, and two young policemen came out and knocked on the door. They asked for him by name and demanded he come out and follow them to the station. What else could he do, but get dressed and go with them? He dressed warmly because he was always scared of cold prison cells and the possibility of being pushed out and taken back to the Bosnian war. The biggest problem for him was he didn't know what Kazo and Refik had told them about him, how he got there, and God knows what else. He was sorry more for his aunt and uncle than for himself because they were honest people who never had problems with the police. He could not forgive himself for their situation. It distressed him more than the possibility that they might send him back to the war. He had wasted thousands of marks traveling from Croatia to Slovenia, and he still owed to his uncle and had vowed to pay it back. Since the war started, their salary was paid in groceries. Every now and then, they received some money in Austrian schillings or German marks.

He was very scared, but now he had some experience riding in police cars and being interrogated.

*If I need to return and fight, so be it*, thought Mooyo in the back seat in police car. *What should I say? What kind of story should I tell to get permission to stay here?* Mooyo tried to devise a story of how he left Turanj and arrived there.

They took him to police station without handcuffs. They asked him for his ID, and he handed them his Ex-Yugoslavian passport, so they could see his picture and all other information although they seemed to already know it. They put him into a small room with two chairs. There he sat until one policeman came in to take him to another office where a middle-aged man in civilian clothes was sitting. He offered him a seat and started with many questions like who drove him over the border, how much he charged him, where he crossed the border of the Republic of Slovenia? Why did he come to Vrhnika? How many days was he there? Who are the people he was staying with?

"Mister, I am the man from that passport, a refugee from Bosnia. I was a refugee in Batnoga, from where I fled to Turanj, and from Turanj over Croatia to Slovenia. From the Karlovac bus station, I came on foot from Turanj, and from Karlovac to your border a Bosnian man took me. Just before the border, he told me to leave his car because he was afraid to take me over even though he wanted to help. He showed me where the check point was, so I walked around the check point. I ended up in a small city that had signs in Slovenian. That's when I realized I was in Slovenia. I came to the bus station, bought a ticket to Ljubljana and arrived there by bus. In Ljubljana, I found bus number three and rode to Vrhnika straight to my aunt and uncle's because I do not have other relatives here. I was not able to go anywhere else. I tried to legalize my presence here, but they didn't give me a refugee ID. I have been here for thirty-five days. They have fed me and given me clothes, so I am very thankful and happy with them, and I do not need anything else." Mooyo finished his story with some truths and many lies.

From the sour look on the inspector's face, Mooyo could tell that he had heard an entirely different story from someone else.

"Listen young man, I know that you know the area well, but I cannot believe that you walked from Turanj and got over our border by yourself. The other thing is that I know the man named Hoky, who you and two young men crossed the border with. That man, your aunt paid one thousand German marks for your transportation from Croatia, from the main station in Zagreb over Brezice to Ljubljana and from Ljubljana to Vrhnika. So, let's not make up any more stories. As you see, we know very well where and how you crossed the border, how much you paid for it, when you came here, who transported you, so we need your confirmation. If you refuse to confirm our story, you will go back to Croatia tomorrow and back to Bosnia, straight to Sarajevo. Therefore, for your own good and to save everyone's time, agree to our version. You need to sign this statement. We have proof from safe sources. If you do, you will be able to get a legal refugee ID to stay here until the war ends." ended the inspector.

Mooyo didn't know what to do. This inspector clearly knew the truth. Was it worthwhile to lose so much already borrowed money, only to be pushed back into the Bosnian mud, misery, injustice, and disrespect for human life? His head hurt. The policeman walked him through a hallway where his uncle and third boy's brother were. He waved to them when the policeman took him to another room. When the policeman opened the door to let him in, he saw Kazo and Refik. The policeman locked the door, and the three refugees were finally alone. Mooyo felt much better because he could learn their made-up stories of crossing the Slovenian border illegally and coming to Vrhnika to their cousins.

"What did they ask you?" asked Kazo.

"They asked me how and why I came to Vrhnika? They made me tell my whole story, and then the inspector told me in detail who drove me, when, how much my aunt and uncle paid for the ride and where. He knew everything, but he asked me to sign and confirm his story. He told me if I refuse to sign it, he will take me back tomorrow to the Slovenian-Croatian border and from there to Bosnia," Mooyo said.

"What did the two of you say during examination?"

"We said that the three of us came on foot to the Slovenian-Croatian border. Then we walked about two kilometers away from the border check point, and we came back to the highway Zagreb-Ljubljana, stopped the car that was heading to Ljubljana, and in that way we came," said Refik.

"Man, you made the mistake of telling them we came together because now our stories don't match. Now, it is too late. He has his own version of it, and his story is the most accurate, and he knows it," added Kazo.

"Boys, I think that someone told on us to the police," stated Mooyo. "Possibly, it was whoever told on Hoky, and we will suffer for it."

"That means, that all of us need to sign the police statement or tomorrow go back to the border?" asked Refik.

For a long time they discussed their situation. During the night, they were called one by one back to the examination room until they finally decided to sign the statement. After that, the police brought Hoky to the police station, and they had to say how they paid him for the ride, but who really drove them they didn't know. What happened with Hoky they never foundout. They were allowed to return to their cousins, with a promise and paper from the investigating officer that they would go to court in the morning.

A few days later, Hoky threatened to fight Mooyo, but nothing happened. They heard how Hoky had been betrayed by his sister-in-law because they had argued about something, and she told the police about his illegal business with refugees. The police searched him and his car, and they found refugee IDs.

Mooyo escaped prison and war once again. It wasn't hard this time because he had learned from his past experiences, but he was sorry he put his aunt and uncle in a difficult situation. When they got back to the apartment, his aunt was crying. He felt guilty for the sorrow he had caused. They ate supper in the middle of the night and went to sleep, but he had a hard time sleeping. When he finally drifted off, he dreamed he was caught and forced in front of a firing squad. He woke up in a sweat feeling sick to his stomach. Being a fugitive was a kind of prison. He was scared to go outside and be checked by the police, and now he was forced to go to court.

The next day, they had a coffee and breakfast and went to court. Snow and ice crunched beneath their shoes as they walked over the main street through the beautiful city.

At the entrance to the court, they handed the paper they received when they left the police station. They sat in the waiting room and waited to be called. Finally, Mooyo was called to stand before the judge.

He entered a room with enormous windows from which he saw a thick and long icicle hanging outside. Beside the judge was his secretary typing his information. The judge was a tiny, old man who was hard to see behind his big table and comfortable chair. He asked Mooyo to sit and started to speak. He emphasized how Mooyo had violated the border of the Republic of Slovenia, and he decided to charge him a fine of eighty thousand tolarjev, Slovenian money. When the judge finished his sentence, Mooyo raised his hand to say something before he finished his verdict.

"Your Honor," said Mooyo in his Serbo-Croatian language, "I do not agree with your verdict. You said that I violated the border of the Independent Republic of Slovenia. First, your Independent Republic of Slovenia until recently was a part of my country too, and this Independent Republic of Slovenia was constructed by my father and many other relatives for more than thirty years. I didn't take any illegal weapons or drugs over your border or anything else that can be against the law. I am merely a war refugee who crossed your border to save my life. Third, I didn't break any store windows during these thirty-five days. In fact, I didn't cause any damage, and I didn't ask anything from this country other than a piece of paper granting me permission to stay here legally and walk in peace in this fine city. My aunt has provided me with clothes, food, drink, and a warm room. And yet, you have sentenced her to pay fines, for what? If you are an independent country as you say, and I know you are, surely you signed the Geneva Conventions in which it states that you must provide and protect war-harmed civilians, and help them find shelter and minimum life conditions. If I survive this war, God will help me and let peace come again to the Balkans. I will tell and write about this inhuman treatment against refugees in all the newspapers and other media. I didn't ask for much from this country, just a piece of paper granting permission to stay here and to live in freedom. Thank you for letting me say these words, and now you can judge me however you see fit," said Mooyo.

The judge listened to him with his head bowed.

"Take the paper out and add a new one," shouted the judge to the secretary. She did it immediately and started typing again. When she stopped and let the judge see, he started to dictate another verdict in a calmer voice. He again said that Mooyo violated their laws by crossing their border. However, this time there was no fine for the violation.

"The same person may live in the Independent Republic of Slovenia for the next thirty days," finished the judge.

He told him to wait in the hallway for the signed and certified verdict. With that paper, Mooyo could walk around the Republic of Slovenia freely for only thirty days, and after that he had to leave without complaint. He would stay there, for there was a very deep snow on the border with Austria. He heard some news about how police on the border shot refugees that tried to cross that border. They killed a sixteen-year-old boy, which symbolized how very strongly that country hated refugees.

When he got back to the hallway, Refik and Kazo were curious to hear what had happened in the courtroom. He told them how he could live in Slovenia for thirty days, but it was not so bad because the judge had removed the fine. He would find some solution for the new situation. He waited in the hallway for his paper, and for his friends' verdicts. Since they all had permits to stay there for thirty days, they walked back to Gradisce fourteen to discuss what they should do next.

Mooyo pleaded with his aunt's neighbor to use her phone to call his cousin Ramo, who lived in Ljubljana. He described his situation and asked him after thirty days if he could move to his apartment until he found a way to go to Austria or Germany. Ramo invited him to his apartment any time, day or night, which pleased him. That day, he called his other cousin Doky, who had left Bosnia just before the war and found a job in Austria. He gave him the number to call him back. Using an outside phone was a little dangerous for him because Hoky could attack him or some of his friends, and if he got in trouble with the police, they would send him straight to the border with Croatia. Doky called him back immediately.

"Godfather, where are you, and where did you call me from?" asked Doky.

"I made my way from Turanj to Slovenia to my aunt, where I am safe for thirty days, but someone reported me because I was here illegally. Therefore, I cannot apply for a permanent refugee permit. That means I have a court order to leave Slovenia after thirty days. I already paid about one thousand two hundred German marks to get here. Most of it was borrowed, so if you know any way to help me cross the Austrian border to come to you or to my sister, I will greatly appreciate it," said Mooyo.

"Do not worry about anything. Stay there and wait until I find a solution," said Doky. "I will call you back at this number when I do."

After that phone call, Mooyo lived in hope. He knew his sister and uncle did not know any way to help him cross the border because they lived quiet, honest lives. His impatience forced him to act illegally.

When his aunt came home that day and heard about his phone call, she cried again.

Every day, he waited for the call from Austria. Snow was falling as if it would never stop, and it was extremely cold outside. He spent his time playing cards with Kazo, his aunt, and her son. His uncle usually slept during the day because he worked the night shift. During the night, they watched television as long as possible to be able to sleep longer in the morning, not to awake their host. He consoled himself planning a backup apartment, if his permit to stay there expired. Sometimes, he listened to the news on Radio Free Europe, but there was only war propaganda, lies, and incitement to murder the innocent.

It was already the middle of January 1995, and Mooyo was losing his faith that Doky could do something for him. Finally, at around one o'clock in the afternoon, at the parking lot in front of his aunt's apartment, he noticed a car with Austrian license plates. He recognized Semo, but he didn't know the other man. It was a spark of hope that Semo was coming with some good news from Doky because they lived and worked in the same city. They got out of the car while Mooyo waited for them.

In the stairway, Semo told him, "Get dressed. We are going to Austria today."

Mooyo didn't know if he was joking or not. The other man was Babic, who knew his father.

"Did you really come to take me?" asked Mooyo.

"Why else would we have come? Here is a passport, learn the information as we will leave as soon as you are ready," commanded Semo.

When he opened the passport, it was Doky's. They looked so different in their faces and hair that a blind chicken could see that Mooyo was different than the man in the picture. Doky had long, orange hair and a very narrow face while he had black hair and a wide face. Although he hadn't had a haircut for months, his hair was long, but it was still the wrong color.

Later, Mooyo realized that Babic had come to collect two kids with his own children's passports and Mooyo with Doky's passport. When his aunt came back from work, she was surprised by the guests and with the news that they were taking him to Austria.

They had coffee and lunch together because Mooyo and Kazo always had lunch and coffee ready when she returned. Mooyo dressed in layers of his pajama, warm socks, shirt, sweater and coat, which his sister brought for him from Austria during the visit.

By around four o'clock, everyone was ready to go. As a precaution, he told them that he would walk to the main street, and they could pick him up from there. On their way, they picked up the two children.

The roomy German Opel Record quickly took them to the highway in Ljubljana, Vienna. However, these men didn't follow the highway with the new tunnels but instead went to an old checkpoint on the border between Slovenia and Austria called Karavanke.

"When we get to the border and the check point, do not be scared. Sit there comfortably, and I will hand the passports to the policeman. It won't be so bad. In this snow and cold, they will not ask us to get out of the car," said Semo.

The information about Doky's birthday was easy to remember, and everything else Mooyo knew very well. Still, he was nervous for himself and Doky. What would happen to him and his passport if the police on a border discovered him using his cousin's passport? He remembered an old song. Whenever they went somewhere and returned over Hadzija's high fence, they put their hands on each other's shoulders and sang, "I have a friend, whose name is sorrow." How nice a childhood they had together.

He was awoken from his thoughts by the lights of the checkpoint. He froze in the back seat and dug his nails in the seat in front of him. There were two cars in front of them, but the Slovenian policeman let them move on without even checking their documents. Possibly it was too cold to open the window of his office. They stopped the car came in front of the window and stopped as a policeman on the border waved them on.

The Austrian policeman was outside because the cars and people were entering his country. He took passports from the passengers in the cars in front of them, checked them, and handed them back to the drivers. Luckily, he didn't ask one to get out of the car. The border station had a little roof. However, there were not many cars and busses to check. The cars in front of them were stopped and motioned to drive over the ramp, where the policeman pressed a switch on the side of his booth.

It was their turn next. Semo stopped the car, opened the window, and greeted the policeman, handing him the three passports. The policeman took the passports and rushed them through, looking through the window to see how many travelers were in the car, and asking if they had someone in the trunk. Semo laughed at that question and turned the car off. He handed his car keys to him to check it by himself. The border policeman laughed, handed the keys back, and said that they could go, lifting the barrier in front of them. Mooyo didn't understand the conversation between the driver and border policeman because it was in German, but Semo told him about it later.

Again he remembered Bucko's words, "Godfather, you have never hurled stones at God."

# CHAPTER 14

## Austria

January 1995

Snow was falling on the wide highway toward Linz. They had crossed one more Western European border without any problem. Whether the refugees would stop there and live happily in this snow-covered, mountainous country, they didn't know. They wished to stop, to be closer to their native land, cousins, and family. But, it didn't depend on them. Everything depended on the regulations for war refugees. Even though it was cold, they hoped there would be stoves to warm them. Laws would protect people forced from the war to their warm hearths. They were ready to earn their own bread and a warm room, without begging what they needed to do for it, just to stay close to their native land.

On the highway, they saw snowplows. Semo wanted to stop and call Mooyo's aunt to tell her that they had made it over the border, but Mooyo told him to get a little farther away from the checkpoint and then call her from a phone booth. When they had traveled about one hour away, Semo stopped the car at a gas station and called her and Doky to tell them they were close to Linz.

"Your aunt cried again because you left her," said Semo when he came back to car. Semo bought coffee for the men and juice for the children, and they happily drove to Linz followed by huge snowflakes. The children fell asleep, so the three men talked about the events in Bosnia.

They arrived at a small town, where they gave the children to their parents. Only Babic went into their apartment while Semo and Mooyo stayed in the car.

Mooyo didn't know where they were, but he thought that they must be close to the suburbs of Linz. When Babic returned, they drove about fifteen minutes to the toll crossing, with a large parking lot, and they parked. From there, the men walked to the elevator and went to the third floor of the building. The hallway was immaculate with many doors. They stopped at number eighty-five and knocked on the door. In front of them stood Mooyo's savior, Doky and his uncle Hasan, who worked for years in Austria. He was his father's stepbrother. They shook hands heartily. Mooyo did not have the words to thank Doky for his sacrifice and risk offering his own passport and visa, which was his permit to stay and work in that western country.

Doky set the table with food and drinks for all of them. There were two beds, two cabinets, and a little sink in the room. Later, Mooyo learned that Doky shared the room with another man who was not there at that time, so he could sleep on his bed. The whole building was like a workers hotel for singles, with showers and restrooms in the hallways.

For a long time they sat, talked, ate, and drank because Doky wanted to know what had happened over the past four years, how Mooyo got to Slovenia, and much more. After an hour, Semo and Babic decided to leave. Hasan asked them how much he owed them for the risky drive Mooyo over the border, but they said nothing. Nevertheless, Hasan gave Babic one thousand schillings for the gas and highway cost. Mooyo expressed appreciation for the wonderful service for them. They said good-bye, and he never saw them again.

Hasan stayed, and they talked about the family and friends Mooyo left behind at the refugee camps.

Thus, he started the hours and days living illegally in Austria. From their conversation, he learned that it was very hard to get permission to stay in Austria as a single man. He guessed that the government only felt pity for refugee families. He realized that they didn't know much about how to get refugee permits to stay there either because they both lived there alone. Doky was not married, and Hasan's whole family still lived in Bosnia.

In the morning, Mooyo noticed the area around the buildings where so many different people lived. For breakfast they bought a pie from an Albanian man who lived and baked pies in his apartment in their building.

Because it was a weekend, Doky was off work. They visited Semo's brother, Baja, who successfully brought his whole family from Bosnia. Mooyo taught some children from that family in elementary school because before the war, they lived in the same area, and Mooyo was a teacher. They welcomed them into their small apartment in Linz, but they didn't know how and where to apply for a refugee permit.

Eventually, Mooyo learned about the life of workers in Austria and Germany. Many of them didn't speak the language of the country where they lived even if they worked and lived there many years. Many of them worked as builders, bricklayers, or carpenters. They learned only as much language as they needed for that job. They worked and slept, living simple lives. During the weekends, they bought newspapers in their language and listened to Radio Free Europe in their language.

After these conversations, he realized that he needed to go further west, and the next country was Germany. He talked with his sister, and they promised him that they would find a guy who was driving a truck across western countries to take him to Munich, Germany, where his uncle lived and worked.

He remembered his first visit in June 1986, when he was a student. His uncle invited him to visit, and he applied for his first passport. After he was done with his military service, he traveled with his uncle on his mother's side. His Uncle Ibrahim didn't charge him for the ride because he was a student, hard worker, and an honest young man. He had the honor of sitting in the front seat next to the driver, and from that seat he was able to see through the big windshield the way to his place and all the places to Munich. It was his first trip outside Yugoslavia. He was in awe when he saw the bridges over the Austrian highways. He was surprised when he saw the lights of a big city like Munich. His uncle Rasim waited for him in front of the main bus station, and he took him to his apartment where he lived with his wife and newborn son, for whom Mooyo would become godfather.

These were unforgettable memories for him. There his uncle had bought him his first cassette radio, a jean jacket, and pants. In the city, he took him to places where his father and uncle used to go.

There at the main bus and train station, Mooyo tasted his first Big-Mac, which was so delicious that he could still taste it.

He remembered his second visit to Munich in 1990, just before New Year's and the war, when he came with his new bride, Fata, on their honeymoon. They bought their first color television and VCR because his uncle gave him his import privilege, so they didn't have to pay import tax on the goods for a year.

*How nice he has it here,* he thought.

The telephone booth was in the hallway in Doky's building, so he was able to call and to be called. He called his uncle and told him about the new situation and the permission to stay in Austria. His uncle told him that it was not a big problem to get permission in Germany because his other cousin had gotten it easily.

These days, being in Doky's room was nice. Doky had some nice books that Mooyo started to read when Doky was at work. He was scared to go outside by himself and get in trouble. He only went outside to the phone booth to call or to answer the ringing. Doky treated him as his dearest guest, but Mooyo wanted to be a free man, who could freely leave without any fear. Those police station examinations and hiding in an apartment were enough for him. He wanted to go to Germany as soon as possible to feel freedom inside and outside. It made him nervous, like the bad news from Bosnian battlefields and thoughts about his son, wife, father, mother, and brother in the war zone. He knew that he needed to calm down because it was important to try to settle in Germany or somewhere else.

From time to time, he talked with his sister and brother-in-law who lived on the border between Austria and Germany, in the small town of Braunau. They promised to find a way to get him over the border. They knew some truck drivers, men from Bosnia and their homeland, who drove trucks all over Europe, and they were waiting for a load for Germany. It gave him hope.

His aunt spoke German well, for she came to Germany at a very young age, and she graduated from high school in German. Mooyo believed that she knew where to apply and get refugee permission to stay and live there. His cousin got the document already. He believed if he could get a legal paper to stay there, he would find a job and earn money to get his son, wife, father, mother, and brother. He was bothered of the money he borrowed from his uncle and eager to pay it back. Dreams of success went with him to bed, and they woke up with him every morning.

On the sixth day of his new life in Austria, his sister called him to say that a driver they knew had a load for Germany, for tomorrow evening, and she said that she would call back to tell Doky the place he needed to drive Mooyo, to meet the driver who would take him over the Austrian-German border.

That news made him very happy, and he told Doky the happy news. Doky was sad that Mooyo could not get permission to stay there with him. He thought of asking his boss to hire Mooyo to do heating which he would teach him because Doky was good at it. Doky graduated from high school in Banja Luka in heating before Mooyo went there for his schooling.

Just before the Bosnian war began, he was visiting their place and invited Mooyo to go with him to Austria, but Mooyo never imagined that such horrors could happen in such a peaceful country. He and his wife had jobs, a little apartment in a school building, and they were building a new home which was almost finished. Moreover, his wife was pregnant with their first child. Mooyo was working at a job in his field. He knew everyone around him. In his mind, he imagined busses taking workers to the west, carrying bags. He could not leave. If only he had known what would happen there, he would have happily left with Doky. It wasn't easy to leave his home, but when a man faces war, it is the darkest thing that can happen in a man's life. Then the man would be ready to leave without any tears of regret.

His last night in Austria, he and Doky reminisced about their childhood. They laughed about their mischief walking to school and climbing neighborhood fruit trees, and all the other beautiful memories they shared. Doky's house was three down from Mooyo's, so they could call each other from their yards.

"Hey godfather, do you remember that one morning we were getting ready to go to the forest Krshnovac to pick some chanterelles, but while you were waiting for me, you took that old thing to cut the grass and ran over a bee hive?" Doky asked.

"How could I forget it? Some bees bit my head because they got stuck in my messy hair. I threw the hand mover and ran to the house. When some of them stung me, I dunked my head in the cow trough with the waste for cows to drink and eat," said Mooyo, laughing.

"Do you remember when Aunt Cimo got married?" asked Mooyo.

"How could I forget? I walked her out from our home, and the groom put faded money in my hand in the dark because there were no electric lights from some reason. You came from somewhere, and I told you that I got a handful of money. We hurried to the grocery store to see how much money I had. Under the lights, we discovered that there was enough money in my hands for two cokes," said Doky.

They both were happy recalling better days. They were so far from their homeland, in the workers hotel.

Together they sang, "I have a friend whose name is sorrow. He is my father and mother. He is hiding very deep in my heart and will always follow me in my life."

They reminisced until late at night when they finally fell asleep.

In the morning, Mooyo woke up early, but he stayed in bed not wanting to wake up his cousin.

Mooyo quietly read the rest of the book he found the first day in Doky's room because he wanted to finish it before he left that night. It was a beautiful winter morning, which reminded him of the mornings before the war.

When Doky woke up, they had coffee, and Doky made them breakfast. Afterwards, they made called Mooyo's sister to confirm the time and place where the truck driver would be waiting. His sister needed to talk with his uncle in Munich to arrange a place where he would be waiting to take Mooyo to his apartment.

It was a busy day because he had to cross another border illegally or be captured. He would feel very bad if someone had trouble with the police like his cousins in Slovenia.

Around four o'clock, they were ready to go in Doky's Mazda. It was snowing, and it was nearly dark outside. They drove outside the city to the highway and stopped at a gas station where they saw green trucks and a couple of small cars. When they met the driver who would take Mooyo over the border, he recognized him from his school. He was a biology teacher in a nearby village. Because of the very low teacher's salary, he got a job as a driver in Austria. Despite the high inflation, he still lived a nice life with the two jobs.

After inflation came to Markovic and tied their money to German marks, salaries were very good. Thus, Mooyo made more money teaching than he could make in Austria. He used his salary to build his house, which he was forced to leave in Bosnia with all his hopes and dreams for a better life.

On his farewell with Doky, they shook hands and promised that they would stay in touch.

"Thank you for everything you did for me," said Mooyo.

"I know that you would have done the same if I was in your situation," replied Doky.

Mooyo climbed into the truck. The truck driver got inside, and the green truck drove onto the highway. The big wipers moved the melting snow from the hot windshield.

The driver saw the worry on Mooyo's face.

"Do not worry. Getting across this border is a cat's cough. I cross it two to three times a week, and it is very rare for someone to ask for my documents," said the driver.

"I know, but I don't want you to get in trouble because of me, the illegal traveler. I hope I will be lucky like other refugees."

"Do not worry. Just sit there, and you will be my co-pilot. Nobody will ask you a question," encouraged the driver.

"I hope everything will go smoothly, but if it goes wrong remember, I stopped you at the gas station and asked you to take me to Munich, where I allegedly live and work, and you didn't know I did not have legal documents. If I get caught, I will be in trouble," said Mooyo.

Two hours of driving passed quickly, and through the snow, they recognized the signs of the checkpoint and border with Germany. There were different lanes for different cars and trucks.

"If you don't mind, I want to go up to your loft, not to risk the possibility of trouble," Mooyo said.

"However you want, it is fine with me," said the driver.

Mooyo climbed up in the bed, which was above the driver's head and got under the blanket waiting to cross the border. Through the tiny window, he saw the trucks slowing down, but they didn't stop between two small booths. A huge German policeman was reading his newspaper, and under his glasses, he motioned for them to go. His heart was pounding with anxiety and happiness that everything was going smoothly.

When they got through the checkpoint, and the trucks speeded up, the driver called, "Come down, the fat man wants to see your papers," joked the driver, with a cup of coffee for Mooyo in his hand.

# CHAPTER 15

## Munich, Germany

January 25, 1995

Downy snowflakes fell on the windshield of the green truck. Mooyo watched them fall. He knew that he was far away from the war. He was floating like the snowflakes and was heading somewhere he would find a new warm home.

He knew for sure that he was welcome to stay with his uncle and aunt, but he felt that his life was a puzzle, which needed to be put together. The biggest problem for him was the new language because in elementary school, he only studied Russian. They had German in high school, but it was hard to start it with other classmates who had already been studying it for the past four years. Who could have predicted he would need it some day? He would have to rely on his uncle and aunt for a while, but if he came to the point of getting a permit to stay there, he was ready to buy a dictionary and start studying the new language.

He thought about many things while riding on the highway toward Munich. The driver so often talked with other drivers over his radio, and he heard that they were planning on stopping at a gas station close to New Perlach. He assumed that his uncle would be waiting there for him. The driver and Mooyo had warm coffee, music in their language, and happiness in their souls, for they had easily crossed the border.

The driver had offered to take him over the border for free, and Mooyo knew that there was no way to change his mind. After the second hour, even over the night and snow, they could see denser patches of houses and businesses. It was a sign that Munich was ahead. Through the windshield, he saw other trucks getting off the highway at the exit and his truck followed.

"Your uncle should be up ahead. If you cannot get permission to stay here, take this number and call me. I will take you to another European country. When I get the load, I will take you for free wherever you want," said this driver, with a wide smile on his face.

"To tell you the truth, I do not know where else to go myself. Here I have cousins who know the language, and I hope they will help me get a visa. If I don't get it, I will call you," said Mooyo.

The trucks stopped slowly at a parking lot, where one car was parked with an open window. Inside the car, two men were smoking, and on both sides of the opened windows came clouds of smoke. When they got out of the truck, Mooyo could see inside the yellow Passat. It was his uncle and cousin, Sabid. They both smoked like Russians, but now possibly more because they were scared about what they were doing even though the truck driver had taken the biggest risk. On their faces, he was able to see they were excited, nervous, and happy at the same time.

They shook cold hands. The other drivers cleaned the ice from the mirrors, when Mooyo's driver spoke to his cousins.

"What do I owe you for this big help?" asked his uncle.

"You owe me nothing. I would do this for any man to preserve his life until that damn war ends," said the driver. Mooyo's uncle insisted on putting one hundred marks in the driver's pocket for drinks and food.

Once more, they shook hands, and then everyone returned to their vehicles.

Mooyo joined his uncle and Sabid and headed to the suburbs of Munich.

The driver and his co-driver smoked heavily all the way, which nearly suffocated Mooyo in the back seat.

When they got very close to his uncle's apartment, they saw a police car behind them. They worried someone told on them to the police. Luckily, the car soon turned the other direction, and they relaxed. The city glimmered in Mooyo's eyes with a layer of snow, and the street's lights made night look like day.

They arrived at a parking lot behind the building where his uncle lived.

When his uncle rang the bell, the smell of that stairway reminded Mooyo of New Year's in 1990, when he had visited with his wife during winter break. His aunt opened the door, and her two kids welcomed him. They hugged each other.

"Here I am again aunt, but this time I do not have cigars, like when I came here during the peace time," he joked.

When he visited them the first time, he came with a full bag because he didn't know it was illegal to take cigars and other items over the border. He was lucky no one had checked his bag. Although his uncle and aunt were very happy, they warned him not to do it again.

"We are happy you made it here, and who ever needs cigars can buy them at the main station," said his aunt.

They sat down in the large living room, where his aunt served drinks and food. They talked until very late in the night.

Mooyo liked German beer, and almost no one cooked as well as his aunt. Her specialties were spaghetti, mixed vegetables and rice, cheese and salami with the spinach.

When they came on vacation to Bosnia before the war, they always brought spaghetti with a special sauce for him, and salami made with cheese. She would cook it in Bosnia and invite him for supper or lunch with a taste of Germany. His uncle would bring beer from Munich, and from the smell and taste of the food and drink, he would feel like he was in Germany again.

Late that night, Sabid went to his apartment, and they decided to stay with them for the night. Mooyo got a warm and comfortable bed with his little cousin.

The cold and frosty morning woke them up before usual. Mooyo wanted to take a shower, to wash off all that smoke from his uncle and cousin.

They let the kids sleep while the three of them enjoyed their morning coffee and planned what to do that day. They wanted to take him to the store even though they brought clothes for him when they visited Vrhnika. They also wanted to show him the place where refugees from Bosnia lived because they were sure that he would be able to get a visa to stay there. After it, they planned to find him a job. That was his wish too as he knew that if he found a job, he could get the rest of his family from Bosnia.

After breakfast, they all took a ride to Centrum, the place "where you can buy everything from a needle to a locomotive." While his aunt shopped, the two men went to a restaurant to eat bratwurst with sauerkraut and to drink a glass of beer like old times.

In the shopping center were so many people walking around, looking in the store windows, going in and out of stores, or eating and drinking in the hallways.

*How carefree, happy, and satisfied these people are*, thought Mooyo. He could not understand what happened to them. How could all that happiness and peace transform into sorrow, shootings, hate, destruction, and death? He could not understand it. He was trying to relax, to put at least a made-up smile on his face, but it lasted just for a moment. His thoughts traveled back to his home, and looking for the answer of what happened to his country?

Finally, his aunt and her children returned, saving him from his thoughts. They spent some more time walking and looking through store windows, and in the end, they stopped to buy groceries. Then, they went back to their apartment on Kurt-Eisner Strasse. His uncle bought a video tape from someone who taped the refugee camp in Batnoga and Turanj, and they spent the rest of the day watching them. When they watched the videos, his aunt cooked something that smelled delectable.

After the meal, Mooyo told them to go sledding on the small hill behind the building. He pulled the sled for them. He enjoyed their happiness and luck, but wondered where his son was at that moment? Was he happy? Did he have something to eat? Were the fighting lines far away from them? He knew that he needed to do something for his small boy, but he was still helpless.

His aunt promised that she would take him to the police station to apply for a visa on Wednesday. It was the first step for him to get his little son.

They played in the snow until he felt cold, and he realized the children must be cold, too. He convinced them to go back to the apartment.

He remembered when his aunt sent her son once to Bosnia to his mother to get two eggs. Because his mother had many chickens and eggs, she gave him four eggs to take home, but he asked her so many times, "Aunt, why do I need to take four, when Mommy told me to bring only two?"

"Take it to your mother as I said," Mooyo's mother told him.

They didn't get any warmer when the bell rang from the entrance door. The children were so happy to have another guest. Soon Mooyo's cousin Nurko, who also lived in Munich, visited. Mooyo was very happy to see him because they hadn't seen each other since the war began, and he thought that he could get information from him about applying for a visa. Nurko told him that he had to go to work in the morning. When he left, he put a hundred marks in Mooyo's pocket. He refused to take it from him, but Nurko insisted.

He shared the same thought with Mooyo's aunt and uncle that there would be no problem getting the refugee visa, which encouraged him that he would soon be free man again.

The rest of his uncle's family was ready to go to sleep. Mooyo waited with his uncle to listen to the news from Radio Free Europe, which was no better than the previous night. Surely, it would be better for both of them not to listen to the news, but they could not help it. The news made them worry more about the family members that were still in the war and suffering. Finally, they fell asleep, but in their dreams came images of war.

Mooyo woke up when the family got up for work and school. He joined his uncle for coffee, and to say good-bye. He was alone with the newspaper his cousin left the previous night. He thought again about his son, wife, father, mother, and brother. He still felt helpless to them.

The day was very long and his thoughts raced. He was so happy when finally someone rang the doorbell. He assumed that the children were back from school. Of course, they came back with red noses and cheeks. They took off their coats and bags, to play before their parents come back. They both spoke their native language so well that Mooyo was impressed. They started working on their homework.

Time passed faster with them around and especially when his uncle and aunt came back. They had coffee and his aunt already filled the pots with something for the supper.

Tomorrow would be another long day for him, and after that, Wednesday was coming at last. He couldn't wait. After taking a bath, he slept dreamlessly. Tuesday was a repeat of Monday.

On Wednesday, his aunt worked a halfday, so she arrived home around eleven-thirty to take Mooyo to the police station in downtown Munich. It was cold, but the streets were cleared of the snow.

Mooyo had his passport and ID. The waiting crowd inside the police station talked in different languages. Mooyo liked the rules in the West. Whenever you arrive, you take a number and wait there until someone calls your number. Mooyo felt better knowing his aunt who spoke good German was there to help him.

After about a quarter hour, they called his number. Mooyo handed his documents to his aunt, and she handed them through window to the clerk explaining. The clerk handed back the form to be filled out. She told him to go to another office where they could do it. In that office, they needed to wait to be called.

They sat there until a nicely dressed lady came through the big metal door and called Mooyo telling his aunt to stay and wait there for him. She would be his translator. Her name was Mrs. Jovanovic.

"Do not hesitate, answer the questions truthfully, and I will say the same answer in German for you," said Mrs. Jovanovic.

So it was in that way. Another woman was sitting in uniform asking questions in German, and Mrs. Jovanovic translated them to Mooyo. He answered them in Bosnian, which Mrs. Jovanovic translated for the policewoman. She wrote the answers on the form in front of her.

She asked about his personal information, who he was, where he was from, when he came to Germany, and why, what his profession was, whether he was married, where his wife and kids, parents and other cousin were, and had he visited Germany before.

Mooyo answered all the questions truthfully except for his arrival date because in Slovenia they told him to say that he had arrived thirty days before. They could not send a refugee back after thirty days in the country.

When they finished the examination, Mrs. Jovanovic translated, "You have three options to go to the refugee camp in Roshtok, Trier, or back to the border. That is what the German government has decided."

"You know that I cannot go back to the border. Can I see the map to find the cities where she wants me to go?" asked Mooyo.

Mrs. Jovanovic translated it to the clerk, who pointed to the big German map on the wall behind his back. He knew that Karl Marx was born in Trier, but he didn't know where it was. On the map, he saw that Rostock was almost on the top of Germany, but trier was on the border with Switzerland but closer to Munich, so he decided to go to Trier.

"Because I don't have a possibility to stay here, where I have cousins who can help me with the language, I would prefer to go to Trier than to Rostock," he said.

"How many days do you wish to stay here with your cousins before they get you a train ticket from Munich to Trier? When you get there, a translator will help you with your needs."

"Please, if can I stay here until Sunday? Then I can go to Trier," he implored.

"Now we need to get a picture and finger prints of you to make the document and the train ticket for Trier," said Mrs. Jovanovic.

"You are free to walk into the waiting room to your cousin to wait for your ID and ticket," said Mrs. Jovanovic.

Mooyo walked back to the waiting room, where he found his aunt and two refugee boys from Bosnia. They were Miodrag from Banja Luka and another boy whose name he didn't remember.

"Well, aunt, I cannot stay in Munich. I need to go to Trier to a refugee camp, and from there, they will send me to live as a refugee. They gave me three locations where I can go: Rostock, Trier, or back to the border. I chose to go to Trier because it is a little bit closer to you than Rostock," he explained.

"Why can't you stay somewhere here in Bayern?" she asked.

"I don't know. The woman gave me only those three choices, but you can ask her when she comes out with my ID and ticket for Trier," he tried to explain.

A young man around thirty-years-old joined them. He told them that his name was Miodrag from Banja Luka, and he was waiting for an exam too, and he was curious to know what the person inside the office asked.

"They don't ask hard questions, just your personal information, your occupation, the time you came to your cousin, and where and when you want to go to the refugee center," explained Mooyo.

"You said you are going to Trier, but which day are you leaving?" asked Miodrag.

"I am leaving on Sunday. They are giving me a new ID and a train ticket," replied Mooyo.

"If she gives me the same options, I will ask for Trier and Sunday too, so we can travel there together," said Miodrag.

Soon after their conversation, Mrs. Jovanovic came out with Mooyo's ID and ticket. She then called Miodrag. His aunt asked her why he could not stay in Bayern, and she said that the refugee camps all over Bayern were full, so the government was trying to send refugees to other provinces.

Nothing could be changed. She and Mooyo knew that. He didn't care where he needed to go. The most important thing for him was the ID card with his information and picture, which made him free and done with hiding, being a shadow, and the fear he would cause someone trouble with the police like he had in Slovenia.

Although he felt guilty for escaping the war, he appreciated the government who would accept, respect, and protect the civilian population of other countries regardless of who they were.

When they left the office, Mooyo once again walked with his head up and greeted people who passed. They returned to the apartment quickly, but the kids were already back from school.

"Your godfather is going to Trier on Sunday. What can we do now?" said his aunt.

"Oh, no, we cannot let you go from us!" the children screamed, hugging him.

"I would be happier somewhere closer to you, but I need to go to the refugee center there," said Mooyo softly.

When his uncle returned from work, he was shocked with the news about Mooyo's leaving for Trier. They called Nurko to tell him the sad news, and he promised he would stop by on Saturday to say good-bye. The news that night from Bosnian or Croatian battlefields was bad. However, his uncle told him that he heard they would be able again to wire money to a bank in Bosnia. Then he could check if it was safe and how it worked. Mooyo had not much money to send to his family, but he was ready to send the hundred that Nurko had given him plus the five hundred schillings that Semo had given him in Vrhnika because he didn't have a place to spend it. His cousins took care of everything.

Three days passed by quickly in the warmth of his aunt's home. On Saturday, they saw Nurko and Sabid, and they had a different topic to talk about. Mooyo got from his aunt an old dictionary, and he started to study German. His aunt was a good teacher.

Eventually, Sunday morning arrived. They had coffee and breakfast together and then got into the car and rode to the main train station in Munich. His aunt made him drinks and sandwiches for a much longer trip than he had ahead of him. In one way, Mooyo was happy to leave, so he could finally take care of himself in that foreign world. However, the children, his aunt, and his uncle were sad because he was leaving, and they could not keep him in Munich.

Mooyo had been to that huge train station many years before with his uncle. They used to buy a newspaper in their language, eat, and drink something or meet someone from their homeland. That day there were many people bundled in the warm coats, hats, gloves and winter shoes. It looked like everyone was there.

They found a big screen with the train number, track number, and time the train would leave for Koblenz. It was his train because he needed to get out in Koblenz and transfer for Trier.

They found his train, and Miodrag from Banja Luka was on the platform, Mooyo was happy to have a fellow traveler that he recognized. They had some time before the train left, so Miodrag told them how he escaped from Bosnia to his sister who lived in Munich, and how the police checked him one late night on the train station and told him he needed to apply for a refugee visa.

During his talk, they realized that he grew up on the cities' streets because without shame, he asked Mooyo's cousins to lend him twelve marks for cigars and a newspaper. He said he would give it back to Mooyo when his sister sent him money to the refugee camp. Mooyo knew that he would never see the money again, but he didn't say anything to his cousins. Mooyo hugged his aunt, uncle, and their children, and he found a seat in a half empty train car.

On his way to the car, he examined his map of the train stations. He counted all the train stations to his destination. When the whistle blew, Miodrag jumped onto the train.

"I almost missed the train because of the cigars," gasped Miodrag.

"You got here just in time. Otherwise, you would have had to change your ticket," said Mooyo.

In that way, he started traveling to Trier. He waved to his cousins, as they disappeared behind the buildings. Then, he settled next to Miodrag.

"You have nice cousins. I met them twice, and they lent me money for cigars, but do not worry, when my sister sends me money, I will pay it back," Miodrag promised although Mooyo still didn't believe him.

Miodrag soon fell asleep, so Mooyo took out the dictionary and tried to make questions like how to ask for the train station, which platform was the train for Trier and so on. The sentences were not exactly grammatical, but he knew that no one would give him a grade, and the Germans were very polite and cultured men who would always help.

Inside, the train was warm, but he was careful not to fall asleep. When he got tired of the dictionary, he watched the beautiful meadows, fields, valleys, forests, and villages or cities covered with a snowy blanket.

His uncle put two beers in his bag, and Mooyo enjoyed the tasty sandwiches. Miodrag slept until the conductor came to check their tickets. The conductor said something in German, "Zuge in Koblenz," which

Mooyo remembered to check in his dictionary. The word "Zuge in" meant transfer to the train for Trier.

The train ride took some hours. He stayed awake to watch all the stations even though the train conductor announced the name of each station they passed. Miodrag was cursing the people who started that evil war. He told Mooyo how he wanted to stay in Munich with his sister and work illegally. Mooyo listened to him while watching the passing stations.

After the long train ride, the conductor finally said, "sitzen Zellen Koblenz," that meant, the next stop and station was Koblenz.

When the train stopped, Mooyo and Miodrag stood in the passageway. It was cold after the warm air inside the train. The train station was very clean. They walked over the train tracks to the number two platform, where another train with only two cars was waiting.

Other passengers got in the car, and after thirty minutes, the train left the station. The train rode between hills. Mooyo could see a beautiful stone castle on the top of the mountain. It reminded him of his own castle in Bosnia, which he hoped to one day see again. During their journey, they followed a small river, sometimes on one side and sometimes on other side of the tracks. The warm train made Mooyo sleepy, but he struggled to stay awake to enjoy the beauty of the German countryside.

The darkness of the night surrounded them when finally they saw a city up ahead. They heard an announcement that the train was at its final destination. They entered the train station with a big white sign for Trier.

Mooyo and Miodrag bought a map of the city. They had the address, which they showed people to guide them to the refugee center. The people explained nicely, but they did not understand what they said.

"I did not understand a thing," said Miodrag.

"It will be harder to find our way in the dark, so we must hurry," agreed Mooyo.

"I don't know how much a taxi will charge, but it's our best choice," proposed Miodrag.

They spotted a couple taxis. They showed the address, and the taxi driver opened the car door for them. Mooyo finally found in the dictionary how to ask the cost, "Was es kostet," before he got in the car. The driver told them that it would be around ten marks which meant the refugee center wasn't far away.

"We can split the cost," said Miodrag.

After about ten minutes, the taxi stopped in front of a big gate with an office in which they found an old man in a police uniform. They handed their papers to the man in the office. The policeman called someone while they stood in front of the reception office. They heard him say, "zwei Bosnische Fluchtlinge," (two Bosnian refugees).

They waited there until another policeman arrived and told them to follow him. They walked passed the reception office, which looked out at something like a military base. The narrow streets and walkways were all around two or three storehouses. He led them to one of them and to a huge room with eight metal bunk beds and small lockers.

"Schlafen hier," he pointed to two beds for them.

"Kommen zu essen," a policeman motioned them to eat.

Again they went to the first floor in the wide room with a kitchen, where many men, women, and children were eating supper. Most of them spoke Bosnian, which made Mooyo feel at home. They met: Adam, Boco, Keti, her daughter and son, and many other refugees from Bosnia, Serbia, Croatia, Monte Negro, and Kosovo.

# CHAPTER 16

## Trier, Germany

February 1995

The first night in Trier, Mooyo met refugees from different places from the Balkans. From their conversations, they all found peace and a place to stay in Germany, which offered them food, drink, shelter, used and new clothes and shoes, hygiene supplies and most importantly, a refugee visa, so they could finally feel free.

Mooyo met a young Albanian boy in the bunk above him. He tried to learn about living in this refugee camp. Albanians knew some German, but he told him that there was an appointed translator who would come the next day to walk them through the center. He will explain them life there and the procedures they needed to follow before they could transfer to somewhere else in Germany. Mooyo hoped that after all the medical and other examinations he would be able to go back to Munich. After his long day of traveling and the warm supper in the new refuge center, he quickly fell asleep.

He woke up early. He tiptoed from to the restrooms and bathrooms where he took a shower and shaved. Mooyo thought of his aunt and uncle. He wanted to find a phone booth to call them and tell them he had arrived safely and that everything was well. He walked downstairs to the kitchen where breakfast was served. There was tea, coffee, and milk.

Around eight o'clock, a young man named Anto arrived. He explained to the new refugees life and procedures in the refugee camp Hajam, until they could get a transfer to another city. He told them how they needed to go through the medical examinations, how they could get new and used clothes, and other supplies they needed for hygiene. He told them that they could not bring alcohol into the center, and the lights would be turned off every night at ten-thirty, so it would not be good for them to return late from the city. Everything was very simple for Mooyo. Anto could not tell them where they should go to get a transfer, but he told them that it would take four to six weeks, until everything was done, and after that, they would be able to leave the camp forever.

"I will inform you about everything because I will come here every morning after breakfast. Be sure not to skip any appointment, to finish every examination on time, and you will be able to get your transfer soon," he told them.

When the meeting was done, Anto took Mooyo to get the new underwear, towels, socks, and a toothbrush. On the way, they stopped by an office where a man in uniform handed each new refugee twelve marks for which they needed to sign a paper. Anto told them to go there every week to sign the paper and take their money, which they could use for hygiene supplies. After that, they were free for the day. Mooyo went to call his cousins in Munich.

The Albanian young man walked with Mooyo to the closest phone box to call his parents, who lived in Germany.

It was cold and snowy, but the streets were clear. He was able to talk with his uncle, who had so many questions about his journey and the living conditions in the camp. He even asked Mooyo to tell him the number of the phone box, so he could call him back, to avoid the cost because their home phone was much cheaper. He told him to come to the phone booth, call them, and they would call him back. After the call, he and the Albanian explored the city before going back to camp.

They stopped by a store, where Mooyo saw a big chocolate bar with hazelnuts, which he could not resist. He thought how he could share it with his son. After he passed examination, he would try to bring him. He knew he must be patient and live for his son, wife, and family.

The city was sat between hills, and it had a strange beauty. Mooyo admired the old buildings, beautiful store windows, clean parks, and all the architecture that made it unique. The bakeries smelled of fresh bread. The restaurants had scents of delicious food. The young man from Kosovo seemed like a good man, but Mooyo had a bad experience from his military time spent with them in Strumica and Stip in Macedonia in the former Yugoslavian, so he didn't trust them much, even that man he explored the city with.

On the way back, he told Mooyo how he got to his mother and father to live in Germany, but he was already eighteen, and not able to stay with them, so he applied for asylum. He remembered that Mrs. Jovanovic, the translator in Munich, had explained that option to him, but Mooyo told them that he escaped because of the war, and after it was over he wished to go back to his native country. The people who applied for the asylum must deny their own country and apply for German citizenship.

By the time they returned, it was lunchtime. He had been given a thermos bottle to refill with coffee and milk. After lunch, they played cards in their room. Kaca, who stayed in her own room with her daughter and son, arrived. She was married to a Bosnian man, but originally she was from Long Village, Croatia. She told them that her husband owned a truck. Her daughter was over eighteen and son around sixteen.

While playing cards, they talked about where they were from and how they escaped the Balkans.

In that way, the refugees spent their time waiting for their examinations and transfers. Some refugees would walk to the city after lunch and come back drunk before lights off. They would start arguments in the sleeping room, blaming each other's region for starting the war. Luckily, they only fought with words because they were scared to hit each other and get sent back to the border without a refugee visa. Mooyo stayed away from alcohol and arguments.

In his bed, he studied his German from a dictionary, writing short sentences because he knew he needed to learn the language.

One day, he thought to call his uncle on his mother's side. He lived in New Ulm, and Mooyo wanted to surprise him about where he was calling. When he reached him, his uncle could not believe that he successfully and illegally came to Germany.

Mooyo told him that he was in a refugee camp until he got a refugee visa, and that he would then transfer somewhere else. During whole conversation, his uncle didn't believe that he was in Germany.

Mooyo worked on a plan to get the rest of his family after he could settle and find a job. He promised his uncle that he would call him again when he got the transfer. When he set the phone receiver down, two coins and eight other coins fell out of the change box. He was up ten marks. He treated himself to a hazelnut chocolate, thinking again about his son.

He heard how they were able to send money to their relatives in Bosnia. He told his uncle to send two hundred marks to his family from him. He knew it would make them happy. It would give them hope that he would get them out soon. It made him happy for the rest of that day. He thought about them, wishing they were next to him in that foggy city on the border.

One night, some roommates came back from the city with some drinks hidden inside their coats, and they drank it in the room. Like usual, they talked about the war, whose was responsible for it, and they argued again. They were members of different armies and faiths.

Mooyo never participated in their discussions, preferring to lay down with his dictionary. He could believe in anything but not how much nationalism got into these young people. When someone pointed to him, he just told men that war didn't interest him. The only thing that occupied him was his family. If they asked him about it, he told them to go back there and fight for their faith and leaders if they wanted. He knew, he needed to put up with their arguments for the next few weeks and he would never see them again in his life.

When he got tired of studying, he played cards with Kaca. She came from a mixed marriage, and nothing bothered her about the war or the leaders in Bosnia. She was looking only for peace for her two teenagers. She often talked about her husband and very happy life she had with him. The war took him somewhere on the streets between Zenica and Tuzla. Sometimes, she cried thinking of him. Mooyo told her that it was possible that he was somewhere in prison, and that she would find him when the war ended. He comforted her with words that there were many wars before, and they ended, and the people were reunited. She wiped her tears, lifting her head to the big windows of their room. It was possible that she prayed to God. He never heard from one woman so many positive and sensitive words about her husband. You could not fit in a poem or book how much love and tenderness was in her words.

Sometimes, the cold days in February were long, and Mooyo took a long walk through the city. When he completed all his examinations, he worried about the city he would transfer to and who would go with him there.

One cold day, Anto came with the news that his transfer would be somewhere farther, Northern with the Albanian man. Mooyo was disappointed with that news because he heard that the Albanian man was caught by the police, because he was dealing drugs, and he didn't want to go farther from Munich either. He was scared that the man would cause trouble for him. He went to Anto's office to talk with him about his situation. Anto very kindly offered to talk with him.

"I came to ask you, if it is possible not to have me transfer with the Albanian man because I don't want to end up in prison in this beautiful and hospitable country. I heard that he was already in prison here because of drugs, and you know if you are with someone like him you become like he is. Please do something, if it is possible and send me to southern Germany, not to the North," Mooyo pleaded.

"I will try to change it, but you may have to stay a couple more weeks, until it is changed," said Anto.

"Once again, I appreciate your understanding, and please let me know as soon as you hear about the new transfer because from now on, I will live here on needles. Until now, I had very nice time here, being welcomed like nowhere else."

During the next few days, Kaca and her children left the camp heading to a small place between Koblenz and Trier like many others who accepted their transfer. Mooyo wished her good luck and thanked her for her friendship. Miodrag went with Jasmin to a place near Neustad. There with him was Boco from Tuzla, Avdi from Prnjavor, Adam from around Zenica because they arrived at the center after him.

There was a parade on Halloween, and they went out to see it in the center of Trier. From the cars and trucks, people threw and handed many different products from their company or farms, beer, and wine. That night, there was a big celebration in the city. Mooyo realized the Germans knew how to be happy because they were satisfied with their lives, peace, and welfare of the country they built from rubble and ashes after World War II, the war they started because they believed in the Nazism. The young generations only wanted peace and freedom to enjoy the life.

"And look at us?" thought Mooyo. "We came from that war torn down, burned, killed, and once again, we didn't learn that it is better to live in peace and freedom like these young German people. There will be few for which the war will make a better life. How much blood and death must we endure before this evil will be done?"

While strangers partied around him, he felt a deep sorry and wished to get drunk to forget all his miseries. He knew it would not help him. Tomorrow, he would have a headache, so he decided to be alone in his room before they turned the lights off.

That night, he dreamed about working action, where young people would build a road in his homeland with a song on their lips. And he was singing, too. He used to like to sing until his classmate, Rasim, died last year somewhere in Pecigrad. From that day on, his songs died on his lips. All songs reminded him of Rasim, who had a speech problem but not when he sang.

After lunch, Anto came to the kitchen to tell him that he got a transfer to Sudlishe Winestrase by Landau with Boco from Tuzla. They would leave camp on March seventh, with a bus, which carried refugees around Germany. He ran to find the map and locate the city. Landau was close to Karlsruhe but far from Munich. However, he could not refuse that transfer, and Boco seemed normal.

Mooyo started counting the days until the transfer. They received a postcard from Kaca, who was happy with her transfer, but in the picture, they realized that she was in a very small town. She wrote that the host welcomed them, that the children enrolled in school and how they received four hundred marks per head for living expenses every month. The furniture and other necessities they got from city hall. She seemed very happy in the new place.

"I hope that we will be as happy in Landau," said Boco when he read the card from Kaca.

Mooyo told his cousin in Munich about his transfer, and they searched the map to see where he was going. When they found it on the map, they were not happy, but they believed he would feel better there.

The time in the camp passed quickly. The first days in March brought more sunshine, but rain as well. The atmosphere in their room after some refugees left felt much better without the fights. The days were almost the same: wake up, morning hygiene, breakfast, study new words, lunch, supper, take a shower, and sleep. His life passed by with him eagerly waiting for his day of departure.

March 7, 1995, dawned sunny and clear, like a proper spring day even though it was still winter on the calendar. The bus was parked in front of the entrance to the camp.

Mooyo woke up very early. All the travelers were ready at nine o'clock. From the kitchen, they got sack lunches for the trip.

Mooyo hoped to find someone in charge to hug him or her for all that excellent hospitality during the past six weeks, but there was only Anto and the porter at the entrance.

"Once again, I appreciate everything you did for me here, and believe me, I will never forget it," said Mooyo, shaking Anto's hand.

"It wasn't much. I just did my job as well as possible. Here is my phone number, if you have there any problems with the language, feel free to call me," replied Anto.

The bus slowly passed through the narrow streets, taking him farther from the refugee camp. When they reached the top of some hills, they saw picturesque meadows and forests.

By afternoon, they reached a plateau with vineyards. They passed villages until they saw the city of Landau. The bus stopped in front of a building with the sign *Auslandbeherde*, which he translated as the office for foreigners. A man walked to the bus with a paper. He read the first and last names of the twelve refugees. They walked inside the building with the clerk.

"Warten Sie hier," said the man.

Some of them sat down, and some of them went outside to smoke. Soon a tall, old man with a yellow envelope and paper arrived.

He read his and Boco's name and added, "komm mit mir," pointing to the entrance door. They followed him to the parking lot. There a yellow car was parked by other cars.

When they got to the car, he introduced himself. "Ich bin Herr Gran aus socialamt Bad Bergzabern," said the man, shaking his hand and handing them their documents.

He opened the door and said, "Bitte."

"Danke schone Herr Gran," thanked Mooyo in German.

They sat in the car and headed back to the vineyards. After thirty minutes, they reached the town of Bad Bergzabern, Sudlishe Winestrasse, where they spotted a castle and a big tower with the German flag.

It was a small town of about sixty thousand residents surrounded by hills, where the homes and buildings were built from the main street on the bottom all the way to the top of hills. Mr. Gran drove his car to the side of hill with the tower. Just under the woods was a parking lot for eight cars. There was another Mercedes.

The man said, "Komen sie, Branka schprechen Yugoslavisch," which meant that one lady spoke their language. He walked with them into a small house, which was beside the parking lot. Branka talked quickly in German about something Mooyo didn't understand.

After a while, she said in their language, "I am Branka, and I know a little bit of Croatian."

# CHAPTER 17

## New Refugees in Bad Bergzabern, Germany

Branka and Mr. Gran showed them two bedrooms in the basement, with a small table and two small cabinets. Everything seemed clean and in order. On the next floor, was a large, a fully stocked kitchen. Boco and Mooyo were satisfied with their new apartment. They got the keys.

Mr. Gran talked while Branka tried to translate for them. She was skinny, with gray hair tied in a ponytail. She was nervous and looked lost in time. She smelled of tobacco and alcohol. Still, they were happy having her there.

The Socialamt (the social service and city hall) was closed that day, but the next day they needed to go there to find Ms. Becker, who would have money for them. They would get an order to buy clothes and one pair of new shoes. Whatever they needed they would find Ms. Becker and Mr. Gran who promised that he would stop by to check how they were settling in their new city.

Mr. Gran left, and the two men listened to the old lady's story about how she came to Germany a long time ago with her mother and stayed there forever. She was living off social services. She lived with Frenky, a German drunk and social case like her. There were two old men, Hajnz and Roby, social cases too. Roby had a car, and he always had beer, cigars, and other strong drinks, which he sold to tenants at one mark for beer and fifty cents per cigar. In another room, lived a man from Kurdistan.

They had enough food from the bag they got in Trier for that night. Boco only lacked cigars, which were very expensive there. There was a phone booth nearby, so Mooyo called his uncle, and Boco called his brother-in-law, who lived in Stuttgart.

They took a walk through the city, which was easy because it was a small town. The main street divided the city on the left and right side behind the buildings and houses. They found the post office, city hall, and all the most important stores.

The city and people seemed friendly. When they reached the edge of the city, they walked back.

The city was full of people walking up to the thermal spas to be healed. There were also green places with lots of flowers, which made the city between two hills like heaven on earth. The streets smelled of bread and other bakery products.

Everything reminded him of Banja Luka, except this one was more modern, cleaner, and more cultivated.

After supper, Mooyo took his dictionary out, and Boco went outside to smoke. When he got back, Mooyo was already asleep. He told him how he had a good time with Branka, Frenky, and Hajnz. They offered him drinks, and he shared his cigars with them.

The sun rose slowly to the little house. When he opened his eyes, Mooyo looked at the cabinets next to his bed. Boco was still sleeping soundly. Mooyo could tell that his roommate had been drunk the night before. He opened the small window, and tiptoed out and walked to the bathroom. He needed to earn money to bring his family. When he got back to their room, Boco was awake in bed.

"What time is it?" asked Boco.

"It is nine-fifteen. We should go to city hall to see what opportunities there are," said Mooyo.

"The people above us are great. I got drunk with them last night," said Boco.

"I felt it in the air this morning. Everything stank of cigars and cognac."

"Branka said that she will take us to city hall to Mrs. Backer if she is able to wake up because she, Frenky, and Hajnz were drunk," said Boco again.

"It would be nice if she would show us where to go. Would you find her and ask?"

Branka arrived carrying a huge cup of instant coffee, asking for Boco when they planned to go to city hall.

"Boco is in the bathroom, and I am ready to go, and ready to eat or drink because we ate everything we got from our refugee camp last night," he told her.

"If you want coffee, there is some left in the coffee machine, and I can give you some sugar," she offered. "I will be in the kitchen whenever you two are ready," said Branka, walking out.

When Boco returned, they locked their room and walked upstairs to find Branka. She was still drinking her coffee and smoking her cigar, and when they came, she offered a cup to Boco. He said that he was out of cigars, and he could not drink coffee without them.

"Let's go to the city hall first, and after that, we will have our first coffee in this heaven," suggested Mooyo.

The three of them walked through the city over the cobblestoned streets to an elegant building, which was city hall. Inside the building, they found the welfare window. Through the small window, a young clerk greeted them and asked Branka about them. Finally, she asked them for their documents. After they signed her forms, she handed each refugee two hundred marks for the next fifteen days. Branka told them the day they needed to come back to get the next check. She told them next time they would get a coupon to buy new shoes. They could get used clothes in the city hall attic.

In less than fifteen minutes, they finished the visit to the welfare center. Branka showed them the cheapest store to buy groceries. They stopped by a coffee shop and sat outside to have a drink, and Boco bought cigars.

Mooyo paid for three coffees while Boco offered cigars to Branka, and they all enjoyed the coffee and cigars and the ambience of the tranquil city.

On the way over the "fusgenga zone," which meant a pedestrian street where only delivery cars and vans could drive. They didn't stop to see what the quaint stores had in them. That would be for another day.

They went to the grocery store and bought food. They made an agreement to split the price of the groceries and drinks, but if someone wanted to drink his share in one night, that was his own choice. However, the first night, they celebrated their new life, apartment, and the welfare help they got.

They bought an extra bottle of whisky, a chicken, and fresh potatoes. Since they didn't have bikes, they walked, carrying the bags two miles back to their apartment. They drank in their room and left their food in the common kitchen.

Back in town, Mooyo stopped in Woolworth's to buy a notebook and markers to write German words with different colors to be easier to remember. On their way back, they saw three young, happy girls windowshopping and laughing. Two of them had black hair, and the third one was blond. These girls caught their eyes because they looked like girls from their homeland, but they could not hear what language they spoke.

"Ciko, I bet my head that these are our girls," said Boco.

"Let's go and ask them," agreed Mooyo.

When they came closer, they recognized their language.

"How are you girls? We assumed by your appearance that you were from Yugoslavia, and now we heard you talking in our language. We are so pleased to know we are not alone in this city. We feel much better now," said Mooyo.

Both men held out their hands to the women, laughing with their luck. The ladies were from Bosnia, somewhere around Tuzla. They were refugees, but they had found jobs, so the boys asked them about job opportunities. The girls promised they would let them know if they heard anything. Radojka gave them her phone number, in case they needed help with the language because she knew some German. The boys told them about their first day in the city, and how they didn't know anyone there. Boco invited them to have a drink, but they said they were in a hurry. They would have a drink with them next time. They parted with the promise to stay in touch.

Boco and Mooyo followed the path and ended up in a park filled with flowers and trees. The park was full of people of all ages. They came to a large lake with ducks and swans. On the side, was a forest with a path. There were some people feeding the ducks and swans with breadcrumbs. Everything looked idyllic.

They returned to their apartment and made their dinner. Boco was very happy with this new beginning. In fact, the two Bosnian refugees were happy and grateful to the Germans hospitality and good care. They drank to celebrate their good fortune.

However, the small party ended soon, for a German named Rosa knocked on their door. The lady bloomed like roses in the fall, but roses don't smell for long. The smell of that fall rose blurred their mind. She, of course, didn't speak their language, but they offered her a drink and food in her language. They thought she was looking for the Kurdish man in the room down the hallway. Maybe she was driven there by the smell of food and drink from their room. They were reminded of the folk saying about how roses bloom only for the rich and happy, but in that moment they felt rich and happy being far away from the war. Sometimes, luck smiled on the unhappy, and it happened to them, too. Rosa enjoyed the rest of their food and drink.

"Ciko, it is unbelievable how well we have done so far in this new city. Please tell her in German to stay here. I wish to smell her at least until the morning," Boco pleaded.

Mooyo asked Rosa to stay until morning with them. She was happy being the rose, that other people could enjoy her smell. She surrendered to the drinks and enjoyed the attention. They weren't sure what time she finally left, for no one looked at the clock. All their senses were satisfied, and they fell asleep without any dreams.

The birds of that green city sang at their small window, so Mooyo decided to put some crumbs for them in an old can. They reminded him of the mornings in his homeland.

# CHAPTER 18

## Life in Bad Bergzabern

That morning, March 9, 1995, Mooyo woke up thirsty but without a headache from the night before. On the table, he saw empty cups and plates. When he drank a mouthful of juice, he felt that something was in his mouth that shouldn't be. He jumped to his feet and ran to the bathroom to spit everything in the sink. In the sink, he saw cockroaches. He vomited everything from the bottom of his stomach, but it was hard to get it out of his mind.

He realized that in the future they could not leave any opened food or drinks in the room, and they must vacuum and clean all the time. He was scared of sleeping with them at night. He was violently disgusted by roaches. When he was at school, they hid in his roommates' books and came out when the lights were off. To keep them from his bed, he always left his light on. His roommates had another system of fighting them. They left opened bottles of beer around their beds, and early in the morning, they would put the cap on them until the roaches all died in the bottle. Then, they threw it out.

His vomiting woke up Boco, who thought he had a hangover. Mooyo told him about the roaches, and what happened when he drank the juice. They had to throw away all the leftover food and drinks that were opened on the table. They started cleaning their room, beds, and cabinets. After they cleaned every centimeter of their room, they had breakfast in the kitchen. In the refrigerator, they discovered some food was missing. They counted everything and wrote the numbers and products on the paper, to see if someone was taking their groceries.

Of course, the refrigerator belonged to everyone, but everyone should only eat own food. That day, Mr. Gran arrived with a small black and white TV and an alarm clock for them. They were very thankful to him for these items. Branka was there as well, and Mooyo told her to ask him if there were any jobs available. Mr. Gran said that he would tell him if he heard anything.

Mooyo spent most of the day studying German. All the things in the room were labeled and color-coded. After lunch, he took another walk around the city. They watched TV and listened to the radio even though they did not understand much.

On the fourth day, they knew for sure that someone was stealing their food from the refrigerator, so they decided to go to city hall to talk with Mr. Gran about the possibility of getting their own used small refrigerator in their room. While they were walking to the city hall, they saw Radojka, who was happy to walk with them. Mooyo spoke in German and explained that someone was stealing their groceries, but it was too expensive for them to eat in restaurants.

"I wrote what I needed to say from my dictionary, but if I get stuck, please be there with us to explain it better. It will be a good exercise for me to use the words I have learned," Mooyo said.

"It is not a problem. I am on my break, and the building is very close," agreed Radojka.

At the welfare window, they saw Ms. Backer. She listened carefully to Mooyo's words about why they came there. She understood his German, but she needed to call Mr. Gran. He came from another office, and he promised to try to find a refrigerator for them soon, expressing regret for the situation. They finished their visit to city hall, and they had hoped the refrigerator would come soon.

Radojka was a short young woman with black bobbed hair. In this foreign land, they were countrymen, regardless on their religion or political affiliation. They needed the help of each other, and everyone fought for survival. Everyone wanted to hear their's native language.

Mooyo knew that ordinary people were not responsible for wars. The guilty ones were the warmongers or men who got profits or high positions in the government or military rank.

The men stopped to buy only bread until they got a new refrigerator. They were finishing lunch when someone knocked on their door. It was Branka and Mr. Gran. Branka told them that they had a new refrigerator, which they had to carry from the parking lot.

"Vielen dank Herr Gran. Sie ein guter Mensch sind," Mooyo said.

They both were thrilled. They opened the box in the parking lot. Branka told them that they could not plug it in the outlet for about one hour, until the solution leveled up inside in the refrigerator. Mr. Gran left because he was busy, and the two young men carried the refrigerator downstairs to their room. Boco collected the rest of their groceries from the shared refrigerator.

They were happy that their groceries would be secured in their new refrigerator, and they decided to walk to Aldi's to buy what they needed for a few days. The beer was cheaper than water. Someone told them not to drink the water from the faucet when they lived in the camp.

They were happy with their apartment. Boco urged Mooyo to find that lady with the smell of fall roses, but he ignored him telling him that old fall roses were not for him.

They passed the days exploring the city. One day, they climbed up the hill above their apartment. They reached the wooden tower with the German flag on top. From there, they could see all the way to Karlsruhe and above the border with France.

On Friday afternoon, when they finished their lunch, they heard words coming from their hallway. The room next to them was empty, so they were suspicious. They opened the door and saw Adam and Avdi, Bosnians from the refugee camp. They could not believe that they were their first neighbors. They were thrilled to see each other again in one place. With them were Mr. Gran and Branka. After they received the keys to their room and the main door, Mr. Gran needed to leave. Branka found them linens and blankets. Then all of them had beer from Mooyo and Boco's new refrigerator.

That night, they decided to have a small party. Avdi said he would cook supper for all of them, and the other three men put together money to buy beer and a bottle of whiskey. Avdi had gotten to Munich before the war to work for one lady who had a construction company, and the war found him there. Before that, he had worked in a construction company in Rijeka, where he did construction and cooking. His wife, son, and two daughters were still in Prnjavor, so drinking eased his sorrow and loneliness. Everyone could see from his weight that he loved kitchens and cooking.

Adam was a waiter and the son of a rich cattle rancher. He left his wife and two kids, as refugees in Tuzla. After all the madness he saw and survived in the war, he decided to live and save his own head. From his behavior and actions, he seemed like a carefree young man. He smoked like Boco. Boco was a Catholic with an Orthodox wife. He had kids, but for some reason, he left Tuzla, too. Taking Branka's advice, he had bought a machine to make his own cigars from ground tobacco because it was cheaper than buying ready-made ones.

The four of them went to a mini-mall to buy groceries and drinks. Avdi bought everything to make a good supper, and the other men bought drinks.

"Aren't you going to buy bread?" asked Boco.

"Bread is so expensive here, and it doesn't taste good," said Avdi.

"How expensive is it in the bakery?" asked Mooyo.

"Do not worry, we have a stove, and we don't need to pay for electricity. Tomorrow, I will buy flour and yeast, and you will see how real bread tastes," boasted Avdi.

"If you want to learn, come tomorrow, and I will show you," Avdi assured him.

The supper he made sent tantalizing aromas all over the house. Branka and Frenky came down to the kitchen, and Avdi shared his stew with them, too. Everyone enjoyed the meal. They sat in Mooyo and Boco's room enjoying the drinks and conversation.

The next morning, Mooyo woke up earlier than usual. The room was smelly from the previous night. He opened the window, but he had an urge to be outside, so he got dressed and decided to run in the woods. He walked to the tower, and he ran through the forest. He ran to the edge of the forest, where the convent was. Because he didn't know that area, he decided to run back. He walked down the hillside.

When he got to the parking lot in front of the house, he sat down to enjoy the beauty of the March morning. He was thinking about his family, when he heard Mr. Gran's Mercedes.

"Guten morgen," said Mr. Gran, turning off his car.

"Willst du zur Arbeit gehen?" he asked Mooyo.

"Ich mochte an die Arbeit gehen," answered Mooyo. He was more than willing to go to work.

"Komm mit mir, Ich habe einen arbeit fur sie," said Mr. Gran.

Mooyo still didn't know where and what kind of job it was. Luckily, Branka heard the conversation. He told him that he found a job at the city swimming pool, and he would take him there. He was out of his mind with joy. Boco was still sleeping, and Mooyo didn't want to wake him to tell him the news. He walked back to the parking lot where Branka was talking with Mr. Gran. Mooyo got in, and Mr. Gran started the car. They drove all the way to the top of the hill where there was a sport's center and a swimming pool. They walked to the basement of a building where they found Mr. Fogel.

Mr. Gran introduced him, and Mooyo and Mr. Fogel shook hands. In the office, he signed the contract for the job. Everything was in German, but he understood from the numbers that he would earn ten marks per hour, but he would get two marks, and the rest would go to city hall for his apartment and social security. He agreed with the contract because he would be able to learn more German. Besides, he was bored of lying around, running, and walking around the city with nothing to show for it. If he worked fifty hours, he would be able to save one hundred from his social help and send two hundred marks to his family back home.

"Komm morgen um acht zur Arbeit," said Mr. Fogel, which meant to come tomorrow at eight o'clock to work at the swimming pool.

Mr. Gran took him back to his apartment, and Mooyo thanked him for the job. Mr. Gran sympathized with the refugees, and later Mooyo learned that the city was occupied by France so many times that most of the people spoke both languages and understood how hard it was to be a refugee. If they helped the refugees find jobs, they would be able to live without the city's help and stand again on their own feet.

When he got back to their room, he told Boco about his job. Boco didn't want to work for two marks, and Avdi and Adam agreed, but Mooyo didn't care about their opinions. He knew that it was better to have something than nothing. Furthermore, he didn't want to live like a tick on the back of city hall. Mooyo's goal was to learn more of the language and then look for a full-time job.

The next morning, he walked up the hill to the swimming pool. He headed out early, so he could find the shortest way to get there on time. He was greeted by the happy, smiling pool owner. Mooyo greeted him in German, and he wanted him to wait for another man to show him what to do. After ten minutes, a skinny man between thirty and forty years old in blue pants and shirt arrived. He reminded Mooyo of workers before the war in the SGP, company from Nova Gorica. On his shoulder, he had a small backpack, which he didn't take off. He greeted Mr. Fogel, who introduced Mooyo to the man named Merling, explaining that they would work together. After shaking hands, Mr. Fogel walked them around the swimming pool telling Mr. Merling what needed to be done before they opened. They needed to wash the big and small pools with brooms and power sprays, take out the trash, cut the hedges, and take care of the parking lot. He then showed them the room with equipment.

Mooyo didn't understand everything, but Mr. Ferling did and immediately took on the role of supervisor. They got to work.

Mr. Ferling was a German electrician who had six kids and a wife who didn't work. Later, he explained why he worked for only ten marks. Working as an electrician, he couldn't earn enough for the apartment, food, clothes, and shoes for the eight of them. With the extra job, he could manage. Mooyo was shocked.

Ferling was the best supervisor Mooyo had ever had in his life. Every thirty minutes, Ferling would call for a break of more than thirty minutes. He listened to his supervisor because no one checked on them. During the breaks, Ferling brought sandwiches and beer for both of them. After two days, he brought a notebook and pencils, and during the breaks, he started to teach Mooyo German. Every day, Mooyo had homework and learned quickly.

There were enough bottles in the parking lot every morning for Mooyo and Ferling to return to a store and buy at least two new beers. Ferling only liked beer in glass bottles with corks, and those were more expensive. Whenever Ferling decided to stop working for that day, Mooyo followed him. Sometimes, they stopped at noon and sometimes at two o'clock. When Mr. Ferling was sick, Mooyo worked eight hours and worked harder, and Mr. Fogel noticed. For his eighty hours, he got a hundred-sixty marks and from social help two hundred, that meant he was able to send some money to his family or pay back to his uncle in Slovenia.

As spring approached, every day began warmer and more fragrant.

One day, Mr. Ferling took him to his house to meet his wife and kids. Mr. Ferling always complained about his wife, and how she refused to do anything like cooking and cleaning, and so he needed to do everything. Mooyo tried to stay out of Ferling's private life because he could not help him with his family. He tried to stay friends with him as long as he could to learn more of the language.

While Mooyo was working, his housemates were hanging out with other refugees from Bosnia, Croatia, and Kosovo. Adam played poker at Tony's Pizzeria sometimes winning money.

It was the time of year when citizens put unwanted items on their curbs. Mooyo and his friends decided to walk around looking for bikes. They found three old bikes that needed only a little work. They worked hard all afternoon to put them together. They were thrilled they finally had transportation.

Unfortunately, happiness for Avdi was short-lived because the streets were narrow, and the pathways around them even narrower. Avdi rode first, and in front of him he saw old woman. He squeezed the brake, but he hit his front wheel, the bike stopped, flipped over and landed on top of him. He sobbed and cursed, as the lady yelled, "Oh, my God, are you okay?"

Avdi was so mad that he stood up and pushed his bike all the way to his apartment, cursing while Mooyo and Adam rode in front of him, laughing.

Boco talked with Miodrag and Ivo, who lived close to Newstad. He invited them to come to visit. One Friday afternoon, they visited and had a small refugee reunion.

By that time, Mooyo had mastered bread baking. Boco helped him bake two chickens and potatoes to feed everyone. They bought a case of beers for after supper. Mooyo was happy to see other people from the camp and talk with them about their lives in their new city.

# CHAPTER 19

## An Effusion of Nationalism

The reunion in Mooyo and Boco's room was followed by quiet music and conversation. Mooyo realized that being far from home in a strange land put these different people together like brothers to remember their former lives. He was happy to have five countrymen in their apartment, sharing food and drinks. Despite their differences, they shared a common history and homeland.

After supper, Boco left and returned with a full box of beer. They played music from their country. After the songs, they discussed who was responsible for their suffering. Mooyo stayed out of it, sitting close to the door because he wanted the guests to have their beds.

Ivo said that Bosnian Muslims were the cause of the war, and Boco supported him. Miodrag said that Bosnians, Catholics, and Muslims were equally culpable, but Avdi and Adam accused Bosnian Orthodox and Catholics. It was a multifaceted matter, and soon the discussion became so heated, it could explode at any moment.

Boco shouted, "All of you, big, small, young, or old Muslims need to be killed or sent back to Turkey." Boco was drunk and out of control but feeling gutsy because of Ivo's presence.

Mooyo could not believe how much nationalism had filled these young men's hearts. He had believed before that Boco was an educated and rational man who understood why the war happened to them.

"Why did you say that? You must have a reason," Mooyo asked, hoping for some reasonable explanation.

"You know when the Ottomans were in Bosnia, every single young bride had to sleep with the Ottoman officers first and then with her husband," explained Boco.

"So, you are blaming the present citizens of Bosnia for something that happened five hundred years ago? Do you know who Omer Pasa Latas was? He was possibly one of the officers who slept the first night with some brides," asked Mooyo.

"He was a Turk, who else?" answered Boco, upset that Mooyo was debating.

"No, my Boco. I thought you were smarter than that. But now I see that you didn't learn anything in school and life. Omer Pasa Latas was a Hungarian Catholic who joined the Turks to become an officer, and those kinds of officers were from all religions and nationalities. I have slept in the same room with you, shared bread with you that I cooked with my hands, so you could save money to have something to smoke, and do you thought that? Shame on you! I am sorry to all of you guys, but if you think and talk that way, take your remaining drinks with you and leave my room. You too Boco! Take your bed somewhere where you can sleep because you have hurt me tremendously. You and I can no longer sleep in the same room and eat same bread. If you refuse to leave, I will call the police and tell them why you cannot share my room. Once more, I am sorry, but please leave this room," asserted Mooyo.

"Let's go, people. We do not need this," said Miodrag, and with his beer and jacket he left the room with Ivo. Finally, Boco took his mattress, pillow, and blanket from the bed and left, too. Adem and Avdi left too. Everyone carried their drinks, and Boco came back to get the box with the remaining beers.

Mooyo silently cleaned the room, opened the window, locked the door, and propped a chair under the doorknob. He felt mad, wounded, and betrayed. Now he realized how much nationalism had soaked into these young men. It felt as if they had all forgotten their classes, and how much blood people lost throughout their history because of nationalism. How could he trust anyone? He knew that evil grew in people and that it was even greater than in his homeland because eventually the war in Bosnia would end, but this prejudice in people's minds could last forever. They didn't know how to think independently. They only believed lies and rumors.

He lay in his bed, crying because he could never have a more beautiful and honorable life as he had in his homeland. Because of the empty-headed people, he would not be able to go back there and live happily ever again. Hate was everywhere, and it was like a sickness from which they all slowly and quietly died, until someone could teach them again how to live in that place together in democracy regardless of their religions.

Mooyo fell asleep with hot tears on his cheeks. In the morning, the songs of birds outside on the bushes and trees woke him up because he had left the window half open, but they did not lighten his spirit. He lay in his bed thinking about what to do in the future.

He decided to ride around other villages and towns on his bike to look for a full-time job in construction. Boco and Ivo were sleeping on mattresses in the hallway.

When he was almost done eating breakfast, Avdi opened his door a crack.

"What are we going to do today?" asked Avdi tentatively.

"I am going to jump on my bike and drive around to any place I see a crane. I'm going to stop and ask if they need a worker," answered Mooyo.

"God be my follower, I am going with you, if you can wait until I eat something," said Avdi.

"Whatever you want. I will wait for you down by the phone booth because I plan to call my uncle in Munich," said Mooyo. He hoped to leave the room before Boco woke up and retrieved his clothes and their shared food in the refrigerator. For his trip, he planned to take his dictionary, but he couldn't find it anywhere in the room. He realized that someone must have taken it last night. He went to Avdi's room and said very loudly that if the person who took hid dictionary did not return it straight away, he would call the police. It awoke Boco and Ivo in the hallway and Adam and Milorag in Avdi's room.

"Are you calling the police for a dictionary? You know that these two should not be here with their "duldung visa," said Adam looking to Mooyo.

"That dictionary means more to me than my only jacket. When I come back from the phone booth, I want to see my dictionary. Last night, I tried to be the best host possible, and you repay my hospitality by stealing from me?" said Mooyo, leaving the room.

He was sullen and hurt. He could not believe that people would act that way. He wished to go somewhere, but he didn't have anywhere to go.

If tomorrow were Saturday, he would sit on a train and go to Munich to be with someone without a corrupted soul and heart.

He was not able to call anyone because he feared he would throw up his breakfast.

"What kind of people are they? They are like animals," he thought.

He walked across the street and sat on a bench. He could not sit there more than about five minutes. He walked back to his room, and on the fridge by the door was the dictionary. Nobody was there, but he heard them from the kitchen where they had coffee and cigars. Mooyo put his dictionary in his pocket and walked out with Avdi where their bikes were locked.

They rode toward Landau, looking around for tall cranes. On their way, in the small villages they saw some construction sites, but they were abandoned because it was Saturday.

"Avdi, we need to come back here on a workday if we want to ask for a job," Mooyo said, pushing their bikes toward the empty building site.

They decided to go back on Monday after Mooyo's job at the swimming pool. He planned to work Monday until twelve o'clock. On their way back, they talked about the events that happened the previous night. Avdi agreed with his reactions.

"Where will Boco sleep now because it is his room, too?" asked Avdi.

"That is his problem, I didn't offend him. If he doesn't find a place to sleep, I will go to city hall on Monday and tell them what happened, and how afraid I am to sleep with a nationalist like him. We will see what they say about it."

Clouds where moving very fast from the French border, which meant rain, so they hurried home. When they arrived in front of their house, rain was pouring down. As fast as possible, they pushed their bikes up the narrow walkway and stairs and entered the building.

All was quiet, but it still smelled of alcohol and cigars. Nobody was in the rooms, and they didn't know where the rest of the refugees were. They decided to make dinner together. With that aroma of a potpie from their country, the house smelled more like home. When they finished eating, Adam came from the city. Avdi invited him to eat because he was so excited to smell that Bosnian dish.

Adam told them how Boco went to his brother-in-law's place in Stuttgart, where he would stay for a while. Adam told them how Boco was sorry for the words he said because he would be hungry and without smoke if Mooyo was not with him. If they did not buy the food together every two weeks when they got money from welfare, he would be short of food because he could not manage his money as well as Mooyo.

"Where did you two go?" asked Adam.

"We went to three villages looking for construction work, but there were no people there on Saturday, so we will go there on Monday when Mooyo comes back from his pool," explained Avdi.

"I will go with you on Monday because we cannot earn enough just sitting around," agreed Adam.

The smell of the potato-meat pie lured Brankica from the third floor with mail for next week for them. Mooyo was surprised of a postcard from Kaca he had met in the refugee camp. Kaca reminded him of a marigold because she smelled and made the male close to her drunk. She invited him to come visit her in her garden where she settled with her kids.

Brankica liked their pie. They decided to buy a broomstick to make a rolling pin, so they could make another pie. They made the next pie for Hasa, the old refugee women from Bosanska Gradishka who came that week to their apartment. After her, came Sakib, who was from Gradishka too. He was a baker and truck owner, but now only a refugee whose family was somewhere in Turkey, and his second wife and daughter were in Austria. He was working on the possibility to transfer her and the girl to Germany. It was not hard for him because he moved many times from Germany to Austria and back. Because he was a master baker, Avdi and Mooyo's bread was not as good as his. He baked huge bread that filled the entire house with the smell of a bakery back home.

Adam and Avdi were bored, and they spent lots of time in the city where they met another big refugee family from Sanski Most.

One night, they were invited to visit the Halilovic family, which lived in a big apartment above Dr. Backer's office. Adam met some Albanian refugees from Kosovo. It seemed that the small city was full of refugees from the Balkan Peninsula.

They were all wounded in their souls, suffering from the loss of their homeland. Worst of all, like Boco, most of them believed the war propaganda and blamed each other for their destruction and suffering. Mooyo told them that the war would stop when the big men around the world stopped it. He thought and prayed to God to save his family. He still was not able to do anything for them, other than sending a little money now and then.

He was still bitter about the night he kicked Boco out of their room. He didn't know what to do if Boco returned from Stuttgart. Could he forgive the words he heard from his mouth and heart? He needed a change of scenery, so he decided to visit Kaca, or the marigold like he called her. He had the address, and he learned how to ask for directions.

On Monday, they rode their bikes along the border with France to a small construction site where they found some Bosnians who promised they would ask the boss to hire them. The constraction company was owned of the Turkish Muslim and the Croatian man. They arranged a meeting for Thursday. They all knew where the village was, and they got Borik's phone number to call before they got there. He promised to bring the work form to fill out. That made them very happy because it was a chance to finally get a full-time job. They rode back to Bad Bergzabern over the bike path. Everywhere they looked, they saw vineyards and orchards but still without any fruit because it was early spring.

That night, they had a visit from the boys from the Halilovic family. They were interested in jobs, too, but they were scared of losing the government benefits because their father already worked in construction. They decided to go to a field the next evening to play soccer and basketball. These boys went to school there, and they were very good in German.

The next day on the field, they met another Bosnian from Zenica. He was there with his pregnant wife. He was a very good soccer player because he had played before the war on some team in his city. The refugees tried to look for any possibility of getting a job and getting off welfare. The soccer game refreshed their souls and wore out their bodies. That night they slept very well.

Mooyo still worked and studied German at the pool with Ferling. He saved marks to send to his family. He knew how much they needed it. He found a Red Cross organization there and asked if they could get his family from Bosnia, but they told him to find a way to get them out and then they would help. He needed help to get them out.

They waited impatiently for Thursday evening, to meet Boric, and they hurried on their bikes to Plajsvajla, the address they had gotten from him. When they arrived at the address in front of a big house with a high fence and locked big entrance door, they didn't know how to get inside because only announced guests were allowed.

Suddenly, from next door came a German man asking if they wanted to buy some wine. They agreed to buy some and find how to enter the house and meet Boric and Safet. When they tasted the wine, Boric and Safet appeared. They were bricklayers who worked for a Turkish man. Boric had work permits, which made them very happy. They had a glass of wine and discussed how to fill the forms and documents. They decided to meet the next day at Tony's pizza, and they would drive to Sar Bricken where their family lived. They all thanked Boric for what he had done for them and got on their bikes to go back and celebrate with the rest of the wine from the farmer.

The boy from the Halilovic family helped them fill out on the forms, and on their way back, they made copies of their visas and crossed their fingers for luck. Adam and Avdi applied for bricklayer jobs and Mooyo applied to be a helper. They didn't ask about the salary because the important thing was working.

That night, Mooyo wrote "Poem to a Blonde Boy" to his son whom he left in Turanj. Thinking of his son, wife, father, mother, and brother, he fell asleep with hope despite the news on Free Europe Radio. Nada Alice from Zagreb lied so much that it was hard to believe a word from her mouth.

Mooyo had terrible dreams that Boco came back repeating words of nationalism and hate. In his dream, he saw houses in Pecigrad in flames. He heard cries and screams of women from the burning houses. He woke up sweaty and panting. He went to wash his face with the cold water. He tried to get the nightmares out of his head, for he had an important day ahead.

He woke up before the alarm. He got ready and packed two sandwiches and two beers in his bag with his homework and walked to the street. He decided to visit Marigold during the weekend when a round-trip ticket was only fifteen marks. He considered going to Munich, but he didn't want his cousins to see the worry on his face.

He didn't tell Ferling about the other job yet. Every Friday, they worked on German's language more than the pool. When the bells on the churches around the city announced that it was twelve o'clock, it meant they needed to leave. They clocked out, and with Ferling's car rode down to the city. Because other people didn't work, they got their money at eight o'clock in the morning when the welfare window opened. When the two men arrived around twelve-fifteen, there was nobody else at the window. They got their money for welfare and for the job at the pool very fast.

Mooyo got two hundred for welfare and from working at the pool one hundred-sixty marks. In front of city hall, they separated. Mooyo planned to go to Tony's by himself to hand his forms and copies to Boric, to take them to the company in Sar Bricken. He met Adam and Avdi, but the Halilovic boys weren't there. They enjoyed sat outside the pizza place, waiting for their man of hope. They watched people walking past and others sitting at tables, ordering food and drinks.

After about fifteen minutes, Boric with Safet arrived and joined them.

When Boric and Safet left, Mooyo walked to the train station and bought his train ticket. From the phone booth, he called Marigold telling her about visiting her small village. She was happy to hear the news.

Mooyo told Adam and Avdi where he was going, in case someone needed him. When he woke up the next morning while he was getting ready, the house was quiet. The city was empty at such an early hour.

He looked forward to his first adventure. With this trip, he wanted to prove his ability to travel by himself, and after this, he planned to visit his cousins in Munich. He finally arrived at Marigold's train station. The taxi to her house passed beautiful landscapes, rolling hills, and scenic overlooks. The villages reminded him of the villages from his home, but the houses were much bigger and more elegant.

When they arrived, and Marigold saw him, her face lit up, and she ran to hug him. He was surprised that someone could be so happy to see him again after just a couple of weeks living in the same refugee center. Marigold gave him the tour of the first floor basement with two bedrooms, a shower, a kitchen, pantry and everything a family needed to live there.

The kids were on the playground when he arrived. Marigold made coffee for them, and they talked about what happened to them after they left the camp. With her kids, she received twelve hundred marks, a paid apartment, electricity, and water, so she used money only for their food and drinks. Her children were already registered for school with free transportation. Mooyo told her about the incident with Boco telling her that it made him very sad and killed his dream of a nice life in their country after the war with that kind of mentality. Marigold listened to him like an old friend, dividing her thoughts about Boco because he had said some unpleasant words to her in the camp about her marriage outside her religion.

"Because of that kind of bubblehead, we came here, and who knows where else we will go? Thank you God for our life and health. Nothing can be worse than war, and it with help from God, it will end soon," said Marigold, sadly.

"I understand that we were all pushed into the war, but I didn't know that nationalism would occupy young men so much that they would be ready to kill everyone who has a different religion," added Mooyo.

"Because of that mentality, those fools will always walk around the world destroying the safety of their own homeland, life, and the freedom which we all shared," added Marigold.

At last, her two children came inside, ending their conversation. They were happy he visited them because they remembered him fondly from the refugee camp. They all sat down and enjoyed a warm soup. She had cooked many different foods, so Mooyo felt like a guest of honor.

After dinner, the children moved to the sofa to play video games while the adults ate more and talked. After lunch, Marigold showed him around the area. It was a big village with large fenced in houses. They had a field for many different sports, but they did not have a grocery store or coffee shop. It was beautiful everywhere, with small hills and valleys. It was fertile land with gardens everywhere and no weeds or broken down buildings.

Marigold told him that she paid for a taxi to shop for groceries and other needs every two weeks when she got welfare money. To travel to the small city they used the bus lines, which were advertised on the bus station in the village. She was very proud of her new place. Mooyo told her how he was working for city hall, and how they had applied for construction jobs to get off welfare and live life like other citizens.

When they got back, they watched a movie, drank some more wine, and reminisced.

It was just what Mooyo needed. He knew that his pain could be pushed away from him. It gave him hope for new days, regardless of where he lived. He felt inebriated, completed, and brought back to life.

Mooyo could only stay a few days. He thanked Marigold for the hospitality, taking him in and got on the bus Monday, and took the first train back to Bad Bergzabern. The smell of the Marigold, he would carry through his life, but he needed to get back to reality and work to reunite his family.

In Bad Bergzabern, Avdi and Adam told him how Boco came back during the weekend to gather his belonging, and he went to work for a company in Russia. He had a Croatian passport which gave him the chance to travel anywhere. He told them how he felt so sorry because he hurt Mooyo's feelings that night during the party.

Life with many refugees in the city on the German-French border went the same way. Mooyo worked and studied with Mr. Ferling. He went out a couple of times with Radojka, Milica, Dragica, and their cousin, who married a German man. He was trying to find any job for them too. Dragica found work in the hotel Garni. It was painting the wood on the balcony and cutting the grass around the hotel. The owner, an older Italian woman, didn't pay much per hour, but it was something he could save and send to his family. She always called him when there was any job. He was scared to work without a work permit, but he had no choice.

In June, Musin arrived with work permits for all three of them. They could start work on a huge building somewhere on the border with France. Musin brought a car for them to ride to work and back and carry the tools. There was one Italian man, without a place to sleep, but Mooyo offered Boco's bed for him because they worked during the day. They opened their bank accounts and told city hall that they would start full-time jobs. They allowed them to get social support until they received their first paychecks. After that, they would be off welfare.

That time of year was very rainy, and it rained night or day, making big puddles and drenching their faces and clothes. Their supervisor was a short, heavyset German man. Adam and Avdi got higher pay per hour because they worked as bricklayers, but when it was time to begin working, it became clear that they had exaggerated their experience. Luckily, Boric and Safet helped them finish on time.

Mooyo did the hardest and dirtiest job, cutting the bricks, wood, and iron for them, yet he did not complain. Adam and Avdi often took the money from the boss in advance, but Mooyo planned to get his salary at once and pay for his family's escape.

His savior at work was his supervisor, who drank two boxes of beer every day. The other men could barely utter a word in German, so it was Mooyo who was sent to buy breakfast and lunch for everyone. It was his only break. Before they started work on the top floor, the supervisor was replaced, but they didn't know why. They continued to work as fast and well as possible. When the first month ended, they accepted their first paycheck, but their salary didn't seem right, which worried them. They had all worked hard to complete the project. The new supervisor was mad at the owner because his salary was inadequate as well, so he chased the cart on the crane to the end and blocked it on the end.

The trucks with concrete arrived, but they did not unload them, which meant the supervisor wanted to be paid for his past hours, but Musin didn't show up with the money. He told them to sit there until the end of the day, when the owner would arrive with the money. The workers were willing to work because the owner owed them one and half month's salary. Mooyo had earned around seven thousand marks. Every worker was happy to work as many hours as possible to earn money to bring their families from the war zones.

At three o'clock, the supervisor signed for their work hours, but Musin still hadn't showed up. The trucks rode back to their base, and the workers rode back to their towns. It was Friday, and they thought the owner would bring their money in the next two days. They waited for their money, but the owner and money never came. They called him and the engineer from Croatia but without success. They became so desperate that many went and got drunk to forget their lost hope. They had two very long days waiting.

Mooyo managed to get the phone number of a former coworker, who promised to help him to get his family. He promised Mooyo that he would take his wife and son from the camp, put them on the bus from Karlovac to ride to Rijeka, where cousins of his wife lived. He didn't know the exact day when he could do it, but he promised it would be soon. For the other members of his family he said he could not do much.

# CHAPTER 20

## On Welfare Again

On Monday, they met at Tony's pizza with their supervisor, who told them that the only way they could get their money was to go to the workman's compensation court because Musin didn't show up with their money. Everyone was shocked and confused. When they left the pizza place, they decided to go directly to city hall to tell them what had happened. The clerk listened to their story and put them back on the welfare because they couldn't get money from unemployment until they had worked for at least six months.

They tried unsuccessfully to reach both men to demand their money. Finally, on Thursday they asked the young Halilovic boy to go with them to the Work Compensation Court in Landau, where they sued Musin and his company for the lost wages.

Mooyo did not know what to do because he had already arranged getting his son and wife to Rijeka. He didn't have the money to send them to live there on their own. Time dragged, and everything had turned to inescapable madness. He decided to go to Munich to visit his uncle, and on the way back, he planned to stop in New Ulm to see his uncle on his mother's side, to ask them if they could help him get his wife and son.

Again on an early Saturday morning, he sat on a train. They were so happy when he arrived, but he soon realized they could not help him. Sunday morning, he rode to New Ulm to see his other uncle. His uncle and his friend Barka welcomed him, and they talked about everything. His uncle had spent much money getting his three sons to Slovenia, where they didn't have refugee permit. For their move to Slovenia, he had paid fifteen thousand marks, which was a fortune for him. Mooyo told him his situation.

Barka gave him one last bit of hope when she promised to ask her cousin in Croatia about the prices for moving people over the borders any possible way. With that shred of hope, he returned to his city.

When he arrived, he called his wife's cousin in Buzet to see if Vlastimir helped them escape from the refugee camp Kuplensko, where Krajishniks had fled the war. He heard the happy voice of his wife's aunt, who put his son on the phone, and after him his wife. Finally, after three years of the war and refugee camps, they had gotten out. Mooyo promised to call the next day.

He was infinitely grateful to his coworker, Vlastimir, with whom he had worked in his native village for five years.

Knowing that his son and wife were in a warm room made him so happy, away from grenades, violence, and war. He was sorry he couldn't get his brother and parents out yet, but he tried not to think about it. He wished to relive the words of his son and wife. He thought that tomorrow would be a new day and the new hope for him and them as well.

Monday dawned with rain, which seemed to be falling from the walkway instead of the sky. By around ten o'clock, the sun was shining again, so everyone forgot the rain. The three men decided to call Boric about a safe job because they still had work permits. Boric promised that he would talk with two young construction engineers who had just arrived from Croatia. They got a job building a big three-story house for a wine man near Landau. They didn't have a car, but they were able to use the bus.

Mooyo took the first step for his son and wife, for he could not leave them with his wife's family forever. He was waiting on Barka to go to Croatia and check with her cousin if he could do something for part of his family.

He didn't have enough money to pay for anything, but he was ready to borrow it in the hope that he would soon get the money from the workers' court. Again, the days became long. Mr. Gran found them some work at city hall where they earned two marks per hour, which only helped slightly. They cleaned some old apartments where the city placed some refugees from Poland. The same people had papers that their ancestors belonged to Germany before, and in that way they could come and live there. Most of them spoke Russian, which could be heard all over the city.

From the time to time, Mooyo called Buzet, Croatia, to talk with his wife and son. They were there illegally and so unable to leave the house. He knew how they felt from his experience in Slovenia. His parents and brother were in a worse place, Kuplensko, but he couldn't help them. It was hard to borrow money from people he knew, and his cousins were very hard off. Moreover, he was already in debt nine hundred marks to his uncle in Slovenia.

They had a lot of free time, so they sat on their bikes and rode deep into vineyards, where they could get different fruit. The dirt in that place was fertile and beautiful.

It was Friday, and the three men were in the parking lot in front of the house, bored when Boric, Vlado, and Milenko arrived in a car with a Croatian license plate. They knew Boric, who introduced other two young men to them.

"What a nice day, and you three are wasting time," said Vlado, laughing.

"We will be happy to work if there is something for us," responded Avdi.

"We just came to end your boredom," said Milenko, reaching out to shake their hands.

"Listen people, we heard what happened with your last job, and we are sorry for that. We know that you will not trust us easily, but we promise that it will not happen again to you. Do your job the best you can, and we will pay you every single mark you have earned on time," Vlado told them. "We don't have anything with Musin. We have our company, and if you are willing to work, you can start Monday morning," continued Vlado.

"We will work hard, but every Friday we want to get some money in advance, for we cannot survive until we get a whole month's salary," replied Avdi.

"That is not a problem. We heard from Boric and Safet how hard you worked, and that is why we will take you," said Milenko.

"In that case, we are willing to work for you," said Avdi, Adam, and Mooyo.

"Boric will stop here on Monday morning to take you to the place, so you need to be ready around eight o'clock in the morning regardless of weather," said Milenko.

They said good-bye and left.

The three men were happy to have full-time jobs again.

Avdi and Mooyo decided to ride into the vineyard and orchard where they could eat fruit and bring some home. They stopped to rest on a bench under a tree, talking about how pleased they were about getting some money every Friday.

After lunch, Mooyo considered buying a cheap train ticket to Munich for the weekend. He really wanted to see his uncle's family. He still remembered his aunt Zaki from when he was a little boy. He bought gifts for all of them.

His uncle was happy to hear the news and gave Mooyo a big welcome. Mooyo wanted to see if they were willing to help him to bring his wife and son. He wanted to go to his cousins and friends because it was always possible to learn something about transporting people over the borders. That weekend, Barka promised to inform him about her cousin from Croatia because she had gone there last week.

He still thought that if he could get money from Workers Court, it would be much easier. The most important thing for him was the new job he would start on Monday. They decided not to go to the welfare office until they got their first paychecks this time.

The trip to Munich took until four o'clock in the afternoon. At the main station, his uncle and family were waiting for him. They hugged him and showed how much they missed him. His aunt took them to New Perlach where they lived. She had prepared an elaborate supper, and his uncle served drinks. They talked about many things. After supper, they called Mooyo's wife and son because it was much cheaper on a home phone. Like before, he promised bring them to him soon even if he didn't know how.

Although his parents an brother were still in the refugee camp, his uncle and aunt visited them. They delivered clothes, shoes, groceries, and money.

Time would tell how better their life would be after the war. Mooyo knew for sure from the folk saying that one person's luck is not built on someone else's misfortune, but it was useless to say to a nationalist zealot.

That night, he and his uncle had some extra drinks. His uncle and aunt planned to visit his other aunt in Vrhnika, so in the morning, he bought some clothes and shoes for them to give his son and wife. The time passed quickly, and he needed to catch the train to Bad Bergzabern.

Around eleven in the afternoon, he got back to his city. The next day was the start of his full-time job. When he woke up, Avdi and Adam were ready for the new job. He quickly dressed, ate breakfast and walked down the street before the eight o'clock. They all wanted to be there before Boric, so he would not need to wait for them. They still had work clothes and tools from the last building site. They sat on a bench when the black Mercedes 190 D stopped in front of them. It was Boric, the bricklayer from Zivinice by Tuzla, a refugee from Bosnia from long before, and he made a nice living working on building sites throughout Germany.

After twenty minutes, they arrived in a small place where Boric parked his car behind the white trail in which they placed their lunches. There they found Vlado, Milenko, and the future owner of the huge house they needed to build. They shook hands and started the foundation work.

The engineers suggested where to put different metal or pipes for the drains. For lunch, the future owner of the house brought six liters of red and white wine for them that he got from his vineyard. He told them to leave the empty bottles by the trail and he would bring full ones for them every day. They all worked until the dark.

Everyone wanted to build it quickly. The workers agreed to work every day for ten hours and earn more money, so the future owner and engineers could put the roof on before winter. Mooyo was the helper, but very soon he learned from Vlado how to operate the crane, and every night how to refill the batteries. The first day, they were surprised when the sun went down behind their city. They put all the tools on the trail, locked the cranes, and happily drove back to Bad Bergzabern. Mooyo wished to return as soon as possible to call Barka, to see if she found a good result for him with her cousin. Avdi wished to celebrate the first day, so they stopped by a store to buy a bottle of alcohol. Everyone chipped in because Avdi promised to cook supper.

Around nine o'clock, Mooyo called Barka. He had some more coins in his hand if she talked too long. He asked her about her trip to Croatia, but she got to the point that he was calling about.

"I talked with my cousin, whom I told you about. He said that he can find a Croatian passport for your wife and son for a thousand marks. He told me that it is the lowest price because he needs to pay someone for the passport and pictures. I know that he is a thief, but he said he cannot do it for less. You need to get their pictures and take them to him. You can pay him after he makes the passports," said Barka.

"Thank you. We will never forget what you have done for us. I started a new full-time job in construction, so I hope I will soon have enough money for the passport, and tonight I will call my wife to make the pictures as soon as possible," he said.

She gave him the name and phone number of her cousin, telling him to say that he was the cousin of Bayo from Germany, and he could make the deal with the man. He bought a phone card to call his wife and tell her about his first workday and that he found someone to get travel documents for them. For a long time after their conversation, he could hear his son's voice. He wished more than anything to hug him, lift him in the air, and feel his little hands around his neck, in his hands, and hair.

He went back to his room happy and satisfied with his whole day. The entire house smelled of the Bosnian food Avdi was cooking in the kitchen. He offered to help Avdi wash the dishes. He waited until supper to tell them about his plan.

The stew was delicious, and they all agreed Avdi was the best cook in the whole city. They washed down the meal with strong brandy.

One day, Mooyo went for wood with Vlado somewhere on the border, which gave him the chance to talk more about everything.

"Do you have family somewhere?" asked Vlado, walking to the storage area.

"I have a wife and son in Buzet, close to Rijeka. They are staying with my wife's aunt. I need to bring them here, but it is slow and expensive. I need to do something soon because they are hiding there without permission," said Mooyo, jumping into the small truck.

"Milenko and I will go to Zagreb for two weeks, and if you get the pictures, you can come with us to Zagreb and ride back too," offered Vlado.

"That would be excellent," replied Mooyo.

That night, he called his wife again to push her to make the pictures and mail them immediately because he had transportation to Croatia. His wife told him that it was already done.

The next days passed rapidly working ten or twelve hours a day. Every day after work, he asked Branka if there was any mail for him. Finally, after seven days the letter arrived. His wife had changed so dramatically in the picture that he was scared she was sick. He called her that same night to see if she was okay. She was skin and bones. She insisted that she was fine, but Mooyo was still worried.

Every Friday, Mooyo and his friends got their paychecks from the engineers without the complaint because they were happy with their progress. Mooyo already had a talk with them about the trip to Zagreb.

He was waiting for it because it was his first trip outside Germany since he had arrived in January. He bought a few presents for people there because he needed a lot of money for the trip there, the passports, and a place to live. Before the trip, he called Barka's cousin to coordinate the place and time to meet. The man said that when Mooyo got there he needed to call him to arrange the place.

No one in the whole world was as happy as Mooyo. He was so close to getting his family back.

Finally, Friday came. They finished work at noon, and they rode back to Mooyo's apartment to get ready for the trip. They only stopped for gas and coffee.

They arrived at Zagreb after dark, so Mooyo could barely see. Vlado invited him to sleep at his mother's house. She made a nice supper for the travelers. She was such a good host that he didn't know how to thank her.

Zagreb drowned in fog. Mooyo awoke early in the morning, but he stayed in bed until he heard others awake.

"Good morning. Did you sleep well?" he asked her.

"Good morning. I sleep fast. How did you sleep?" asked the old woman, smiling. On the kitchen table was enough food for at least five hungry people. Soon Vlado came to the kitchen to join them.

When they were done, Vlado brought the phone for Mooyo to call his contact. They decided to meet at the main train station. Mooyo explained what he looked like, so the man could recognize him.

"Okay. I will be there in an hour," said the man, hanging up the phone.

"The main station isn't far from here," explained Vlado. "We have plenty of time. Have some more coffee."

When it was time to leave, Mooyo thanked Vlado's mother and him for the hospitality, and they drove down the sleepy Zagreb streets to the station. Mooyo had phone numbers of both engineers. He told them where they would pick him up on Sunday afternoon because he wanted to visit his aunt in Vrhnika too. Once more, he thanked Vlado for everything and they parted in the parking lot.

Mooyo remembered the day he came to the station as an illegal traveler, sitting in a small Reno with an unknown driver and three Bosnian refugees. They were hard memories, but he still owed his aunt nine hundred marks for it. He hoped that after this new thousand he needed to pay for a passport, he would be able to save money and start paying back his debts. This time, he wasn't scared of being asked for his documents, but he was aware that once again, he was doing something that was against the law. There was no other choice. He had asked institutions like the Red Cross in Germany to help him bring his family, but to no avail.

At the station, he saw travelers and salespeople, who never closed their stores. He walked inside a restaurant and sat at a table by the door. He ordered an orange juice. In his pocket he had the pictures of his wife and son and their information.

After about ten minutes, a tall man walked into the restaurant, dressed in a leather jacket and jeans. He greeted Mooyo with a good morning and asked, "Are you Barka's friend and Bayo's cousin?"

Mooyo stood up and shook hands. "Pleased to meet you and I am happy we found each other. Barka and Bayo say hi. Let's have a seat and drink together. Then we can talk about the business," said Mooyo kindly.

The man ordered coffee and brandy, and Mooyo ordered one for a toast.

"How long have you been in Germany?" asked Barka's cousin.

"Since January of this year, I arrived illegally, and now I am trying to get my son and wife who are hiding in Croatia in my wife's aunt house," said Mooyo.

Mooyo pulled an envelope with the pictures and information. Just then, the waiter returned with drinks, and they toasted to success with the business between them.

"Call me in a week to check if I finished the passport because the process can sometimes take a long time," explained the man. He seemed to be in a hurry to go somewhere.

"How about one more brandy for the road?" asked Mooyo.

"No, thank you. I have some other business to finish, and I need a clean head for it," replied the man.

Together they walked outside the restaurant, shaking hands and promising to keep in touch. Mooyo thanked him for the help.

"Do not worry. Everything will be perfect," said the man.

Mooyo bought a bus ticket to Rijeka, but he had about an hour before the bus left, so he bought a newspaper and some pies, one made with cheese and the other with minced meat and onions. He wanted to have some food for the trip. Then, he walked to the platform and sat inside the bus reading the newspaper. The bus slowly filled and left the station. Mooyo read his newspaper until he fell asleep.

He awoke at a bus station in Karlovac. At the bus station, he didn't see many travelers, like before the war. The people looked serious, with sorrow and exhaustion in their eyes, they stood patiently waiting for their bus. Some of them smoked, and some of them drank something from bottles or cups.

At the outskirts of the city, Mooyo saw fresh signs of war on the buildings. He tried not to think about it. He tried to focus on seeing his wife and son, in a couple of hours.

Somewhere along the road, the bus stopped by a little restaurant with a parking lot on both sides. The driver announced a twenty-minute break. This time, Mooyo got up and walked to the parking lot where some ladies were selling honey, cheese, and brandy. The prices were high in the new currency. He wished that the bus would take off as soon as possible to get to Buzet.

Finally, around noon, they got to Rijeka. He exchanged one hundred marks for Croatian money, and at the first kiosk with the newspapers asked for phone cards to call one of his wife's young cousins, as was the agreement before he left Germany. Luckily, when he dialed the number, the girl answered. She told him to get on the bus headed for Pula, and to take off on the fork Pula-Rijeka-Buzet, and wait there until she went to pick him up. He thanked her and turned to look for the bus to Pula.

The ride on the narrow, winding road was as long as a day because he was so anxious. He saw houses and buildings squished on little hills above the Adriatic Sea. He knew that somewhere his cousin and some people from his neighborhood lived. They had escaped before the war. There lived a girl named Guzla from his elementary class. She was taller, stronger, and heavier than all other kids in his. It was nice to remember after a long time. He was so lost in memories of his childhood, thinking about people, days and events that he almost forgot where he was. Luckily, the bus driver stopped and told him to get out at the fork. The conductor didn't walk through the bus, so he was surprised he was already at the place he needed to go. He thanked the driver and got off.

The bus disappeared from view, and he walked down the road. Only a few cars passed. He searched for the car that would take him to his loved ones. Suddenly a small, white Fiat stopped near him. He recognized his wife's cousin. He opened the door and greeted her.

"Sorry, if you waited long. It was rush hour when I left the city," explained Sena with a smile on her face.

"Don't worry about it. The most important thing is you are here. Through my experiences, I have learned to be patient," Mooyo said.

They talked about life in Rijeka, about his son, how he was for them like a toy, how he lit the cigars and pipes for her parents, and how he listened to everyone. Finally, she arrived at their destination.

During their conversation, they came to a small city with narrow streets and sharp corners, and then in front of a big house. When the small car stopped, Mooyo's wife and son ran outside to meet him. Almost ten months without each other, the son and father hugged each other so hard, as if they never wanted to be apart again. The boy looked fine, and more grown than Mooyo had remembered. His wife was as skinny as a woman in a prison camp. Her hair was longer than Mooyo remembered. He couldn't believe she could lose that much weight in ten months. Nonetheless, everyone in the house was happy to see each other.

Over coffee, they caught up. He told them how he took the picture to Zagreb for the passport, which would be done soon, and he would try to get them to Germany. His son sat on his lap and wouldn't get off. He had his father back, and he didn't want to get out of his arms. The two of them were always so close and listened to each other. When Mooyo and Fata wanted to go somewhere without him, it was very hard for him to let them go.

They talked until late in the evening. He told them how he had worked in construction for a month and a half but didn't get paid for it. He trusted the new company with the two young engineers from Zagreb, whom he came to Zagreb with the previous night.

All three of them lay in the same bed like before the war. He and his son scratched each other until his son fell asleep happy and safe in his father's arms. The rest of the night, Mooyo and Fata clung to each other hugging and whispering. They wished the morning would never come, but the hours passed too quickly, and the sunrise brought a new day and new obligations.

By eight o'clock, everyone was sitting around the table drinking coffee. His wife's aunt had already checked the time the train was leaving. How could Mooyo leave his loved ones again? He hoped to return soon to get them. He told them that it would be in the next two or three weeks. With this thought, they parted, and Kemal took him to the small train station. His son and wife stayed there, sad but hoping for his speedy return.

The train from Rijeka-Buzet-Ljubljana was already there. Mooyo thanked Kemal for everything he had done for him and his family and stepped onto the train. He found a seat in a nearly empty car. He took off his jacket, and looked through the window at the fields covered with pine trees. When they reached the border with Slovenia, the border policemen of the Republic Slovenia arrived to check the travelers' documents. When he saw Mooyo's Bosnian passport with a German visa, he stared at Mooyo like a ghost. When he came to his visa, he folded and folded the passport, checking if it was fake one. He spent a long time checking the information in his computer, but when he didn't find anything wrong, he handed the passport back to him.

Mooyo watched him with joy, laughing inside because this time he was a free man and had nothing to fear. He wanted to show the policeman, that he is not the man they interrogated with ugly questions last winter, the man they forced to pay a high amount of money to "cross their border of Independent State" and said a civil war refugee must leave their country within thirty days.

From the main station in Ljubljana he walked to the bus station for Vrhnika. He bought a ticket and found a free seat in the bus happy he was traveling the same roads and proud he had overcome his bad experience with that country and places. His aunt was waiting for him.

Vrhnika was always dear to him, especially because he had spent his summer breaks as a young boy with his aunt. The ride was very short, and he walked to where his aunt lived. She cried with joy and hugged him like her own son.

Over coffee, they talked about many things. They talked about other refugees from their family who lived in camp Kuplensko. Because they knew he was coming, lunch was ready. He had enough time to eat with them and ride back to Ljubljana to the main bus and train station where the engineers would pick him up. Of course, his aunt didn't let him go back to the bus because they had a car, so they could take him to the main station, and he could stay longer.

The car ride was fast because it was a weekend. He bought a Bosnian newspaper and patiently watched for the engineers. In a short time, the white Pezo appeared. They greeted each other and started the drive home. Mooyo thanked them for driving.

"No problem. We went to our house, and now we are going back there. If the seat in the back is empty or full, it is the same. Was your family happy to see you after such a long time?" asked Vlado.

"I can't describe it, but everything was rushed. Everything was like a dream, but never were people better and nicer. Because of it, I am thankful to you. I do not have enough words to express that," said Mooyo happily.

"If everything goes to plan, with God's help in two or three weeks, I will be able to try take them to Bad Bergzabern," added Mooyo.

"That means you did everything for the man in Zagreb?" asked Milenko.

"The man looked earnest, and the money I will take and hand him when I see the passport in my hands. The only thing is I need to work hard and earn one thousand for the passport and some extra for the trip to Croatia and back to Germany," explained Mooyo.

"The first of the month will be payday, and before you leave, you can take something in advance," added Vlado.

"Thank you guys. Without the two of you and the job, all this would be impossible," said Mooyo.

There wasn't a lot of traffic, and the custom officers and border guards checked their passports and quickly returned them to Milenko who was driving and handing the passports to them through the driver's window. The ride through Slovenia and Austria was interesting. Like other boys, they talked about women and drinks during the ride.

When they arrived in Germany, it was already dark. While Vlado was driving, Mooyo fell asleep.

After midnight, they came to the parking lot above Kurtal Strasse. They walked downstairs to Mooyo's room quietly and slept the rest of the night. The engineers shared Boco's bed.

The slamming doors of Adam's room and the bathroom awoke them around seven o'clock the next morning. It was hard for them to get up, but they had no choice. Avdi noticed they were back, so he cooked a huge pot of black Bosnian coffee for all of them. They drank coffee and ate breakfast, talking about their trip to Croatia and back. At eight o'clock they all were done with breakfast when Boric with Safet came from Sar Bricken, so in two cars, they drove to their construction site.

The fall days in Sudlishe Weinstrasse were very beautiful, with less rain than during the summer time. The building was rising quickly. Everyone was happy, from the people who the building belonged to, to the young engineers, and the workers. The man who owned the building visited the site every day with three liters of white wine and three liters of red wine for them. Mooyo helped all the masters unload and load the materials with a crane, deliver and drive materials from and to the construction site, which made him very busy all the time. He asked his uncle if they could drive him down to Zagreb when the passport was done and drive them back to Germany. They made the deal to do it, but they planned to visit the refugee camp Kuplensko to see the rest of their family and relatives. Another man from their neighborhood would go with them. He had been working and living in Munich for many years. Once again, he talked with Barka to implore her to call her cousin to make the passport in the best way.

The salary was on the time, but the engineers couldn't promise further work because winter was coming. Mooyo wasn't worried about it. He had enough money for the passport and the trip to Croatia and back. He was finally able to communicate in German, which would open up possibilities for other jobs. He kept the job in Wisenburg in the hotel with an older Italian lady. Little by little he established his new life. His wife begged him to hurry every time he talked with her. Her aunt had some flood damage in her warehouse, so they planned to leave Croatia and move back to Bosnia where they had a house. For that reason, he found another place for them in Rijeka, where his cousin lived.

All Mooyo could do was wait for the call that the passport was ready. He gave his wife his cousin's phone number, but his wife was disappointed.

Throughout his life, he had learned to be patient, knowing that a new day never comes before sunrise.

# CHAPTER 21

## Smuggling over the Border

Two weeks passed since Mooyo had visited Zagreb and met Barka's cousin when he decided to finally make a call to see if the passport was done. He was nervous, so he took his time and slowly walked to the phone booth. He had spent a lot of money in that phone booth talking with people since he came to that city.

For good luck, he stepped inside the booth with his right foot, he held the receiver with his right hand, and then he dialed the numbers for Zagreb. After the third ring, the man answered. He introduced himself as Barka's friend and Bayo's cousin. He was always suspicious that someone was spying on the phone. He asked him if he was done with the job for him, again skipping the words about the passport.

"Do not worry. Everything will be done this Friday. If you want to be sure, call me again on Friday night, and I will tell you if the document is done and if I have it with me," said the man.

"Please, try to make the seal over the pictures as we talked about, and I will come to get it if not this Saturday, then the next one because I need to arrange transportation with someone," Mooyo replied.

"Okay. We will talk again on Friday night," said the man.

Mooyo was ready to go the next week, but he needed to double check with his aunt and Visoki if they could go or not. He needed to know a week in advance if the passport was done. He called his uncle in Munich to tell them that the passport might be done that week.

"That is great. If the passport is done by Friday, you can go there next week because you need to travel here during the day on Friday. From Zagreb, you need to go to Kuplensko if the police let you enter the camp to meet a refugee," said his uncle.

"All right, my uncle. Say hi to everyone there, and I will call you Friday night when I know if the passport is done," Mooyo said.

Mooyo's uncle warned him of scary scenarios because it was dangerous to have someone illegally transported. His uncle and aunt were nice, honest working people who never did anything against the law. Mooyo knew it and hid his fears inside, but there was no other way. He wouldn't put them in danger with the law.

If the passport was good for the first two borders, they didn't need to be worried about the next two borders because they would have valid passports. Inside, just false pictures and names. The girls went shopping often in Trieste, Italy, and they had good experiences with border controls. They both had Croatian passports. He was sorry to put them at risk too, but he needed help, and he didn't know anyone else to ask.

He felt stomach cramps when he got back to his room, but Avdi invited him for coffee, and on the table was an open bottle of German brandy.

"Want some spice?" asked Avdi, sipping the coffee.

"Of course, I can have two Avdi. Everything is painful in my stomach, like I will throw up," said Mooyo.

He had one more coffee with brandy, and they played cards. They played until Avdi remembered to turn on Radio Free Europe. Avdi sometimes cursed and swore, and then he sighed, sipped another brandy to feel better.

"Thank you for the coffee and brandy Avdi. Everything was so good. I am going to take a shower and go to bed. We are off tomorrow. If you want, we can ride our bikes to the orchards," said Mooyo.

"Do not thank me. Tomorrow night we can drink in your room. Everything makes me nervous, so I need to drink. My feet hurt me so bad during the night, and if I have some brandy, I cannot feel it," said Avdi.

When he got in the bathtub, he remembered the day he went with Bucko to the main train station in Zagreb and started his journey illegally traveling to the west, when Bucko had told him, "You, my Godfather should never throw stones at God, so you will arrive wherever you plan to go." The words gave him hope.

Saturday morning dawned gloomy. The house was quiet. He decided to walk through the forest above the house. He thought he could gather chestnuts, so he took a small bag with him. When he climbed up the hill, he felt that everything around him was sleeping. The quiet was disturbed only by a car passing below the hill or an occasional bird call. Leaves fell on the ground in the different colors and shapes. He passed the tower with the German flag. He wouldn't climb up because it was too windy. He carried leafs, loading them without a sound on the forest ground to its cousins and neighbors related species of trees.

Before the edge of the forest, he saw meadows all the way to the castle where nuns lived and worked. He saw the chestnut trees he had discovered during his walks through the forest. He and Avdi had discovered different kinds of fruit trees around the castle, and knowing the months in which they would ripen, they went to pick and eat cherries, apples, grapes, and plums. Nobody said no to men. They would eat some and take some home with them.

In the woods, Mooyo used a small stick to move the leaves right and left, and under the leaves, he found many chestnuts, so after about thirty minutes, his plastic bag was full. Winter was coming, and he enjoyed collecting fruit like in his homeland. He wanted to have something when his son and wife arrived. He had the feeling they would be there soon to collect chestnuts, walk around, and ride the bikes around that beautiful vineyard.

"If they would only come," he thought, walking down the hill with his bag of chestnuts. Avdi was awake, so Mooyo offered to make coffee for them. Adam was still sleeping. They decided to ride their bikes to the orchards where they found tons of apples and pears on the ground. On their bikes, they had small baskets, but they took their light backpacks to carry beer in case they got thirsty. On their way, they met other people walking or riding bikes through the vineyard and the beautiful place close to the French- German border.

"Avdi, do you see how smart these Germans are to plow and plant all the dirt they have and make something valuable. We needed to run many kilometers away to save our own heads and lives, leaving our fruit and land to who knows who," said Mooyo, biting a juicy red-yellow apple.

They returned before the lunchtime because the apples they ate were like a good meal. In his room, Mooyo again felt nervous and crushed between two walls. He ate just a couple of bites and walked back out to the city to see what else he could buy and take to his family in the refugee camp. The best and cheapest store was the mini-Woolworth, where he was always able to find useful and nice things for his family if he was be able to get to them. His sister and brother-in-law visited them and took some things they needed there.

Mooyo passed by happy, nicely, dressed pedestrians, who couldn't have been visitors or locals. Many of them were patients from the rehabilitation clinics, enjoying the thermal spas or tourists who were enjoying the beauty of the vineyard, sampling good food and wine.

On his way back, he saw a soccer player from Zenica, and they talked about going to the field to play soccer. It was the best solution for him to play soccer, get tired, and sleep away his worry and impatience. Many other refugees from Bosnia, played soccer there until the dark covered the hills. Soccer made them tired.

After the game, he went home and listened to Radio Free Europe where the speaker talked about peace signs in Dayton and the Peace Conference in the USA, where Cuzman (how his uncle called him), Slobo, and Aljo signed a treaty with Americans for Bosnia and Herzegovina. The speaker talked about new maps and borders between the new Federation to which belonged the Bosnian Catholic and Muslim people and Serbian Republic in which belonged the Bosnian Orthodox people.

"I do not care about their drawing of the border lines. How many will be there even if every village will have their own border? My only care is to stop the war and violence. If they want to make a black Arab president just to stop the shooting and not kill more of humans, I will be thrilled," thought Mooyo, laying in the dark.

The days got shorter and shorter but not for him burdened with so many thoughts and hopes about everything that needed to be done the next week. Luckily, there was a lot of work to do on the construction site, which made his days easier. He was patient until Thursday, when he decided to call his man and ask if the passport was done. He ambled to the phone booth on Kurtal Strasse. The man answered.

"Good afternoon. This is Barka's friend from Germany," he told the man.

"Good afternoon. It is good you called. I have the passport for you, and you can come this weekend to get it."

"Excellent. I will try to be there on Saturday morning in the same restaurant at the main station, but I will call you when I arrive. I have the money, which I will give to you when I see the passport," explained Mooyo.

"Do not worry. Everything is as we discussed. When you come, just call me, and I will be there, and you can check it. I couldn't have done it better. Then, good night we'll see each other here soon."

"Good night and thank you for everything," added Mooyo, hanging up.

The receiver was shaking in his hand. Again, he tossed the card into the phone and dialed his uncle in Munich to tell him that the passport was done, and if his aunt was ready, they could go to Croatia on Friday night. His uncle seemed happy but worried about his wife going against law. Still he wanted to help even though he was scared they would be discovered, and get in trouble. His uncle told him to call back in a half hour when he talked with Visoki and his wife. When they hung up, he called Vlado to ask if he could take off work the next day, and if they could give him another five hundred marks until the next paycheck. The engineer promised to stop by eight o'clock with the money, and he excused him for one day of work.

Mooyo then went to his room to change out of his work clothes. From the excitement of the last thirty minutes, he felt like his heart would jump out of his chest. He took a shower to calm his nerves and once again went to the phone booth, this time he talked with his Aunt Pasima. She and Visoki were ready to go with him Friday afternoon after work. He needed to return to Munich the next day. He told her that he would take the first train in the morning.

He still had money on his phone card, so he was able to call his wife in Buzet to tell her that he would arrive on Saturday. Fata was very happy and wished to talk more with him. He told her that they could talk until the phone card ran out.

He went back to his room. He packed clothes and shoes to take to his mother, father, and brother in case he could see them. His documents and other things he needed he packed in the small bag. When he was done packing, he went to Avdi and Adam's room to tell them that he would be off work tomorrow because he had to go to Munich and then to Croatia. They both wished him safe travels and good luck in his business.

That November morning was cloudy with impending rain or snow. At seven-thirty in the morning, Vlado came with the money. Mooyo thanked him and apologized for missing work that day. Vlado drove him to the train station. They tightened their hands together, and Vlado wished him good luck.

Mooyo bought a ticket just to Karlsruhe because he wanted to check the driving routes and the prices of different trains. In Karlsruhe, for a ticket to Munich, he needed to pay a hundred-thirty marks, which seemed very expensive since before he rode for only fifteen marks round trip during the weekend. During the ride, he passed the time reading and napping and enjoying the scenery. At the main station, he walked down to the underground station for Uban, which went to New Perlach, where his uncle and family had lived for a long time. From that station, he walked to the Kurt-Eisner Strasse.

When he arrived, his relatives were all still at work or school, so he decided to sit on a nearby bench and wait.

By two-thirty, all the walkways came to life again with school children and workers leaving the first shift. He immediately recognized two of the children. It was his uncle, aunt and their children. His uncle made coffee, and they talked about the plans. His aunt made everything for the trip, but they still needed to wait for Visoki to get in the car and on the road. Mooyo could tell his uncle was worried but was trying to hide it and stay positive. Until supper was done, they talked about the news and the Peace Conference to stop the war because the nationalist leaders, under American pressure, had finally decided to agree on new names, maps, and most importantly a ceasefire. His uncle always listened to many different kinds of news from his small radio, so he was well-informed about the events in their homeland and the world at large.

The kids were playing around them because tomorrow they didn't have school. By the time Visoki arrived and they had loaded the car with bags, it was eleven o'clock, almost midnight when they got on the highway toward Salzburg.

They switched drivers during the night. The highways were not crowded, but they knew that it would take at least seven hours to reach Zagreb. Luckily, there wasn't snow, and the highways were dry. Slovenia was foggy, and the fog followed them all the way to Zagreb. At around seven o'clock in the morning, they got off the highway to the city and the main bus and train station. At that hour, it was easy to find a parking space.

Mooyo had a phone card from his last visit. They walked to a pay phone, from which he called his man to tell him he was in the restaurant waiting for him. The man told him he would be there in thirty minutes.

The morning coffee tasted delicious. The restaurant was nearly empty, but slowly, it began to fill with customers getting their morning coffee. Mooyo tried to guess if any were undercover policemen. He was suspicious of everything. Luckily, after thirty-five minutes Barka's cousin arrived. He greeted everyone and sat down. Mooyo waved to the waiter who brought the coffee and brandy for the man. The man pulled an envelope with a passport out of his pocket. Mooyo warned him that people might see, so he put it back in his pocket.

"I will go to the restroom, and you can come a minute later because we must be careful," said Mooyo, standing up from the table.

"Okay," agreed the man.

Mooyo waited a moment for him in the restroom. The man arrived, handing him the envelope with the passport.

"Do not worry, everything was done to precision," said the man.

Mooyo nodded and checked the passport. It had a Croatian name Ivana, and the pictures of his wife and son, over the right corner was a small seal. Everything looked perfect. Mooyo had a thousand marks, which he handed to the man.

"How did you come here?" asked Mooyo.

"I came in a tram. Why do you ask?" the man asked, surprised.

"O.K. we will take you to your address where you live, and you can hold the passport in your pocket until we get there, and when we come to your address, I will give you the money, and you can give me the passport because you never know if someone is spaying on us or you."

"Okay. There is no problem. For me, it is easier to go back with you than in the tram," said the man.

They finished their coffee, and Mooyo told his aunt and Visoki they would take the man back to his home. He waved to the waiter, paid the bill, and they all walked to the parking lot. The man told Mooyo's aunt the directions.

"Please count the money to make sure everything is there," said Mooyo.

"Everything is there. I wish you good luck and a safe trip. Call me when everything is done."

They shook hands, and the man got out of the car.

They got back on the highway to Karlovac. The ride wasn't long. Mooyo hid the passport in the bottom of his small bag. The police there sometimes stopped and searched cars, and if they found the passport without the person, they could put them in prison, and who knew what would happen then.

They rode through Karlovac and toward Kuplensko. The city was still demolished Turanj, but there weren't check points from the UN, HVO, or SAO anymore. The road was still overgrown with bushes and weeds. They almost never passed civilian cars on their way. They just passed occasional police cars. Everything seemed neglected and abandoned, as if no one had lived there in years. There were ruined houses, and it was difficult to find nice ones like before.

They drove slowly, until they got to the police checkpoint just before the camp Kuplensko, where a police officer stopped them.

"Where do you wish to go?" asked the policeman.

"We want to take some clothes and shoes to our families in the refugee camp", his aunt answered politely.

"Right now you can't go there because they had a problem there. Until it is solved, you need to wait here," replied the policeman.

"How long it will take?" asked Visoki.

"We can't tell you exactly, but at least two hours," said the policeman.

They tried to bribe him with cigarettes and money to get permission to pass, but he insisted they had to wait on the side, and when the control there was done, he would take them there. The minutes were like years, but they stayed and waited.

Eventually, a couple of other cars came with the same wish to go to the camp, but they needed to park on the side and wait for permission, too. They could see through the window that everyone offered presents and payoffs, but they still needed to wait there. Luckily, they had enough sandwiches and drinks, so they didn't need to drive back to buy anything.

At around one o'clock, they got permission to pass the police checkpoint and drive to refugee camp. Everything would be fine, but in front of the refugee camp was another checkpoint with police, which they needed to pass to enter the camp. Once again, they tried payoff presents of money and cigarettes, but they were told to stay there. At the entrance, they found some people they knew.

Mooyo's father, mother, brother, uncle and many other relatives rushed to meet them. There were many hugs, tears, and questions. His mother and father wanted to know where his son and wife were. He told them that his plan was to get them today if everything went smoothly. Mooyo was sad when he saw the rest of his family, so he had a hard time talking. All the refugees other than his brother looked like people made of clay. The living conditions for them were terrible. There was no place for personal hygiene, washing clothes, or taking showers, and the food was bad and suspicious in origin. Snow was on the way, and they didn't have wood or stoves to heat their rooms. The reality was so bleak that it was hard to believe.

During their conversation, he told them that he was going to Buzet, where his wife and son were. From there he would take them to Germany. In the end of the visit, he told his parents to go back to their home because some kind of peace was signed in Dayton, which ended the Bosnian war. He told his brother to stay there because they would still use him as a soldier, so it was better to stay in the camp for the time being. Mooyo thought if he successfully got his wife and son, he would try to get him out, too. He left some money for them.

The policeman who was standing behind them pointed to his watch. It was time for them to leave the refugee camp. They were scared that someone would overthrow them, or maybe he wanted more money from them. Separation was painful, with tears and hugs, but everyone needed to return to their side. They walked back to the police checkpoint where they had left the car. Lost in their own thoughts, they drove back to Karlovac. Mooyo couldn't erase the images of the people he saw there, women and children covered in soot with dirt smeared on their faces.

Visoki drove from Karlovac to Rijeka. They only stopped once to get something to eat. The road was narrow with many twists and turns. So speeding was dangerous. There were police on the road, and if they drove over the limit, they would have to pay a large fine. The day was almost over. When they got to Buzet, they had to plan their next move.

When they reached Rijeka, it was already dark, and they still needed to reach Buzet. The narrow streets and darkness made it harder for them to find the address where his wife and son lived. They drove about half an hour until they finally found the right place. They were exhausted from the trip and especially from the heart-wrenching meeting with their relatives in the camp, so they wanted to stretch their legs and sleep. Mooyo's son was happier than anyone else.

The original plan was to take his wife and son over the first two borders on Saturday. The border checkpoints would be busy that day, and the border guards would be unable to pay attention to so many travelers. Because everything had taken longer than expected, the only solution was for Mooyo to stay there until Wednesday, another shopping day, and girls would take his wife and son to Trieste and then take a train to Austria and finally Germany. His aunt and Visoki needed to return home as they couldn't wait until Wednesday. Mooyo would stay until Wednesday. He needed to ask for more time off work. He had no choice.

Mia and Kamil were very good hosts, offering food, drinks, and a place to sleep that night. Mooyo was much happier with the new plan because he would put fewer people at risk.

His son woke up first, happy that his father was sleeping in the same bed with him. He entertained all of them with songs and stories of his careless happy childhood. Slowly, everyone got up. Kamil came back from the bakery with bread and a newspaper, and they had breakfast crowded in the kitchen. At around ten o'clock in the morning, Mooyo's aunt and Visoki were ready for the road.

The images from the refugee camp worried Mooyo, but he believed that his father and mother would take his advice and return to their home. The same day Kamil's cousin came from Germany. When he heard the plan for transporting Mooyo's wife and son over the borders, he offered to drive Mooyo behind the girls' car. They would follow them, so they would know immediately if border guards discovered or captured them. They practiced his son's new identity, Ivan, that his father worked and lived in Germany, and he and his mom Ivanka were going to visit him. The boy learned it fast, almost as if he understood how hard it was to travel illegally. His wife practiced the information and the signature, and they were ready for the journey. They waited for Wednesday like a birthday. There were worries, but they needed to trust chance and the value of the false passport and God.

Three days passed quickly. The girls were ready at nine o'clock. The coffee and breakfast were done. Everyone tried to tease his son, calling him Ivan. Kamil and Mia had a hard time letting him go. They were used to his childish games, conversations, and songs. The sisters sat in front, and Mooyo's wife and son sat in the back. Kamil and his cousin sat in front and Mooyo sat in the back seat of the other car. Thus, the journey began.

The ride to the border wasn't long, but for Mooyo it took a lifetime. On the border between Croatia and Slovenia, the guards waived to the girls. When the Slovenian guard took the passports, he checked them and handed them back to the girl driving. All three men in the second car were relieved when they passed the first border. They reached the next guards who took their passports and checked them for fifteen minutes because the car had a German license plate, the driver had a German passport, his front passenger was Croatian, the man in the back had a Bosnian passport with a German visa, and all three had Muslim names. They were as suspicious as could be. They took the passports to check on the computer, and they doublechecked the pictures with their faces.

Finally, they returned the passports because they couldn't find anything wrong. The same scenario happened at the Slovenian border, but the travelers in the second car didn't care because their passports were legal and the girls passed through eventually.

At the Slovenian-Italian border, they had the same situation. The girls passed through easily, but the second car had trouble. When they got their passports from the Italian guards, they drove to the parking lot where the girls were waiting for them, happy and making fun of their difficulties at the borders. At the parking lot, they got out of the cars, and after wishing them good luck, Mooyo got into the girls' car to drive them to the train station in Trieste. The two men in the second car drove back. Mooyo needed to buy tickets to Karlsruhe for himself, his wife, and his son. They thanked the girls for the huge help and they said good-bye. This part of the trip they could do alone.

They needed to sit on the train bound for Tervisio on the Austrian border, but by mistake they got on the train headed to Tervisio, Italy. They left that train at the first station, and rode back to Trieste to find the correct train for Austria. The conductors didn't understand German, and Mooyo didn't speak Italian. In the end, they found the correct train and started again. They sat in two different cars to avoid the suspicion of border guards since they were traveling with different passports.

Mooyo and Fata agreed that if they discovered her and took her and their son back, not to mention him because he would find another way to get them later. If they discovered about him, there would be no help for any of them.

The train was slowly moving through the majestic Alps. Snow looked like a white hat on the top of the mountains. Throughout the ride, Mooyo watched the train car where his wife and son sat. When they left Italy, nobody checked on the travelers. Mooyo wasn't sure when they crossed the border. It was dark when the train stopped at a large train station. He tried to identify the city. He decided to find a conductor to ask if this was the right train for Karlsruhe. The conductor told him that their car was going farther to Salzburg, but they would remove some of the train cars.

He told him that there they needed to find another train for Munich, and from Munich to Karlsruhe. On his way back to his seat, he told Fata to stay there because they would catch the train to Salzburg.

"At least we are in Austria. Do not worry. If they check you in the train, give them your passport and look them straight in the eyes."

The locomotive made noise, switching cars, until the train left the station and headed into the darkness. They were still nervous and scared of the border check guards. They came to a large train station in Salzburg. They walked outside together to find the train to Munich. At the well-lit station, many people were rushing in all directions. To be sure they were in the right train, Mooyo found the first man in uniform and asked because he could communicate in German. The conductor directed him to the correct platform, where the train for Munich sat. They walked over the bridge to the platform. They entered the car, and like before, they sat in different seats. His wife and son sat in the middle of the car, and Mooyo took the last seat in the car.

One more border and then he could drink champagne.

The train left the station. After a short ride, a border guard came into their car to check their tickets and passports. One heavy German policeman had a computer on his shoulder in which he checked the passports of all the travelers trying to get to Munich. Mooyo sank in his seat, crossing his fingers, when the guard got to his wife and son and took her passport. He put it in his computer and politely handed it back to Fata. No one was happier in the world then him at that moment. The guard came to his seat. He scanned his passport and visa and handed it politely back to him. Because Mooyo was the last passenger in that car, the guard left the room. He knew at that moment that her passport was correct, and he walked to the seat behind them.

"Now everything is okay. This was the last passport check before Bad Bergzabern," said Mooyo, encouragingly.

When the cart arrived with drinks, they ordered drinks to celebrate getting through all the borders. Soon they would be safe in his cozy room on Kurtal Strasse. Their son was sleeping well as they drank coffee until they arrived at the main station in Munich. They didn't have to change trains until Karlsruhe. From Karlsruhe, they changed trains for Winden and from there to his refugee city.

The city was sleeping peacefully under the stars, and there were barely any cars on the street. From the city train station, he carried his son in his arms. His happy and satisfied wife walked at his side. The house on Kurtal Strasse smelled of cigars and alcohol like always. The house was very quiet. He unlocked his door and put his son in Boco's bed. He and Fata shared his bed embracing and happy to be together again, side by side, after almost a year of separation.

# PART III

## Leaving A Second Home for the U.S.

In the morning, Mooyo woke up like the happiest man on the Earth. Even though he was a refugee in a foreign land, he once again lived with his wife and son. He got himself ready for work like before, but today he was able to drink his morning coffee with his wife. His son woke up too, and he introduced them to Adam and Avdi. They went to their job. Despite the cooling temperatures, they had finishing touches on the building they were constructing.

On Friday, it rained, which later turned to sleet, so they were not able to work. Mooyo used the day to take his wife and son to register at city hall. They told him to take them to the Office for foreigners in Landau to register them, which he did the same day. In Landau, they gave him the address of the collection center for refugees in Newstad, where they needed to register and complete a health screening.

They went to the stores because they were not in hurry. They didn't have enough money to buy what they needed, but still they found some needed things for a start. After shopping, they got on the train home. They invited Adam and Avdi to their room to have a drink to celebrate their happy arrival.

Saturday morning, they slept in, finally having no place to go. They could relax at last.

Suddenly, a knock on their door warned them to get out of bed.

Mooyo asked, "Who is there?"

From the other side of the door, Branka said, "I am with Mr. Gran."

They were surprised, and Mooyo wondered what was going on. He slowly opened the door to see what was wrong, and Branka told them that he came to move them to their new apartment because he needed their room for another refugee from Sarajevo. They would have a four-room apartment with a kitchen and bath on Koenig Strasse, across from City Hall. They couldn't believe their ears. They were even more surprised when Mr. Gran showed them the new apartment. It was on the first floor. From the stairway, they walked straight to the kitchen and from there to the other three rooms. Through the biggest room, they entered the bathroom with its own laundry machine. In the biggest room, there was a king-size bed, with two dressers. The other rooms were still empty. He told them he would bring a bed for their son. Because they didn't have many groceries or other belongings, it was easy for them to move the same day. Their luck was now even greater.

December brought more cold rain and snow, so they had difficulty to finish the work on the building until the roof people were finished. Still, despite the cold days, they completed the job just before the Christmas.

They shared the hope that their bosses would have a new job for them in a spring. In the meantime, Mooyo took his wife and son to Newstad to register at the collection center for refugees. Because they already had a two-bedroom apartment, they assumed it would be done expediently.

However, it took a long time because as far as the German government was concerned, the Bosnian war was over. The Germans wanted the refugees to go back to their country. However, for Mooyo's family, going home didn't make any sense because they had just gotten the apartment. They didn't understand why the government was making it so hard to get the transfer papers, so they could legally stay in the apartment. His wife and son completed the health screening, but they kept them in the center. The little boy became bored and cranky. Fata tried to entertain him, but he cried, and Mooyo became frustrated.

He tried to talk with the officials in the center but without success. They told him that his family could stay with him, but they needed to report to the center every Monday. When the application and pleas didn't help, he asked them for the address and phone number where they could file an appeal. He got the address and phone of Minister for the Foreign Business. Then Mooyo called his aunt in Munich and told her everything, asking her for help because she was fluent in German.

She called and explained his situation, and finally, after three months, they got the transfer and a six-month visa, which solved their last hurdle.

In March, his visa expired, and when he went to renew it, he got a duldung visa like his wife and son. With that visa, it was very difficult to find a new full-time job. The German Government issued them partial working visas, so they were only able to find part-time jobs. Mooyo found a part-time job in Arbeit Samaritar Bund delivering food to diabetic people. His wife got a cleaning job with other Bosnian Orthodox girls in the Thermal Bad. They signed their son up for the Kindergarten, where he was able to learn the new language. Knowing the language and new culture allowed Mooyo to find jobs around the city.

Luckily, his parents returned to their damaged and looted home and again live under their own roof. With his help and the help of other relatives and friends, they repaired the damage and rebuilt their lives on their own property. The best part of all was that there was no more shooting. His brother moved to a refugee camp in Obonjan, Croatia, where he had better living conditions than in Kuplensko. There he applied for a visa to move to another country.

In November of 1996, Mooyo's brother arranged to move to Saint Louis, Missouri and started his new life. Mooyo and Fata had made new friends and had enough work. They were refugees, but they had many nice days in the city with many flowers, healthy water, kindly people, vineyards, and greenery. Their main problem came with the letters the German government sent to them about returning to their country. Mooyo got back only half the money he had earned on his first full-time job. He paid back the money to his aunt in Slovenia. He also sent some money to support their parents in Bosnia when they could, but they worked hard and saved money to have something when the day came for them to return to their country.

The government first deported single refugees who had applied for asylum but didn't get it, and after them families who didn't work and lived entirely on government support. Knowing how destroyed and filled with land mines their Bosnia was, and fearing government corruption, many people found ways to move to third countries like Canada, Australia, and America. They wanted to go somewhere they would be able to stay longer. Mooyo's family had a visit from his sister's father-in-law who worked and lived in Germany. He was friend with the new minister for education in their city, and he brought the call for Mooyo to return to Bosnia.

"I talked with Raskom, and she said she has a job for you in Rajnovac," said Dzeko.

"I need to go to Rajnovac and have school in front of my house? Is she crazy?" asked Mooyo, outraged.

"I am just telling you that she said they need educated people in the city and country," he replied, seeing how Mooyo had become so mad at the new minister. In addition to the minister, there were the national parties, which were in charge of opened job; who could work, where they could work, and how safe and welcomed they could be in their own country. Again he needed to decide whether to go back home or somewhere else in the world.

When they were free, they went for a walk, enjoying the beautiful scenery, vineyards, and orchards, green and full of different fruit. They talked about their dilemma.

Together, they decided to put an application for a third country because with it they would extend their permission to stay in Germany, where they could earn money and have a fresh start. From some friends, they got the application forms for Canada, but they found they didn't qualify for that country. They didn't have relatives in Australia. Their only choice was to go to America.

They talked with Halil, and he promised to send them the warranty letter, which he would sign to take care of them until they found jobs and could stand on their own feet. Through an organization called Raphaels Werk they got all the forms that needed to be filled out.

When they received the letter from Halil, they sent the forms and letter to the American Embassy in Frankfurt, after two weeks, they got the confirmation that their application was complete and being processed. From then on, every time their visa expired, they could take the confirmation letter and their passport to the Office for Foreigners in Landau, and they could extend their visas.

Meanwhile, unmarried people were pushed back to Bosnia. One family soon got a visa to move to Australia. Another family they knew moved to Canada. Then, other families that didn't apply to move to a third country were pushed back to their hometowns or somewhere in Bosnia to be refugees there too as they were not able to go to their old homes.

Time passed with Mooyo and Fata working part-time jobs, hanging out with new friends they met, and waiting for the appointment for their health screening or interview. One day in 1997, they got an appointment for the first health screening in Frankfurt. After that, they got the letter to attend a cultural seminar about life in the USA, which was held in Karlsruhe. There they were told about life, habits, customs, and American culture. It appeared like they would get visas to go there.

Mooyo had mixed feelings, still dreaming about his castle and homeland. He thought about learning yet another new language. That made him even more apprehensive. Still, walking through the lush vineyard above Bad Bergzabern, he thought about the history of Bosnia and Herzegovina. When he went through the history from the beginning of Bosnia, he realized the truth. His small country was more often occupied by different empires, armies, and wars, than it existed in peace and wealth. He thought of his long dead ancestor, Mooyo, who worked so hard to build the castle and protect its people only to have death and misery surround him and his family. In this just ended, bloody war, approximately one hundred-fifty thousand people had died or vanished, over sixty percent of homes were destroyed, and over sixty percent of industry was gone. One million people had left that region and found new homes around the world.

"If I go back what will my family and I find there, and how long will peace last this time?" wondered Mooyo.

"Do I need to walk, drive, or fly as far as possible from my country, or will we once again be pulled into war's cruel vortex?" In that moment, a scared bird, from a nearby grape plant flew to the woods nearby. At the same time, he decided to fly as far as possible from Bosnia. He would leave his parents, cousins, neighbors, habits, house, language, his earned degree and students who were waiting for his return.

They continued talking with Halil. He told them that he was happy in the new world. He and his wife had jobs, which gave them the opportunity to have a nice life.

By the beginning of 1999, they finally passed their last exam. They got permission to go to Saint Louis, Missouri to be with Halil. They didn't receive final word of their flight until the organization Raphaels Werk signed the contract with them. They would have to pay for the tickets after they found jobs in America. But after that final decision, everything moved quickly. They signed the contract for the airplane tickets and their itinerary from Frankfurt to America.

Before their flight, they wished to visit their parents in Bosnia. They went again in the Office for foreigners to ask for a special visa, to travel outside Germany and come back.

It was a bittersweet visit with their parents, neighbors, and friends filled with sadness about the war that should never have happened.

Finally, they needed to leave Bosnia and their relatives to go back to Germany and then relocate to America. To their relatives, America was at the end of the world. They left with tears and hugs.

Mooyo's coworkers made a small going away party for him. They had a special lunch, where he received a card with wishes for a good trip and good luck in the new country. They had even collected money for his new life.

Finally, on July 12, 1999, Mooyo's friends and neighbors sent him off from Bad Bergzabern, and Heinz. The German man, for whom Mooyo had worked for a long time, drove them to the airport in Frankfurt. It was their first flight in an airplane.

At the airport parking lot, they said their final good-byes to their friend. At the gate, they found many Bosnians who were flying on the same airplane to America and some of them to Saint Louis. They met Koka, her husband and daughter, just a little bit older than their son. They were going to Saint Louis.

Their first stop was in Chicago, Illinois. They huddled in their seats, until the stewardesses explained what to do in case of a crash or fire. It frightened Mooyo's family even more. Then they heard the noise of the aircraft engines. Someone told them to open their mouths wide until the airplane reached the needed height. They did it even though they didn't know why.

Mooyo sat in the window seat, so he was able to see the city fade away under their airplane. The airplane engines were so powerful that they didn't know when the wheels left the runway, and for a few seconds climbed high above the Frankfurt's skyscrapers. After that, soft white clouds covered the beautiful German landscape. Mooyo and his family were so thankful for the incredible hospitality of the Germans during his stay. That kind of hospitality he couldn't find in countries like Croatia, Slovenia, or Austria, where he was an illegal traveler even though those countries were members of the Geneva Convention. He wished that one day he could pay back the city of Bad Bergzabern, its kindly and hospitable people, and the whole country of Germany for everything they had done for him and his family and many other Bosnian refugees.

# EPILOGUE

## From Refugee to Writer

Life in the new country has brought limitless possibilities. Everything surrounds you, and you can succeed with your hands as long as you are willing to work, study, create, and enjoy life in peace, freedom, and wealth. From the immense airport in Chicago where I landed, high above the enormous St. Louis Arch, the doorway through which I entered this city, all places, cities, and towns offered me the opportunity to visit or live there and enjoy their beauty. Hundreds and hundreds of kilometers on each side of the country have attracted my curiosity to explore all these places I have read about in books and seen in movies.

The first year, I traveled through many cities with my brother Halil in his eighteen-wheel truck. That same year, we visited some cousins in Waterloo, Iowa and more cousins in Chicago, Illinois. They lived and worked happily and as satisfied as we were in St. Louis.

At my job, I tried to learn more and more of the new language whenever I had the chance. I found a job in a small company where the workers were mostly Bosnian men with little or no English. I started working and translating for them when necessary. The job wasn't hard, so I soon became bored. The worst part was that the hall was too hot, and the smell of chemicals, paint, and drying plastic was unbearable.

One day, while visiting my cousin, Mersa, a godsend arrived. He was an American who spoke nearly fluent Bosnian. He helped many Bosnians settle. Once, he told me he had visited Bosnia, I realized that I had met a kindred spirit. He told me where he had visited, and he mentioned the name of the school where I used to work. I told him that I had been a student, teacher, and principal there.

"Where and what do you do now?" he asked.

"I am working in a plastic company," I told him.

"Do you want to work in a school again?" asked he.

"I'd love to, but I don't know enough English to teach in America" I replied.

"Mister, your language is good. If you give me your address, I will send you all the information and applications with an address to send it with a copy of your certification translated into English," he responded.

After a while, I received all the forms. I translated my index and diploma at an International Institute. I eagerly filled out the forms and mailed them out. I was not too hopeful because I was worried about my language skills.

In the fall, Halil and I sent the warranty letter to our mother to come and visit us for three months although our father refused to come. Everyone was overjoyed by her visit, especially my son. While she was here, I got called for an interview for the job in the school. I was scared to death of that interview, but it was my chance to escape the smell of the chemicals. At that time, our father became ill and was hospitalized in Bosnia, so our mother needed to return before the expiration of her visa. We cried when the jumbo jet took her far over the fertile fields of Missouri, across the vast Atlantic Ocean back to Bosnia.

My first interview went amazingly well, and soon they invited me to a second one. After that interview, I had an accident at my job where another man hit my hand and damaged my pinky. Luckily, I had surgery, so I didn't lose it.

After the second interview, I was sent to an elementary school to have an interview with the principal. There, I met a very tall, elegant, and refined man with a German last name. We talked about teaching, the place I came from, and about his last name. I asked him if he knew what his last name meant in English. He didn't. I explained to him that it meant castle for the pigeons. He smiled from the bottom of his soul. He shook my hand and told me to go to the main office to complete paperwork, and on Monday, I could start the new job in the school.

I was the happiest man on the Earth because I would be in a clean school with kids. I even got the position of assistant and translator for students, parents, teachers, and administrators. The salary was a little less than in the company, but it included health insurance and a pension. Moreover, I was pleased that I got a job in this city of two million people and just a couple of miles from my apartment. Thus, by the beginning of February, 2001, I was working in the profession I had been born to have.

In the fall of that same year, I got the opportunity to sign up for the Base program and started to take classes at college for free. That year, everything worked well, until one night.

When I got back from my evening class at college, I found several pairs of shoes in front of my apartment. I couldn't believe that many people had come to visit unannounced. When I opened my door, they told me the saddest news. My mother had died. I wasn't able to talk with the people who told me. I immediately called my father in Bosnia to see if it was true. It was. From that moment, I felt I had a wall around me, through which I could see people and things, but I couldn't and feel them. I told my father I would try to go to her funeral.

In the morning, Halil and I bought tickets for Zagreb. In Detroit, the flight to Frankfurt was cancelled, so I had to wait there until morning. I was devastated. I told them where and why I was going, and they found a flight headed for Amsterdam. When I arrived in the morning, I found that the flight for Zagreb was four hours late. That meant I couldn't be on time at my mother's funeral. I called my father the news. I sat at the airport in Amsterdam and prayed for my mother's soul. When I arrived late that night, the house was still full of our family, cousins, and friends. I cried like a child, but my tears couldn't bring her back. I found one cousin with his wife and little baby to stay and help my father.

I returned to my job on Monday, but from that time, something had changed inside me. The death of my mother had taken something from me. I was depressed and wounded for many years. During that time, I wrote poems about the past and published a book of poetry dedicated to my mother.

The next year, I got an offer to teach Bosnian at Saint Louis Community College. In my classroom were policemen, firefighters, nurses, doctors, teachers, principals, and many others who must deal with and do business with Bosnians. It was something new, so one night, a local television and newspaper reporter came for an interview. The next morning, my picture was in the first page of the newspaper. Someone from my class recommended me to another college, and after a while, I got four classes in Bosnian, two beginning and two advanced.

I was surprised how I, a foreigner, could move quickly from one job to another in a new country despite the new, very hard language.

In that way, I convinced myself that here, in this freedom-loving place, you can become whatever you wish if you work hard and dream of something better.

The American dream is not a fantasy. Within a couple of years, we had two cars. We have gone on vacations to Bosnia and have visited friends and cousins in Germany and Austria. We went on vacations to the Lake of Ozarks, Florida, the Gulf of Mexico, and all the way to the Adriatic Sea. Nothing was too far or unavailable.

Eventually, we had another child, a beautiful daughter. We decided to buy our own home. Our son grew up and started his first part time job, and when he celebrated his sixteenth birthday, we bought him a car. We were truly living the American dream.

After ten years of living in the new country, we were able to buy our new castle. This one wasn't as strong or tall as the one we left in our old country, but it was better because this one isn't in danger of destruction, fire, invasion, or war. We prayed for good health. We had everything else, like so long ago in our country before the war. Only the war dreams ruined our happiness.

"Hi Mooyo, where have you been for so many years?" said my school friend in our city during our summer vacation in Bosnia.

"I was in so many places that it is a very long story, but now I live in St. Louis, Missouri," I answered.

"If you have time, let's have a drink because I am so happy to see you again after all these years after the war," said Laki, who was the trendy boy in high school.

"Where do you want to go?" I asked.

"Let's go to our Old Castle. My cousin has a coffee shop there," added Laki proudly.

The castle more beautiful than I remembered surrounded by pine trees, flowers, and to my surprise, a monument in the front showing my ancestor Mooyo Hrnjica on his jogat with a long rifle on his shoulder and a falcon in his hand. I was so pleased. I couldn't remember the last time I had enjoyed the view of the castle.

"I didn't know they had installed the sculpture that was sitting in the basement of City Hall for so many years," I said, bursting with excitement.

"I knew that you would be surprised because I remember how you always talked about and draw this sculpture during our school days, and how you sang the lines from collection of "Poems of Mooyo Hrnjica" collected from our folks of that Austrian's student before WWI," said Baki, with a big grin on his face.

"When did all this happen, and how did they get the permission and money to install it?" I asked him still thrilled with the sight.

"I don't know who provided the money, but today everything here is possible. Some people are enormously rich, but the rest are on the edge of poverty. This is not the same place and system you and I lived before. Here we have a new corrupt system with parties, war profiteers, after war profiteers, war privileged officers, families, drugs, weapons, and people smugglers and everything else that came from the West.

We sat on the terrace talking and enjoying our drinks when a huge explosion shook our table, spilling our drinks. It exploded in the room beneath us. We ran downstairs, where at least six young people where lying down in pools of blood. I was screaming for the help.

When I woke from this dream, my wife was holding me in our bed.

"You had another bad dream. Drink some water, and you will be fine. You must be tired of all the work you have done since last summer. We need to go on vacation to relax and erase all these dreams," said my wife, still holding my sweaty head and neck.

"You are right. After any of our vacations, I feel better with fewer nightmares. This one had been a trick because it had started out so nicely."

After sipping some water, I told her what was the dream about.

So many times the nightmares of the war haunt us, but when we open our eyes, we realize the hard times although carved in our memories are past.

I had my small dream of a monument of my great-great grandfather Mooyo. It was built but never installed. The communists in the former Yugoslavia didn't allow our community to install it during their time.

The summer of 2008, when summer school was almost over, Fata was off, so we decided to go somewhere on vacation. We found someone had cancelled tickets for a trip to Jamaica. We landed at a small airport in Kingston City. We stayed at a hotel on the beach. Very soon, night fell and supper was served. We got the keys of our apartment and enjoyed delicious food like never before.

We stayed for a week on the beautiful sandy beach, under the blooming tropical trees and palms, the clear and warm ocean water and tasty drinks and food everywhere.

215

There on the beach were many tourists from all around the world who calmly enjoyed free time. My daughter and I built sand castles, turtles, and roads. Building the sand castles brought back memories of the castle of my ancestry, but I knew that the castle I would build in the new country would be in a better place than one that is always attacked, destroyed, or usurped by someone.

After seven unforgettable days on the Jamaican beach, we went back to St. Louis. Our daughter was very happy to be back with her brother because she missed him so much that she had refused to eat because he was not with us. We had many July days left to relax in our castle and swimming pool.

The hot summer was at an end. We all returned to our jobs, schools, and everyday life. Fall came quickly, and with it the Thanksgiving holiday. We fried the turkey in my yard behind the house with my brother and friends. Every year in America, we had much to be thankful for. That year, the day was so cold that we set the tables in our basement, where we enjoyed good food, drinks, and conversed until midnight. The next day, we were off work. I woke up early and decided to run through my neighborhood. When I returned, I was thinking about my mother's words when she visited us.

"It is nice for you here. If Asim agrees to come and stay here, I will be happy to join you. I am going back there with joy in my heart and soul knowing that you have everything you need for yourself and your families. From now on I will not be sad you left us." I gave a prayer for her because she was the best mother ever. I made coffee and tea thinking about hers words and set empty cups on a tray.

I sat at the kitchen table and thought about this beautiful country, about the appreciation of these people, the laws and regulations, which let you touch the stars if you work hard. My ancestors over eight generations bled for love of their homeland.

I knew that in that moment she thought about all the suffering, tears, and farewells to our closest friends we left in the homeland. Her wounds were healed by our new found, freedom, equality, and the wealth which was on all four sides of this country.

Her words pushed me to write my story for others to read and learn from and to justify her confidence in my abilities. I wanted to make my dream come true with words of my friend from my childhood, that I still hear in my ears, "Godfather you never throw stones at God." It can come true for every human in this beautiful United States of America, my new homeland.

———

Made in the USA
Monee, IL
07 July 2021